Edward Smith

William Cobbett

A Biography. Vol. 1

Edward Smith

William Cobbett
A Biography. Vol. 1

ISBN/EAN: 9783337012175

Printed in Europe, USA, Canada, Australia, Japan

Cover: Foto ©Raphael Reischuk / pixelio.de

More available books at **www.hansebooks.com**

WILLIAM COBBETT:

A BIOGRAPHY.

By EDWARD SMITH.

IN TWO VOLUMES.

VOL. I.

London :

SAMPSON LOW, MARSTON, SEARLE, & RIVINGTON,

CROWN BUILDINGS, 188, FLEET STREET.

1878.

" It is not by his faults, but by his excellences, that we measure a great man."

G. H. Lewes (*On Actors, &c.*).

" Fear never but you shall be consistent in whatever variety of actions, so that they be each honest and natural in their hour. For of one will, the actions will be harmonious, however unlike they seem."

R. W. Emerson (*Essay on Self-reliance*).

" My good blade carves the casques of men,
My tough lance thrusteth sure,
My strength is as the strength of ten,
Because my heart is pure !"

Tennyson (*Sir Galahad*).

NOTE.

THE following pages need no Preface, with regard to their subject.

I am unwilling, however, to let the work go forth to the public without a renewed word of thanks, to those who have given me any sort of encouragement or assistance. My acknowledgments are especially due to the venerable daughter of Mr. James Swann, for the use of some letters; to the author of the "Handbook of Fictitious Names," without whose apt teaching in the art of Bibliography, the work might have wanted the interesting appendix; to Mr. Job Swain, one of the last survivors of Cobbett's personal friends, for some reminiscences; and to Mr. Ellis Yarnall, of Philadelphia, for copies of several letters, and for some suggestions which have enabled the author to throw additional light on the " Porcupine " days.

E. S.

London : *November*, 1878.

CONTENTS.

CHAPTER I.

1762–1784.

CHAPTER II.

1784–1791.

CHAPTER III.

1792.

CHAPTER IV.

1793–1794.

CHAPTER XI.

1800–1801.

CHAPTER XII.

1802.

CHAPTER XIII.

1803–1805.

WILLIAM COBBETT:

A BIOGRAPHY.

———•———

CHAPTER I.

"I LOOKED BACK WITH PRIDE TO MY WAGGON-DRIVING GRANDFATHER."

WILLIAM COBBETT was born in the parish of Farnham, in the county of Surrey, on the 9th of March, 1762.

The town of Farnham is a hop-garden. It had, in olden days, one of the most important corn-markets in the south of England. Before that, it was a great clothing mart; and, early in Parliamentary history, was called upon to send representatives to the "Collective Wisdom." But, at last, the mercantile spirit proper, as was the case with many towns in Surrey, Kent, and Sussex, fled from Farnham; granaries took the place of workshops; and manufactures declined. With the extinction of the iron-furnaces of the Weald expired the once-flourishing trade of the south of England; and agriculture became the staple pursuit of the still-prosperous people, all over the fertile country which lies between the Thames and the English Channel. Corn-fields took the place of extensive sheep and cattle pastures; new grazing-downs succeeded to the burnt-up forests, whilst hops took the pick of the land, upon which they throve in a hitherto-unexampled manner. And Farnham, with its deep, rich, light-brown soil, found itself with a title to give to the best hops grown in England.

So Farnham is, to this day, a big hop-garden. In spite of a railway-station and 10,000 inhabitants, and the proximity of a garrison, the impression is, all around, the same. You enter the town from London, and the first church you come to is nearly surrounded with vines; the last building, at the other end of the long street, is an oast-house. You may take a lodging down by the river-side, and find a forest of hop-poles immediately outside your window, in the morning; or taking stand on any elevation, you will see all the uplands around, either in their luxuriant summer dress of vine, or else, so many square miles of poles placed tent-wise, taking their winter rest, looking like nothing so much as the encampment of a monstrous army.

They must have been clever enough in their generation, who planted and built hereabouts nearly two thousand years ago; but he who did the most on behalf of this part of Surrey was he who planted a small field of hops on the upland towards Crondell, somewhere about the year 1600. By the middle of the eighteenth century the hops of Farnham were already distinguished—"always at the top of the market;" and the agricultural writers of that day wax eloquent over the praises of the pleasing, fertile vale, and its "hazel-coloured," loamy soil, and the yearly-increasing number of acres given up to hop-culture. Arthur Young calls the district between Farnham and Alton the finest in England.

The scenery around Farnham is not, in itself, unique; so far, that any well-cultivated English river-valley is like almost any other, with its low hills crowned along their summits with the evidences of prosperous farming. But, from the top of one of these eminences, the eye soon discovers certain characteristics, which compel a deep impression upon the mind of singularity and beauty. The best view is, perhaps, to be obtained from

Hungry Hill, near Aldershot ; the most prominent object being Crooksbury Hill, rising from above the woods of Moor Park and Waverley Abbey. A very odd-looking hill, covered with tall Scotch firs, the like of which it would be difficult to name ; a wide expanse of sandy heath, now partly cultivated, stretches for many miles beyond, until broken up into a tumultuous range of heath-clad hills ; and these, again, succeeded by the distant blue outlines of the Sussex and Hampshire downs. The river Wey courses down the vale, passing through the lower part of Farnham town ; and after spinning merrily through the meadows and hop-fields below, bends abruptly round in the direction of Guildford.

The inhabitants of this district, one hundred years ago, were almost out of the great World. The turnpike-road to Winchester and the south-west bounded their earthly aims ; upon it was situated the weekly goal for the produce of their farms ; and along it was, at a toilsome distance, either the great metropolis at one end, or Portsmouth and her marines at the other. With strong native prejudices, and a character for inflexible honesty, the farmers (generally speaking) lived remote, "equal enemies to improvements in agriculture and to relaxations in morals ;" the smallest occupiers sharing the hardest toil with their labourers.

Before the great scarcity and dearness set in, in the last quarter of the century—when the clocks and the brass kettles began to disappear from the parlours, and the visions of general pauperism began to appear—the spirit of the peasantry in the remoter parts of Surrey was high and in-dependent—chill penury was then uncommon with the able-bodied. In the receipt of only seven or eight shillings a week of average money wages, such was the cheapness of food, and so light were the burdens which Prudence had to bear, that the labourer was healthy, cheerful, and contented; whilst he could often explain clearly enough, from his own observation and reflection, the merits or demerits of the different systems and practice upon the neighbouring farms.

Of this class was the grandfather of William Cobbett.

" With respect to my ancestors, I shall go no further back than my grandfather, and for this plain reason, that I never heard talk of any prior to him. He was a day-labourer, and I have heard my father say, that he worked for one farmer from the day of his marriage to that of his death, upwards of forty years. He died before I was born, but I have often slept beneath the same roof that had sheltered him, and where his widow dwelt for several years after his death. It was a little thatched cottage with a garden before the door. It had but two windows ; a damson-tree shaded one, and a clump of filberts the other. Here I and my brothers went every Christmas and Whitsuntide, to spend a week or two, and torment the poor old woman with our noise and dilapidations. She used to give us milk and bread for breakfast, an apple-pudding for our dinner, and a piece of bread and cheese for supper. Her fire was made of turf, cut from the neighbouring heath, and her evening light was a rush dipped in grease."

George Cobbett, son of this old couple, appears to have much improved his condition in life ; and he lived to see all his boys gradually rising in the world. WILLIAM was the third (out of four), and he gives vivid sketches of their daily course of existence.

"My father, when I was born, was a farmer. The reader will easily believe, from the poverty of his parents, that he had received no very brilliant education : he was, however, learned, for a man in his rank of life. When a little boy, he drove the plough for twopence a day, and these his earnings were appropriated to the expenses of an evening school. What a village school-master could be expected to teach, he had learnt, and had besides considerably improved himself in several branches of the mathematics. He understood land surveying well, and was often chosen to draw the plans of disputed territory: in short, he had the reputation of possessing experience and understanding, which never fails, in England, to give a man, in a country place, some little weight with his neighbours. He was honest, industrious, and frugal; it was not, therefore, wonderful, that he should be situated in a good farm, and happy in a wife of his own rank, like him, beloved and respected.

"So much for my ancestors, from whom, if I derive no honour, I derive no shame.

"A father like ours, it will be readily supposed, did not suffer us to eat the bread of idleness. I do not remember the time when I did not earn my living. My first occupation was driving the small birds from the turnip seed, and the rooks from the peas. When I first trudged a-field, with my wooden bottle and my satchel swung over my shoulders, I was hardly able to climb the gates and stiles, and, at the close of the day, to reach home was a task of infinite difficulty. My next employment was weeding wheat, and leading a single horse at harrowing barley. Hoeing peas followed, and hence I arrived at the honour of joining the reapers in harvest, driving the team and holding the plough. We were all of us strong and laborious, and my father used to boast, that he had four boys, the eldest of whom was but fifteen years old, who did as much work as any three men in the parish of Farnham. Honest pride, and happy days! . . . ."

"I have some faint recollection of going to school to an old woman, who, I believe, did not succeed in teaching me my letters. In the winter evenings my father taught us all to read and write, and gave us a pretty tolerable knowledge of arithmetic. Grammar he did not perfectly understand himself, and therefore his endeavours to teach us that, necessarily failed ; for, though he thought he understood it, and though he made us get the rules by heart, we learnt nothing at all of the principles."

No, the book-learning was not to come yet. That was to be left until the little world of his birthplace had become too small to hold him. Nearly sixty years after these simple times, Mr. Cobbett is riding in the neighbourhood, accompanied by one of his sons, and the two go out of their way to visit the spot where he received " the rudiments of his education."

" There is a little hop-garden in which I used to work when from eight to ten years old ; from which I have scores of times run to follow the hounds, leaving the hoe to do the best that it could to destroy the weeds ; but the most interesting thing was a sand-hill, which goes from a part of the heath down to the rivulet. As a due mixture of pleasure with toil, I with two brothers, used occasionally to disport ourselves, as the lawyers call it, at this sand-hill. One diversion was this : we used to go to the top of the hill, which was steeper than the roof of a house ; one used to draw his arms out of the sleeves of his smock-frock, and lay himself down with his arms by his sides; and then the others, one at head and the other at feet, sent him rolling down the hill like a barrel or a log of wood. By the time he got to the bottom, his hair, eyes, ears, nose, and mouth, were all full of this loose sand; then the others took their turn; and at every roll, there was a monstrous spell of laughter. I had often told my sons of this while they were very little, and I now took one of them to see the spot. But, that was not all. This was the spot where I was receiving my education; and this was the sort of education; and I am perfectly satisfied that if I had not received such an education, or something very much like it; that, if I had been brought up a milksop, with a nursery-maid everlastingly at my heels, I should have been at this day as great a fool, as inefficient a mortal, as any of those frivolous idiots that are turned out from Winchester and Westminster School, or from any of those dens of dunces called colleges and universities. It is impossible to say how much I owe to that sand-hill; and I went to return it my thanks for the ability which it probably gave me to be one of the greatest terrors, to one of the greatest and most powerful bodies of knaves and fools, that ever were permitted to afflict this or any other country."

In such manner the merry, sturdy, little life went on. At tying hop-poles, or scaring birds, almost as soon as he could barely stand, a trifling share was given to the family efforts; whilst the vigorous, healthy senses were already open to the keenest enjoyment of nature, and to the unexpected moments of fun which enter into the days of boyhood. Look at this, for example (written at nearly seventy years of age).

" When I was a very little boy, I was, in the barley-sowing season, going along by the side of a field, near Waverley Abbey; the primroses and blue-bells be-spangling the banks on both sides of me; a thousand linnets singing in a spreading oak over my head; while the jingle of the traces, and the whistling of the plough-boys saluted my ear from over the hedge; and, as it were to snatch me from the enchantment, the hounds, at that instant, having started a hare in the hanger on the other side of the field, came up scampering over it in full cry, taking me after them many a mile. I was not more than eight years old; but this particular scene has presented itself to my mind many times every year from that day to this. I always enjoy it over again, &c."

Cobbett's political writings, during his whole career, were largely illustrated by the incidents and occurrences of his life. This was the line taken by his own peculiar egotism, and we are indebted to it for numerous pictures similar to the above. Of this particular period there is only space here for the following capital story :—

" When I was a boy, a huntsman named George Bradley, who was huntsman to Mr. Smither, of Hale, very wantonly gave me a cut with his whip, because I jumped in amongst the dogs, pulled a hare from them, and got her scut, upon a little common, called Seal Common, near Waverley Abbey. I was only about eight years old; but my mind was so strongly imbued with the principles of natural justice, that I did not rest satisfied with the mere calling of names, of which, however, I gave Mr. George Bradley a plenty. I sought to inflict a just punishment upon him; and, as I had not the means of proceeding by force, I proceeded by cunning in the manner that I am presently going to describe. I had not then read the Bible, much less had I read GROTIUS and PUFFENDORF; I, therefore, did not know that God and man had declared, that it was laudable to combat tyranny by either force or fraud; but, though I did not know what tyranny meant, reason and a sense of justice taught me that Bradley had been guilty of tyranny towards me; and the native resources of my mind, together with my resolution, made me inflict justice on him in the following manner:—Hounds (hare-hounds at least) will follow the trail of a red herring as eagerly as that of a hare, and rather more so, the scent being stronger and more unbroken. I waited till Bradley and his pack were trailing for a hare in the neighbourhood of that same Seal Common. They were pretty sure to find in the space of half an hour, and the hare was pretty sure to go up the common and over the hill to the south. I placed myself ready with a red herring at the end of a string, in a dry field, and near a hard path, along which, or near to which, I was pretty sure the hare would go. I waited a long while; the sun was getting high, the scent bad; but, by and by, I heard the view-halloo and full cry. I squatted down in the fern, and my heart bounded with the prospect of inflicting justice, when I saw my lady come skipping by, going off towards Pepperharrow; that is to say, to the south. In a moment, I clapped down my herring, went off at a right angle towards the west, climbed up a steep bank very soon, where the horsemen, such as they were, could not follow; then on I went over the roughest part of the common that I could find, till I got to the pales of Moor Park, over which I went, there being holes at the bottom for the letting in of the hares. That part of the park was covered with short heath; and I gave some twirls about to amuse Mr. Bradley for half-an-hour. Then off I went, and down a hanger at last, to the bottom of which no horseman could get without riding round a quarter of a mile. At the bottom of the hanger was an alder moor, in a swamp. There my herring ceased to perform its service. The river is pretty rapid, I tossed it in, that it might go back to the sea, and relate to its brethren the exploits of the land. I washed my hands in the water of the moor; and took a turn, and stood at the top of the hanger to witness the winding up of the day's sport, which terminated a little before dusk in one of the dark days of November. After overrunning the scent a hundred times, after an hour's puzzling in the dry field, after all the doubles and all the turns that the sea-borne hare had given them, down came the whole *posse* to the swamp; the huntsman went round a mill-head not far off, and tried the other side of the river: '*No! d— her, where can she be?*' And thus, amidst conjectures, disputations, mutual blamings, and swearings a plenty, they concluded, some of them half-leg deep in dirt, and going soaking home at the end of a drizzling day."

The little life, that was destined to be such a cruel thorn in the sides of Authority, was very near being summarily extinguished about this time; on occasion of William getting out of his depth while bathing in the river Wey, and from which he was "pulled out by the foot, which happened to stick up above the water."

By the time of his reaching ten or eleven years of age he is already getting useful, in his way, and he takes his turn with his brothers of going the annual visit to Weyhill Fair with their father. The fair at Weyhill, though still considerable, is not what it was then; the hop-growers now run off to Worcester, or Burton-on-Trent; but in those days, long before the railways, Weyhill in October was the grand centre for sheep, hops, &c. There the yearly hirings took place, and there the bucolic gathering from all the neighbouring counties had an annual dissipation. We shall presently see that it was at one of these trips Cobbett made his first acquaintance with American politics. But the following incident—which has often been told, but cannot on that account be omitted here—presents his first recorded look-out upon life.

"At eleven years of age, my employment was clipping of box-edgings and weeding beds of flowers in the garden of the Bishop of Winchester, at the Castle of Farnham, my native town. I had always been fond of beautiful gardens; and a gardener, who had just come from the King's Gardens at Kew, gave such a description as made me instantly resolve to work in these gardens. The next morning, without saying a word to any one, off I set, with no clothes except those upon my back, and with thirteen halfpence in my pocket. I found that I must go to Richmond, and I accordingly went on, from place to place, inquiring my way thither. A long day (it was in June) brought me to Richmond in the afternoon. Two pennyworth of bread and cheese, and a pennyworth of small beer, which I had on the road, and one halfpenny that I had lost somehow or other, left threepence in my pocket. With this for my whole fortune, I was trudging through Richmond, in my blue smock-frock, and my red garters tied under my knees, when, staring about me, my eye fell upon a little book in a bookseller's window. 'TALE OF A TUB,' price 3*d.* The title was so odd, that my curiosity was excited. I had the 3*d.*, but then I could have no supper. In I went, and got the little book, which I was so impatient to read, that I got over into a field, at the upper corner of Kew Gardens, where there stood a haystack. On the shady side of this, I sat down to read. The book was so different from anything that I had ever read before; it was something so new to my mind, that, though I could not at all understand some of it, it delighted me beyond description; and it produced what I have always considered a birth of intellect. I read on till it was dark, without any thought about supper or bed. When I could see no longer, I put my little book in my pocket, and tumbled down by the side of the stack, where I slept till the birds in Kew Gardens awaked me in the morning; when off I started to Kew, reading my little book. The singularity of my dress, the simplicity of my manner, my confident and lively air, and, doubtless, his own compassion besides, induced the gardener, who was a Scotchman, I remember, to give me victuals, find me lodgings, and set me to work. And it was during the period that I was at Kew, that the present King (Geo. IV.), and two of his brothers laughed at the oddness of my dress, while I was sweeping the grass-plat round the foot of the pagoda. The gardener, seeing me fond of books, lent me some gardening books to read; but these I could not relish after my 'Tale of a Tub,' which I carried about with me wherever I went; and when I, at about twenty [24] years old, lost it in a box that fell overboard in the Bay of Fundy, in North America, the loss gave me greater pain then I have ever felt at losing thousands of pounds."

How long the employment at Kew lasted, and how he got home again, does not appear. The life at Farnham was probably resumed before the approach of winter; for, either the year before this, or that immediately succeeding, he mentions being sent down from Farnham to Steeple Langford, in Wiltshire, with a horse; remaining at the latter place "from the month of June till the fall of the year."

Cobbett must have been about fourteen years of age at the time alluded to in the following incident:—

"My father used to take one of us with him every year to the great hop-fair at Weyhill. The fair was held at Old Michaelmastide, and the journey was to us a sort of reward for the labours of the summer. It happened to be my turn to go thither the very year that Long Island was taken by the British. A great company of hop-merchants and farmers were just sitting down to supper as the post arrived, bringing in the 'Extraordinary Gazette,' which announced the victory. A hop-factor from London took the paper, placed his chair upon the table, and began to read with an audible voice. He was opposed, a dispute ensued, and my father retired, taking me by the hand, to another apartment, where we supped with about a dozen others of the same sentiments. Here Washington's health, and success to the Americans, were repeatedly toasted, and this was the first time, as far as I can recollect, that I ever heard the General's name mentioned. Little did I then dream that I should ever see the man, and still less that I should hear some of his own countrymen reviling and execrating him.

Although we have learned, not only to look with complacency upon the results of the attempt to coerce the Colonies, but, also, to wonder that there could have ever been English statesmen so deluded as to expect anything but disaster from the contest; it has not been sufficiently observed, that the immediate effect was the partial ruin of the labouring poor in this country; that it is from that period that their prosperity has declined, and their comforts have become fewer and fewer. And what is more, before their impoverishment made it obvious to everybody, the common people and the tradesmen showed, by their abhorrence of the war, that they were, for once, gifted with a truer political sagacity than their precious rulers; and that there must have been some vague general anticipation of the consequences to them, and to their families. Prices rose, whilst wages remained stationary; and, from the very outset, the privations of the poor were aggravated to an intense degree. But from that date arose the thirst of the labouring classes for political information, which has since resulted in their possessing so general a share in representation.

So, down at quiet Farnham, the people had hitherto been, "like the rest of the country people in England," neither knowing nor thinking much about politics. The "shouts of victory or the murmurs at a defeat," would now and then break in upon their tranquillity for a moment; but after the American war had continued for a short time, the people began to be a little better acquainted with subjects of that kind. Cobbett says, that opinions were pretty equally divided concerning the war, at first; whilst there grew up a good deal of pretty warm discussion, sometimes :—

"My father was a partisan of the Americans : he used frequently to dispute on the subject with the gardener of a nobleman who lived near us. This was generally done with good humour, over a pot of our best ale ; yet the disputants sometimes grew warm, and gave way to language that could not fail to attract our attention. My father was worsted, without doubt, as he had for antagonist a shrewd and sensible old Scotchman, far his superior in political knowledge; but he pleaded before a partial audience : we thought there was but one wise man in the world, and that that one was our father. He who pleaded the cause of the Americans had an advantage too, with young minds : he had only to represent the King's troops as sent to cut the throats of a people, our friends and relations, merely because they would not submit to oppression, and his cause was gained."

Old George Cobbett remained a staunch American in politics; but, as to whether he was right or wrong, his son admits that he never, at that period, formed any opinion. His own notions were those of his father, which would have been as warmly entertained if they had been all on the other side. The short autobiography of which the above forms a part, was written during the early part of his pamphleteering career in the United States; at which time he found it necessary to explain that he had not been nursed in the lap of aristocracy, and that he did not imbibe his then "principles or prejudices from those who were the advocates of blind submission." The story of this pamphlet will come in its proper place, when its author was upwards of thirty years of age.

Here we have, then, probably as much as we shall ever know, of William Cobbett's early years. The utter obscurity of his father's social status is, of itself, sufficient reason why there were no admiring friends to detect precocity, and to record its achievements: until the age of twenty his life was made up of the ordinary occupations of a country lad. Fairs, cricket-matches, and hare-hunts filled up the joyous periods of recreation; and it was not till the year 1782, that an incident

occurred, which, bringing him into the bustling
activity of town-life, had the same effect upon him,
that a similar change of scene has had upon many
an ardent, healthy spirit ; and which estranged
him from the sequestered vale of life, for ever.

There can be little doubt, however, that a very
great mental stimulus was acquired by the trip to
Kew, and the reading of Swift's wonderful satire.[1]
The poor ploughboy, very probably, read and re-
read the laughable story of Peter and Martin
hundreds of times without understanding the real
drift of it ; but there was enough in the book,
with its entertaining accounts of grotesque fashions
and weak-minded characters, to furnish such an
impressionable spirit as Cobbett's with an inexhaustible store of odd ideas concerning the world
outside him.   Readers of his works will notice his
frequent quotation of Swift : " The celebrated Dean
of St. Patrick somewhere observes, &c., &c." is
the opening sentence of the autobiographical
sketch ; and the " Political Register," in after-years,

---

[1] It is a noteworthy circumstance that Moor Park and "my
grandmother's cottage " should be almost within hail of each other ;
for it was among these very scenes that Swift spent some of his
earliest and best years—a nice little item for any ingenious believer
in "affinities."

When Cobbett wrote "The Life and Adventures of Peter Porcupine," he was not aware of this coincidence, otherwise his humour
would have happily played around the topic.

continued to manifest evidences of the source and character of Cobbett's early reading. Cobbett's literary ·style, however, was not exactly that of Dean Swift; of which the former's ignorance, and even contempt, of Latinity is sufficient explanation. But his alternations of sweetness and acrimony,—his ever-ready images,—the picturesque manner of his describing individual characters,—his constant tendency to satire,—cannot but be ascribed, in great measure, to the little book whose loss "cost him greater pain than losing thousands of pounds."

So there is, now, some difference. A head and shoulders above the average of his mates, his mind is, likewise, on a higher level. Not so high, but as yet to be infinitely dark as to any purpose : a healthy spirit in a healthy body, there stood, working as hard and as cheerily as ever ; but ready for the first impulse—which impulse came, in no uncommon way ; in no more romantic style than that which sets a ball rolling, upon the impact or the foot.

"Towards the autumn of 1782, I went to visit a relation who lived in the neighbourhood of Portsmouth. From the top of Portsdown, I, for the first time, beheld the sea, and no sooner did I behold it than I wished to be a sailor. I could never account for this sudden impulse, nor can I now. Almost all English boys feel

the same inclination : it would seem that, like young
ducks, instinct leads them to rush on the bosom of the
water.

"But it was not the sea alone that I saw; the grand
fleet was riding at anchor at Spithead. I had heard of
the wooden walls of Old England; I had formed my
ideas of a ship and of a fleet, but what I now beheld so
far surpassed what I had ever been able to form a con-
ception of, that I stood lost between astonishment and
admiration. I had heard talk of the glorious deeds of
our admirals and sailors, of the defeat of the Spanish
Armada, and of all those memorable combats that good
and true Englishmen never fail to relate to their children
about a hundred times a year. The brave Rodney's
victories over our natural enemies, the French and
Spaniards, had long been the theme of our praise, and
the burthen of our songs. The sight of the fleet brought
all these into my mind; in confused order, it is true,
but with irresistible force. My heart was inflated with
national pride. The sailors were my countrymen, the
fleet belonged to my country, and surely I had my
part in it, and all its honours; yet, these honours I had
not earned; I took to myself a sort of reproach for
possessing what I had no right to, and resolved to
have a just claim by sharing in the hardships and the
dangers.

"I arrived at my uncle's late in the evening, with my
mind full of my sea-faring project. Though I had walked
thirty miles during the day, and consequently was well
wearied, I slept not a moment. It was no sooner day-

light than I arose and walked down towards the old castle on the beach at Spithead. For a sixpence given to an invalid I got permission to go upon the battlements; here I had a closer view of the fleet, and at every look my impatience to be on board increased. In short, I went from the Castle to Portsmouth, got into a boat, and was in a few minutes on board the 'Pegasus' man-of-war, commanded by the Right Honourable George Berkeley, brother to the Earl of Berkeley.

"The Captain had more compassion than is generally met with in men of his profession; he represented to me the toils I must undergo, and the punishment that the least disobedience or neglect would subject me to. He persuaded me to return home, and I remember he concluded his advice with telling me, that it was better to be led to church in a halter, to be tied to a girl that I did not like, than to be tied to the gang-way, or, as the sailors call it, married to Miss Roper. From the conclusion of this wholesome counsel, I perceived that the captain thought I had eloped on account of a bastard.

"I in vain attempted to convince Captain Berkeley,[2] that choice alone had led me to the sea; he sent me on shore, and I at last quitted Portsmouth, but not before I had applied to the Port-Admiral, Evans, to get my name enrolled among those who were destined for the service. I was, in some sort, obliged to acquaint the Admiral with what had passed on board the 'Pegasus,' in conse-

[2] Afterwards Admiral Sir George Berkeley. He entered the navy at twelve years of age, and saw a good deal of service, including the glorious 1st of June. Died 1818, æt. sixty-five.

quence of which my request was refused, and I happily escaped, sorely against my will, from the most toilsome and perilous profession in the world.

" I returned once more to the plough, but I was spoiled for a farmer. I had, before my Portsmouth adventure, never known any other ambition than that of surpassing my brothers in the different labours of the field, but it was quite otherwise now; I sighed for a sight of the world ; the little island of Britain seemed too small a com-pass for me. The things in which I had taken the most delight were neglected ; the singing of the birds grew insipid, and even the heart-cheering cry of the hounds, after which I formerly used to fly from my work, bound o'er the fields, and dash through the brakes and coppices, was heard with the most torpid indifference. Still, how-ever, I remained at home till the following spring, when I quitted it, perhaps for ever.

" It was on the 6th of May, 1783, that I, like Don Quixote, sallied forth to seek adventures. I was dressed in my holiday clothes, in order to accompany two or three lasses to Guildford Fair. They were to assemble at a house about three miles from my home, where I was to attend them ; but, unfortunately for me, I had to cross the London turnpike-road. The stage-coach had just turned the summit of a hill and was rattling down towards me at a merry rate. The notion of going to London never entered my mind till this very moment, yet the step was completely determined on, before the coach came to the spot where I stood. Up I got, and was in London about nine o'clock in the evening.

" It was by mere accident that I had money enough to defray the expenses of this day. Being rigged out for the fair, I had three or four crown and half-crown pieces (which most certainly I did not intend to spend), besides a few shillings and half-pence. This my little all, which I had been years in amassing, melted away like snow before the sun, when touched by the fingers of the inn-keepers and their waiters. In short, when I arrived at Ludgate Hill, and had paid my fare, I had but about half-a-crown in my pocket.

" By a commencement of that good luck, which has hitherto attended me through all the situations in which fortune has placed me, I was preserved from ruin. A gentleman, who was one of the passengers in the stage, fell into conversation with me at dinner, and he soon learnt that I was going I knew not whither nor for what. This gentleman was a hop-merchant in the borough of Southwark, and, upon closer inquiry, it appeared that he had often dealt with my father at Wey Hill. He knew the danger I was in ; he was himself a father, and he felt for my parents. His house became my home, he wrote to my father, and endeavoured to prevail on me to obey his orders, which were to return immediately home. I am ashamed to say that I was disobedient. It was the first time I had ever been so, and I have repented of it from that moment to this. Willingly would I have returned, but pride would not suffer me to do it. I feared the scoffs of my acquaintances more than the real evils that threatened me.

" My generous preserver, finding my obstinacy not to

be overcome, began to look out for an employment for me. He was preparing an advertisement for the newspaper, when an acquaintance of his, an attorney, called in to see him. He related my adventure to this gentleman, whose name was Holland, and who, happening to want an understrapping quill-driver, did me the honour to take me into his service, and the next day saw me perched upon a great high stool, in an obscure chamber in Gray's Inn, endeavouring to decipher the crabbed draughts of my employer.

" I could write a good plain hand, but I could not read the pot-hooks and hangers of Mr. Holland. He was a month in learning me to copy without almost continual assistance, and even then I was of but little use to him; for, besides that I wrote a snail's pace, my want of knowledge in orthography gave him infinite trouble: so that for the first two months I was a dead weight upon his hands. Time, however, rendered me useful, and Mr. Holland was pleased to tell me that he was very well satisfied with me, just at the very moment when I began to grow extremely dissatisfied with him.

" No part of my life has been totally unattended with pleasure, except the eight or nine months I passed in Gray's Inn. The office (for so the dungeon, where I wrote, was called) was so dark, that on cloudy days, we were obliged to burn candles. I worked like a galley-slave from five in the morning till eight or nine at night, and sometimes all night long. How many quarrels have I assisted to foment and perpetuate between those poor innocent fellows, John Doe and Richard Roe! How many times (God forgive me!) have I set them to assault each other with guns, swords, staves, and pitch-forks, and then brought them to answer for their misdeeds before our sovereign Lord the King seated in his Court of Westminster? When I think of the saids and soforths, and the counts of tautology that I scribbled over; when I think of those sheets of seventy-two words, and those lines two inches apart, my brain turns. Gracious Heaven! if I am doomed to be wretched, bury me beneath Iceland snows, and let me feed on blubber; stretch me under the burning line and deny me thy propitious dews; nay, if it be thy will, suffocate me with the infected and pestilential air of a democratic club-room; but save me, O save me from the desk of a pettifogging attorney!

" Mr. Holland was but little in the chambers himself. He always went out to dinner, while I was left to be provided for by the *laundress*, as he called her. Those gentlemen of the law, who have resided in the inns of court in London, know very well what a *laundress* means. Ours was, I believe, the oldest and ugliest of the officious sisterhood. She had age and experience enough to be Lady Abbess of all the nuns in all the convents of Irish-Town. It would be wronging the witch of Endor to compare her to this hag, who was the only creature that deigned to enter into conversation with me. All except the name, I was in prison, and this Weird Sister was my keeper. Our chambers were to me, what the subterraneous cavern was to Gil Blas: his description of the Dame Leonarda exactly suited my Laundress ; nor were the professions, or rather the practice, of our masters altogether dissimilar.

"I never quitted this gloomy recess except on Sundays, when I usually took a walk to St. James's Park, to feast my eyes with the sight of the trees, the grass, and the water. In one of these walks I happened to cast my eye on an advertisement, inviting all loyal young men, who had a mind to gain riches and glory, to repair to a certain rendezvous, where they might enter into his Majesty's marine service, and have the peculiar happiness and honour of being enrolled in the Chatham Division. I was not ignorant enough to be the dupe of this morsel of military bombast ; but a change was what I wanted ; besides, I knew that marines went to sea, and my desire to be on that element had rather increased than diminished by my being penned up in London. In short, I resolved to join this glorious corps ; and, to avoid all possibility of being discovered by my friends, I went down to Chatham, and enlisted into the marines as I thought, but the next morning I found myself before a captain of a marching regiment. There was no retreating : I had taken a shilling to drink his Majesty's health, and his further bounty was ready for my reception.

"When I told the captain (who was an Irishman, and who has since been an excellent friend to me) that I thought myself engaged in the marines : ' By Jasus, my lad,' said he, ' and you have had a narrow escape.' He told me that the regiment into which I had been so happy as to enlist was one of the oldest and boldest in the whole army, and that it was at that moment serving in that fine, flourishing, and plentiful country, Nova Scotia. He dwelt long on the beauties and riches of this terrestrial Paradise, and dismissed me, perfectly enchanted with the prospect of a voyage thither."

CHAPTER II.

"WHEN I HAD THE HONOUR TO WEAR A RED COAT."

FROM the point of view which Englishmen usually take, in speaking of success in life, it may remain an open question as to whether the hero of this story ever really attained it. But let such question be narrowed down to a point, from which is excluded all notions of wealth, and personal aggrandizement : the placing of one's feet upon a given spot from which others have been ousted—the thing becomes clearer. The attainment of objects upon which one has set the heart, from time to time, can alone be called SUCCESS.

Now, this reflection is hazarded, because it is necessary for the reader of William Cobbett's history to observe a leading feature in his character, from this stage onward ; consisting in what may be called the instinct of discipline. Money-making (as such) was ever with him a process which he treated with contempt ; the whole future, as it stood before him year after year, was to promise only the comfort of his family, and the welfare of his countrymen. All the blunders which he committed, in the untiring pursuit of this twofold object, were the result of undue impetuosity, the rashness of the soldier in the heat of strife : the temporary derangement of discipline, in the rear of a discomfited enemy. But in spite of ridicule and opposition, and long-deferred anticipation, and, besides, slanders of the foulest character, one after another were the dearest wishes of his heart fulfilled ; and at seventy years of age he could write :—

"I HAVE LED THE HAPPIEST LIFE OF ANY MAN THAT I HAVE EVER KNOWN. NEVER DID I KNOW ONE SINGLE MOMENT WHEN I WAS CAST DOWN ; NEVER ONE MOMENT WHEN I DREADED THE FUTURE."

So, if we think of the soldier's career ; what it is for the idle and the devil-may-care ; what it is to the mere adventurer ; what it is to the drudge ; and what it is, as a last resource, to the outlaw ; and, then, what it is to him who deliberately makes it a school of self-discipline, then we shall have some likelihood of understanding why this man, only twenty years after leaving the plough-tail, had become the Mentor of English statesmen, and wielded a pen so powerful that no price could buy it.

It cannot be said, however, that there had been any want of parental control in the little household at Farnham. In the foregoing chapter are clearly to be found traces, on the part of Cobbett's father, of his duty in this respect; and to the gentle discipline of home must be ascribed the readiness, with which the sterner apprenticeship of army life was undertaken. All the sons of George Cobbett did well in after-life. Whilst this WILLIAM, going into a rougher school than his brothers, and submitting for a term to its rough lessons, not only with a good grace, but with a happy foresight, distances them all.

His own testimony to the quality of his early moral training is, by-the-bye, worth quoting :—

" When in the army I was often tempted to take up the cards. But the words of my father came into my mind, and rescued me from the peril. . . . . During this part of my life I lived amongst, and was compelled to associate with, the most beastly of drunkards, where liquor was so cheap, that even a soldier might be drunk every day; yet I never, during the whole time, even *tasted* of that liquor: my father's, and especially my mother's precepts were always at hand to protect me."

But there is one other factor to be taken into

account. It seems that among his few acquaintances in London, was a young man who could give him friendly counsel, from a superior social standpoint; and consequently, with a far better knowledge of the world upon which they were both emerging ;[1] and Cobbett declares that it was to his advice that he owed all that he ever possessed beyond the lot of a common soldier. For after the enlistment,—

" Upon being informed by me of what I had done, he began his answer to me in somewhat these words :— 'Now then, my dear Bill, it is for you to determine whether you shall, all your life, yield an abject submission to others, or whether you yourself shall be a guider and leader of men. Nature has done her part toward you most generously ; but her favours will be of no avail without a knowledge of grammar. Without that knowledge you will be laughed at by blockheads ; with it, you may laugh at thousands who think themselves learned men.' The letter was long, full of urgent recommendation, and seasoned with the kindest of ex-

[1] This was Mr. Benjamin Garlike, who afterwards became envoy to two or three foreign courts. He died in 1815, unmarried, ætat. forty-nine. For a notice of him, *vide Gent. Mag.* lxxxv. 564. Cobbett met him again, when in the full tide of fame, and says that "he had lived so long in courts, had so long had to do with superior power, and had so long lived in submission to the mandates of others, that he became nervous when he heard my ordinary talk, about men in place and authority."

pressions, all which I knew to be sincere. I was, at
that time, much more intent upon the beauty of my
cap and feathers, than upon anything else; but, upon
seeing my friend afterwards to take leave of him, he
renewed his advice in such a strain as to make a
thorough impression upon me ; and I set about my study
in good earnest."

Not, then, of mere chance, nor even because he
possessed certain advantages in the shape of a
robust, elastic frame, and a healthy mind therein
dwelling, did this man eventually put such a powerful shoulder to the wheel of liberty. Without the
personal influence of his noble peasant-father, the
affectionate firmness of his friend, the soldier's round
of duty cheerily performed, and supplemented by
self-discipline, these natural advantages were value-
less ; and he no leader and guider of men !

The year 1784 opened, with England at peace.
The American States had achieved independence,
or as it is sometimes euphemistically put, King
George had granted it to them. Soldiers were
getting their discharge, or were being sent out to
colonize New Brunswick. Recruiting was comparatively sluggish work, and there was little need to
complement the full strength of regiments on
foreign stations. The 54th, that in which William

Cobbett found himself, was then serving in Nova Scotia, whilst the depôt was in garrison at Chatham; and here he remained about a year. Of this life at Chatham, learning his drill, &c., there are abundant materials for a picture, as Cobbett never tired of referring to this period, when in after-years he would, again and again, point a moral from his own career. The story was told at seventy years of age, to the young men of England, as it had been told to his irritated American neighbours, in 1796.

" My leisure time, which was a very considerable portion of the twenty-four hours, was spent, not in the dissipation common to such a way of life, but in reading and study. In the course of this year I learnt more than I had ever done before. I subscribed to a circulating library at Brompton, the greatest part of the books in which I read more than once over. The library was not very considerable, it is true, nor in my reading was I directed by any degree of taste or choice. Novels, plays, history, poetry, all were read, and nearly with equal avidity.[2] Such a course of reading could be attended

---

[2] Some clever *lecturer* has said that " he had but little knowledge of books, and even less of other men's thoughts." We find, however, in " Porcupine's Works " (1794—1800), quotations from, or references to, Swift, Shaftesbury, Pope, Sterne, Butler, Dryden, Shakespeare, Somerville, Racine, Montesquieu, Le Sage, Cervantes, Congreve, and Bishop Watson, besides minor names. But such is the way of these clever historical lecturers—cooking a man's reputation in their own pot, and taking the skimmings for truth.

with but little profit : it was skimming over the surface
of everything.   One branch of learning, however, I went
to the bottom with, and that the most essential branch
too, the grammar of my mother-tongue.   I had experienced the want of a knowledge of grammar during my
stay with Mr. Holland; but it is very probable that I
never should have thought of encountering the study of
it, had not accident placed me under a man whose friendship extended beyond his interest.

" Writing a fair hand procured me the honour of being
copyist to Colonel Debbieg, the commandant of the
garrison.   I transcribed the famous correspondence
between him and the Duke of Richmond, which ended
in the good and gallant old colonel being stripped of the
reward bestowed on him for his long and meritorious
servitude.[3]   Being totally ignorant of the rules of

[3] Colonel Debbieg was himself no ordinary man, and had seen
active service in various parts of the world.   He entered the army
in 1746, at the age of fourteen, served in the Low Countries, and
afterwards in North America under General Wolfe, whose friendship and entire confidence he soon acquired.   He was gazetted
Colonel-Commandant of the Engineers early in 1783, but retired in
a year or two ; gazetted Major-General, 1798, General 1803.   He
died in 1810, at an advanced age, having employed his retirement in
ingenious studies in fortification.   The circumstance in the text
refers to certain letters of Debbieg (who was a high-spirited fellow)
which were addressed to his superior officer, the Duke of Richmond,
then Master-General of the Ordnance.   The Duke took offence, and
demanded a court-martial on Debbieg, " for using indecent and dis-
respectful expressions towards him, and injurious and groundless
expressions imputing partiality and oppression in the discharge of
his duty."   The Colonel was found guilty, and reprimanded in open
court, and ordered to apologize to the Duke, which he did, and his
arrest was then terminated.   It is pretty clear that this affair, how-

grammar, I necessarily made many mistakes in copying, because no one can copy letter by letter, nor even word by word. The colonel saw my deficiency, and strongly recommended study. He enforced his advice with a sort of injunction, and with a promise of reward in case of success. I procured me a Lowth's grammar, and applied myself to the study of it with unceasing assiduity, and not without some profit, for, though it was a considerable time before I fully comprehended all that I read, still I read and studied with such unremitted attention, that, at last, I could write without falling into any very gross errors. The pains I took cannot be described; I wrote the whole grammar out two or three times; I got it by heart; I repeated it every morning and every evening, and, when on guard, I imposed on myself the task of saying it all over once every time I was posted sentinel. To this exercise of my memory I ascribed the retentiveness of which I have since found it capable, and to the success with which it was attended, I ascribe the perseverance that has led to the acquirement of the little learning of which I am master. This study was, too, attended with another advantage: it kept me out of mischief. I was always sober and regular in my attend-

ever, did him no injury ; and it is not unlikely that there was some ground for the "expressions" which he had used. No doubt the members of the court felt bound to protect the Duke in his official character, even if they thought that Colonel Debbieg had right on his side ; and Cobbett must have very early learnt that military discipline did not always go along with even-handed justice. The sequel will show what opinion he acquired concerning the impartiality of military courts.

ance ; and not being a clumsy fellow, I met with none of those reproofs which disgust so many young men with the service."

These efforts at self-education would be wonderful enough, in a person surrounded with the comforts of life, but when we recollect what the life of a private soldier was, until very recently, with the temptations presented by poverty, and by dissolute associates, and by the almost utter want of sympathy between the soldier and his aristocratic superiors, the extreme difficulty of the case is evident.

" Of my sixpence nothing like fivepence was left to purchase food for the day. Indeed not fourpence. For there was washing, mending, soap, flour for hair-powder, shoes, stockings, shirts, stocks and gaiters, pipe-clay and several other things, all to come out of the miserable sixpence ! . . . . The whole week's food was not a bit too much for one day. It is not disaffection, it is not a want of fidelity to oaths, that makes soldiers desert, one time out of ten thousand ; it is hunger, which will break through stone walls ; and which will, therefore, break through oaths and the danger of punishment. We had several recruits from Norfolk (our regiment was the West Norfolk) ; and many of them deserted from sheer hunger. They were lads from the plough-tail. All of them tall ; for no short men were then taken. I remember two that went into a decline and died during the year; though when they joined us they were fine hearty young men. I have seen them lay in their berths, many and many a time, actually crying on account of hunger.

"The edge of my berth, or that of the guard-bed, was my seat to study in ; my knapsack was my book-case ; a bit of board lying on my lap was my writing-table. . . . . I had no money to purchase candle or oil; in winter-time it was rarely that I could get any evening light but that of the fire ; and only *my turn* even of that. . . . . To buy a pen or a sheet of paper I was compelled to forego some portion of food, though in a state of half-starvation : I had no moment of time that I could call my own; and I had to read and to write amidst the talking, laughing, singing, whistling, and brawling of at least half a score of the most thoughtless of men, and that, too, in the hours of their freedom from all control. Think not lightly of the *farthing* that I had to give, now and then, for ink, pen, or paper. That farthing was, alas ! a great sum to me. I was as tall as I am now; I had great health and great exercise. The whole of the money, not expended for us at market, was *twopence a week* for each man. I remember (and well I may !) that upon one occasion I, after all absolutely necessary expenses, had, on a Friday, made shift to have a halfpenny in reserve, which I had destined for the purchase of a red-herring in the morning ; but, when I pulled off my clothes at night, so hungry then as to be hardly able to endure life, I found that I had lost my halfpenny ! I

buried my head under the miserable sheet and rug, and
cried like a child."

And yet the life had its amenities.   Tender
recollections come up, when he visits Chatham
again, nearly forty years after, of the pretty girls of
his "cap-and-feather days."   How they evinced a
sincere desire to smooth the inequalities of life ; and
particularly to serve out the beer more fairly than
their masters or husbands.   His superior officers,
too, inspired him with a certain amount of respect
and affection ; whilst the Colonel's discovery of the
willing horse was, undoubtedly, a fount of pleasure
and gratification to the young recruit.

Cobbett tells, somewhere, of a poor little
drummer-boy who gambled.   He gambled away
all his pay, his shirts, his stockings, and all his
necessaries, even to his loaf, which was served out
to him twice a week.   At last, to prevent him from
begging through the streets of Rochester and Chatham, the men were compelled to take his loaf from
him, to serve it out a slice at a time, and to see that
he ate it.   Here is about the lowest depth of
degradation to which a private soldier could
descend ; but the moralist will see, in this anecdote,
only one other instance in which the weight or the
deficiency of moral stamina is dependent, whether
in private soldier or in prince, upon the habit of

mind acquired in childhood. Beneath the parental roof must the parental duty be done; no "prayer," and no idle talk of reliance on providence (so very, very often put forth, when only a plea for laziness and indifference) will avail, unless the dictates of common prudence are heeded, and a straight-forward principle, in example, daily shown. The riff-raff of society, in all grades, is composed of those whose childhood was neglected.

Early in 1785, a detachment from the depôt at Chatham was forwarded to head-quarters, and the event is thus described in the autobiography :—

"There is no situation where merit is so sure to meet with reward as in a well-disciplined army. Those who command are obliged to reward it for their own ease and credit. I was soon raised to the rank of corporal ; a rank which, however contemptible it may appear in some people's eyes, brought me in a clear twopence *per diem*, and put a very clever worsted knot upon my shoulder too. . . . . As promotion began to dawn, I grew impatient to get to my regiment, where I expected soon to bask under the rays of Royal favour. The happy day of departure at last came : we set sail from Graves-end, and, after a short and pleasant passage, arrived at Halifax in Nova Scotia. When I first beheld the barren, not to say hideous, rocks at the entrance of the harbour, I began to fear that the master of the vessel had mistaken his way; for I could perceive nothing of that fertility that my good recruiting captain had dwelt on with so much delight.

"Nova Scotia had no other charm for me than that of novelty. Everything I saw was new : bogs, rocks, and stumps, mosquitoes and bull-frogs. Thousands of captains and colonels without soldiers, and of squires without stockings or shoes. . . . . We stayed but a few weeks in Nova Scotia, being ordered to St. John's, in the province of New Brunswick. Here, and at other places in the same province, we remained till the month of September, 1791, when the regiment was relieved, and sent home."

Cobbett repeatedly declared, in after-life, that during these eight years he was never accused of the slightest fault. As his numerous opponents, in all their violence and unscrupulousness, never succeeded in raking up anything, in the smallest degree, derogatory to his high character as a soldier, the statement is, probably, as perfectly true as need be. But he also boasts that he never wilfully disobeyed his father or his mother. These two things are so interdependent (in the mind of the biographer), that the reader must once more be recalled to the idea presented in the early part of this chapter, of the prominence due to the illustrious results of self-discipline. An idea, which is *only* an idea with the great majority of mankind, to their latest hour. An idea, which gains prominence in some minds only just in time to enable them to warn their younger fellows, of the certain consequences of its neglect. An idea, which is eagerly embraced by some few, who, by a happy inspiration, note that the world has been led and guided, and governed, by the men who first put the bit and the bridle upon their own unruly selves.

So William Cobbett goes to his regiment. And while others are swilling, or gambling, or idling, he is continually training. Rapid promotion is the result. At the end of little more than a year, he is Sergeant-Major, having been placed in that proud position over the heads of fifty other sergeants.

While, however, he was only corporal, he was made clerk of the regiment, a post which brought him in an immensity of labour, a great deal of which was due to the ignorance or unworthiness of his superior officers. The studies, too, were not neglected :—

"I was studying at one and the same time, Dr. Lowth's *Grammar*, Dr. Watts's *Logic*, the *Rhetoric* of some fellow whom I have forgotten, a book on *Geometry*, ... Vauban's *Fortifications*, and (*ex-officio*) the famous Duke of York's *Military Exercise and Evolutions*, explaining these latter by ground-plans. . . . . Never did these cause me to neglect my duty in one single particular; a duty of almost every hour in the day, from daylight till nine o'clock at night." . . . . "When I was sergeant-major . . . . I found time to study *French* and *Fortification*. My *chef-d'œuvre* in the latter was the plan of a regular sexagon with every description of outwork. When I had finished my plan, on a small scale, and in the middle of a very large piece of drawing-paper, I set to work to lay down the plan of a siege, made my line of circumvallation, fixed my batteries and cantonments, opened my trenches, made my approaches, covered by my gabions and fascines,—at last effected a mine, and had all prepared for blowing up the citadel." . . . . "When I was in the army, I made, for the teaching of young corporals and sergeants, a little book on *arithmetic;* and it is truly surprising in how short a time they learned all that was necessary for them to know of that necessary department of learning. I used to make each of them copy the book."

Those were days when a man might rise above the rank-and-file.[4]   Cobbett himself had the pro-

[4] "When I was in the army, the Adjutant-general, Sir William Fawcett, had been a private soldier; General Slater, who had then recently commanded the Guards in London, had been a private soldier; Colonel Picton, whom I saw at the head of his fine regiment (the 12th, at Chatham) had been a private soldier; Captain Green, who first had the command of me, had been a private soldier. In the garrison of Halifax there were no less than seventeen officers that had been private soldiers. In my own regiment the quarter-master had been a private soldier; the adjutant, who

mise of an ensigncy, when he came to make application for his discharge. As a matter of course, such officers, through their skill, prudence, and general knowledge, became the crack men of their regiments; the best practically-instructed men, perhaps, in the army. For the rest, the average officer must have been a curious make-up; sent into the army, often as early as fourteen years of age—without any special training—he was there for his social position ; and, except when on active service, passed a frivolous sort of existence; often so ignorant of his professional duties (*i. e.* everything beyond daily routine) that they were habitually shirked, excepting when the colonel was a Tartar, or when a clever *factotum* could be found among his subordinates.

Such a *factotum* was the new clerk to the 54th regiment :—

"In a very short time, the whole of the business, in that way, fell into my hands ; and at the end of about a year, neither adjutant, paymaster, or quartermaster, could move an inch without my assistance. The *military* part of the regiment's affairs fell under my care in like manner. About this time, the new *discipline*, as it was

was also a lieutenant, had been a private soldier. No man of sense need be told what powerful motive there was here for good conduct in the soldiers."

called : (that is to say, the mode of handling the musket, and of marching, &c., called *Dundas's System*) was sent out to us, in little books, which were to be studied by the officers of each regiment, and the rules of which were to be immediately conformed to. Though any old woman might have written such a book, though it was excessively foolish from beginning to end, still it was to be complied with ; it ordered and commanded a total change, and this change was to be completed before the next annual review took place. To make this change was left to me, who was not then twenty [24] years of age, while not a single officer in the regiment paid the least attention to the matter; so, that when the time came for the annual review, I, then a *corporal*, had to give lectures of instruction to the officers themselves, the colonel not excepted ; and, for several of them, if not for all of them, I had to make out, upon large cards which they bought for the purpose, little plans of the position of the regiment, together with lists of the words of command, which they had to give in the field. . . . There was I, at the review, upon the flank of the grenadier company, with my worsted shoulder-knots, and my great, high, coarse, hairy cap, confounded in the ranks amongst other men, while those who were commanding me to move my hands or my feet, thus or thus, were, in fact uttering words which I had taught them; and were, in everything excepting mere authority, my inferiors, and ought to have been commanded by me."

Several references to this period are made in the " Advice to Young Men ;" and need not be reproduced here. But the following racy story (from the " Political Register" of Dec. 1817) must be laid under contribution to illustrate this period of Cobbett's life.

"The accounts and letters of the Paymaster went through my hands, or, rather, I was the maker of them. All the returns, reports, and other official papers were of my drawing up. Then I became the sergeant-major to the regiment, which brought me in close contact at every hour, with the whole of the *epaulet* gentry, whose profound and surprising ignorance I discovered in a twinkling. But I had a very delicate part to act with these gentry; for, while I despised them for their gross ignorance and vanity, and hated them for their drunkenness and rapacity, I was fully sensible of their *power ;* and I knew also the envy which my sudden rise over the heads of so many old sergeants had created. My path was full of rocks and pit-falls ; and, as I never disguised my dislikes or restrained my tongue, I should have been broken and flogged for fifty different offences, given to my supreme jackasses, had they not been kept in awe by my inflexible sobriety, impartiality, and integrity, by the consciousness of their inferiority to me, and by the real and almost indispensable necessity of the use of my talents. First, I had, by my skill and by my everlasting vigilance, eased them all of the trouble of even *thinking* about their duty; and this made me their master,—a situation in which, however, I acted with so much prudence, that it was impossible for them, with any show of justice, to find fault. They, in fact, resigned all the discipline of the regiment to me, and I very freely left them to swagger about, and to get roaring drunk out of the profits of their pillage, though I was, at the same time, making preparations for bringing them to justice for that pillage, in which I was finally defeated by the protection which they received at home.

" To describe the various instances of their ignorance, and the various tricks they played to disguise it from me, would fill a volume. It is the custom in regiments to give out *orders* every day from the officer commanding. These are written by the adjutant, to whom the sergeant-major is a sort of deputy. The man whom I had to do with was a keen fellow, but wholly illiterate. The orders, which he wrote, most cruelly murdered our mother tongue. But, in his absence, or during a severe drunken fit, it fell to my lot to write orders. As we both wrote in the same book, he used to look at these. He saw *commas, semi-colons, colons, full-points,* and *paragraphs.* The questions he used to put to me, in an obscure sort of way, in order to know why I made these divisions, and yet, at the same time, his attempts to disguise his object, have made me laugh a thousand times. As I often had to draw up statements of considerable length, and as these were so much in the style and manner of a *book,* and so much unlike anything he had ever seen before in man's handwriting, he, at last, fell upon this device : he made *me* write, while he pretended *to dictate!* Imagine to yourself me sittting, pen in hand, to put upon paper the precious offspring of the mind of this stupid curmudgeon ! But here a greater difficulty than any former arose. He that could not *write* good grammar, could not, of course, *dictate* good grammar. Out would come some gross error, such as I was ashamed to see in my handwriting. I would stop; suggest another arrangement; but this I was, at first, obliged to do in a very indirect and delicate manner. I dared not let him perceive that I saw, or suspected his ignorance; and, though we made sad work of it, we got along without any very sanguinary assaults upon mere grammar. But this course could not continue long, and he put an end to it in this way: he used to tell me *his story*, and leave me to put it upon paper; and thus we continued to the end of our connexion.

" He played me a trick upon one occasion, which was more ridiculous than anything else, but which will serve to show how his ignorance placed him at my mercy. It will also serve to show a little about Commissioners sent out by the Government. There were three or four Commissioners sent out to examine into the state of the provinces of Nova Scotia and New Brunswick. Their business was of a very extensive nature. They were to inquire into the number of the people, the extent of their settlements, the provisions expended upon them, and a great variety of other matters. Upon all these several heads they were to make *a Report*, and to subjoin to it a detail in figures. It required great ingenuity to frame these tables of figures, to bring the rude and undigested materials under general heads, dividing themselves into more particular sections, and then again subdividing themselves, and so on, and showing, at last, a sort of total, or result of the whole. To frame this appendix to the Report, and to execute in any moderate space of paper required a *head*, an *eye*, and a *hand ;* and to draw up *the Report itself* was a task of a still superior order. The Commissioners, the name of one of whom was Dundas. . . . who or what he was besides, I know not; and I have forgotten the names of the rest. But they closed their work at Fredericton in New Brunswick, where I was with my regiment. As the arrival of every stranger was an excuse for a roaring drunk with our heroes, so this ceremony now took place. But the Commissioners had their *Report* to make. And what did my ass of an adjutant do, *but offer to do it for them !* They, who in all likelihood, did not know how to do it themselves, took him at his word; and there was he, in the sweetest mess that ever vain pretender was placed in. He wanted to get some favour from these Commissioners, and relied upon me, not only to perform the task, but to keep the secret. But then, the part he had to act now was full of difficulty. The Report of these fellows was no concern of mine. It could not, by any contrivance, be hooked in amongst my *duties.* He therefore talked to me, at first in a sort of ambiguous manner. He said that the Commissioners wanted him to do it,—and, d——n them, he would not do it for them. Then, when I saw him again, he *asked* me something about it, showing me their rude mass of papers at the same time. I now began to find what he would be at ; but I affected not to understand him, turned the matter as soon as I could, and so we parted. At this time I had long been waiting to go and see an old farmer and his family, and to shoot wild pigeons in the woods ; and, as the distance was great, and a companion on the journey necessary, I wanted a sergeant to go with me. The leave to do this had been put off for a good while, and the adjutant knew that I had the thing at heart. What does he do now, but come to me, and after talking about the Report again, affect to lament, that he should be so much engaged with it, that there was no hope of my being permitted to go on *my frolic*, till he had finished the Report. I, who knew very well what this meant, began to be very anxious for this *finishing*, to effect which I knew there was but one way. Tacked on to the pigeon-shooting the report became an object of importance, and I said, '*Perhaps I can do something*, sir, in putting the papers in order for you.' That was enough, Away he went, brought me the whole mass, and tossing them down upon the table : ' There,' said he, ' do what you like with them; for, d——n the rubbish, I have no patience with it !' Rubbish it really was, if we looked only at the rude manner of the papers ; but the matter would to me, at this day, have been very interesting. I d——d the papers as heartily as he did, and with better reason ; but they were to bring me my week's frolic; and, as I entered into everything with ardour, this pigeon-shooting frolic, at the age of about 23 [27], was more than a compensation for all the toil of this Report and its appendix. To work I went, and with the assistance of my shooting-companion sergeant, who called over the figures to me, I had the appendix completed in rough draft, in two days and one night. Having the detail before me, the Report was short work, and the whole was soon completed. But before a *neat copy* was made out, the thing had to be shown to the Commissioners. It would not do to show it them in my handwriting. The adjutant got over this difficulty by copying the report; and having shown it, and had it highly applauded,—'Well then,' said he, 'here sergeant-major, *go and make a fair copy.*' This was the most shameless thing that I ever witnessed. This report and appendix, though I hated the job, were, such was my habit of doing everything well, executed with so much neatness and accuracy, that the Duke of Kent, who afterwards became Commander-in-chief in those provinces, and who was told of this report, which was in his office at Halifax, had a copy of it made to be kept in the office, and carried the original with him to England as a curiosity; and of this fact he informed me himself. The duke, from some source or other, had heard that it was I who had been the penman upon this occasion, though I had never mentioned it to anybody. It drew forth a great deal of admiration at Fredericton, and the Lieutenant-governor, General Carleton,⁸ asked me in plain terms, whether it was I who had drawn up the Report. The adjutant had told me

⁸ General Carleton, a "very wise, mild, and just man," as Cobbett said of him. The General, many years afterwards, renewed acquaintance with his quondam subaltern. He was created Baron Dorchester in 1786.

that I *need not say* but it was he, *because* he had promised
to do it himself. I was not satisfied with his logic; but
the pigeon-shooting made me say, that I certainly would
say it was done by him if any one should ask me. And
I kept my word with him; for, as I could not give the
question of the governor the *go-by*, I told him a lie at
once, and said it was the adjutant. However, I lied in
vain; for, when I came to Halifax, in my way from the
United States to England, *ten years* afterwards, I found
that the real truth was known to a number of persons,
though the thing had wholly gone out of my mind; and
after my then late pursuits, and the transactions of real
magnitude in which I had been concerned, I was quite
surprised that anybody should have attached any importance to so trifling a thing."

It appears that the Duke of Kent, who was
Commander-in-chief at that station a few years
later, was one of the "persons" who got wind
of this affair; and in 1800, when Cobbett was
returning to England the second time, the Duke
saw him, and showed that he had kept the
veritable copy as a curiosity, having had it transcribed for the use of the Governor. Further—

"When I told him the whole story, he asked me *how*
much the Commissioners gave me; and when I told him
not a farthing, he exclaimed most bitterly, and said that
thousands of pounds had, first and last, been paid by
the country for what I had done."

It must be noted, too, that there were individual cases of benefit arising from the example of our very smart sergeant. Several men caught the "grammar"-fever, whilst an increasing zeal appeared, in the performance of duty, on the part of many of his comrades. So far, indeed, that his services to the regiment were at last recognized in public orders. When the regiment was relieved and sent home in the autumn of 1791, Cobbett applied for his discharge; which he obtained, accompanied by a flattering testimonial from his major,⁶ to his "good behaviour, and the services he had rendered the regiment."

And, with all his duties, Cobbett found time for his share of sports ; skating, fishing, shooting, and even gardening, took some portion of his hours of liberty. He could work, and he could play, but could never be idle for a minute.

It must have been in the year 1787, when Cobbett was about twenty-five years of age, that he first saw his future wife. She was the daughter

---

⁶ Major Lord Edward Fitzgerald. Cobbett declared that Fitzgerald was a really conscientious and humane man. He makes repeated testimony to this effect. In point of fact, he was one of the most amiable of men, besides a very promising young officer. His unfortunate end, a few years after this period, is matter of history. (*Vide* his "Life," by Thomas Moore.)

of an artilleryman, and then only about thirteen, and, although so very young, won the heart of our sergeant in a twinkling. Her character, too, had been moulded by careful and untiring parents; and when the lover came by, there was the promise of a genuine helpmeet for one, who required in that respect a woman of unquestioned propriety, of great industry, and of unfailing discretion. How quickly he prospered, and the whole story of his courtship, with the one great risk that it ran of being annulled, is all told in the "Advice to a Lover;" suffice it to say here, that not only was there never a moment's regret, but that Cobbett, to the last day of his life laid all his fame and all the earthly prosperity which he had enjoyed, to the happy choice which he had made in his wife. The first trial came, early enough in the history of the affair, to be a real trial, when the artillery were sent home, and carried the sergeant's hopes along with them, besides 140 or 150 guineas of his savings in the girl's pocket.

CHAPTER III.

"I HAVE ALWAYS SHOWN MY ENMITY TO EVERY SPECIES OF PUBLIC FRAUD OR ROBBERY."

SEVEN years of army-life had completed the drill of William Cobbett. Master of himself, in every sense of the word, his campaign was now to begin. Putting off his red-coat, of which he had been proud enough withal, he entered upon the last stage of that educational process which, sooner or later, was to bear some fruit. He had studied men in the world of books, and he had seen something of them in the circumscribed arena of one class, viz. the military. But of mankind as a whole he knew almost nothing: and he would blunder on, for long years, before getting that sort of wisdom.

However, he came back from Nova Scotia with two closely-linked ideas uppermost in his mind—an intense affection for the soldiery and for the classes from which they were drawn, and the deepest disgust at the peculation which added to their natural privations. He had never read the newspapers, and was ignorant of politics; he did not know that the public service was at that period eaten into by corruption as far up as the Treasury Bench, and that the specimens of venality that he had witnessed were only examples of a system that pervaded all classes of officialism. In point of fact, he did not know that returning to England and obtaining his discharge, with the determination to expose peculation, he had set his foot upon a track which would in after-years give him the distinction of having mainly contributed to the disgrace, the utter confusion, of "the race that plunder the people." Beyond all, he did not know that, far from getting any credit from any soul upon earth, the sure reward for raking up the misdeeds of the "public plunderers" was contumely and malignity to the bitterest degree.

The first thing, of course, which Cobbett attended to upon reaching England in December, 1791, was his love affair with ANN REID. He found her in service, with his money unbroken; and "admiration of her conduct, and self-gratulation on this indubitable proof of the soundness of my own judgment, were now added to my love of her beautiful person." So that matter was settled, from that moment, and on the 5th of February, 1792, they were married at Woolwich. They appear to have lived in London for a few weeks. Here is one anecdote of the period—

" I was about two months in London; and some one led me to spend two or three evenings in the week at Coachmakers' Hall, where there was a debating society[1] that held its regular sittings. The 'Cruelties of the Slave Trade' was the standing subject; it was the fashionable cant of the day; the country was in peace and in great prosperity, and this was a sort of overflowing of the idle feelings of the nation. The hall used to be crowded to excess, and with as many women as men. It did not require much talent to be eloquent upon such a subject, especially as there was perfect *freedom as to facts*, and as to *contradiction*, that was nearly as much as a man's life was worth. . . . . In consequence of the *intense* oratory of the Coachmakers' Hall, and of little lying books, and delightfully-disgusting pictures . . . my *wisdom* decided that my wife and I should never more use sugar or coffee, these being, as the orators assured me, highly impregnated with the sweat and blood of the poor blacks."

The young couple adhered to this resolve until some time after they had settled in Philadelphia.

---

[1] This was The Society of Free Debate, one of several which had just been set on foot. For some interesting particulars of these societies *vide* " Memoirs of John Thelwall " (London, 1837).

The debating societies in London had other subjects, too, to occupy their minds; the progress of the French Revolution 'having strongly excited the popular mind. In May a proclamation was issued against meetings and seditious writings, and as the year went on there was increasing ferment. Although the country was at peace, His Majesty's ministers were really contemplating war against France; and the Government had enough on its hands, endeavouring, at one and the same time, to quell these feelings and to humour the military and naval forces. It was found necessary, early in the year, to make some important changes in the Navy Victualling Department, in consequence of wholesale corruption, and prostitution of the public money, being unexpectedly brought to light.[2] The sister service had also its grievances, a stringent warrant having been issued regulating the soldiers' equipment, and reprobating extravagance and waste.[3] In February, a curious item appeared in the discussion on the estimates of the year, in the shape of an additional allowance to the soldiers' pay, which was distinctly a bait thrown out to humour the private soldier, victim of the said extravagance or something

[2] *Public Advertiser*, April 10, 1792.
[3] *Scots Magazine*, Jan., 1792.

worse.—Concerning which item in the estimates we shall see presently.

Meanwhile, William Cobbett was spending his honeymoon in completing the plans he had designed several years before, for bringing certain officers of the 54th Regiment before a court-martial. And, as to the history of this affair, we must have full details, because we cannot otherwise see very clearly how he came to fail in this his first on-slaught upon public fraud.

Rapid writers have been content to say that he was bought off; that he carefully avoided all reference to the affair ; that no trace of any allusion to it occurs in his subsequent writings ; that there was something unpleasant which would tell against himself, and so he stopped short, &c. Indeed, the paragraph-monger began it ; for the *London Chronicle* of the 28th March, after mentioning the holding of the court-martial, adds that "the person who was to have prosecuted the above officers was formerly sergeant-major of the regiment. It is said that he has fled to France on account of some misconduct."

No such thing at all, paragraph-monger ! And, no such things at all, ye rapid writers ! You don't know this man. You don't know how he retires from the unequal conflict with money, prescription,

aristocratic influence. Let him flee from anticipated vengeance, and see him return one day,
himself always incorruptible, with such a budget,
such a quiverful!—come back and tell you, with
absolute calmness, that he lays his account with
" being calumniated, and with being the object of the
bitterest and most persevering malice." And why?
Because he has made the war upon CORRUPTION
his own particular business, and has found out that
the cruelties which wounded his earnest soul, in
those hapless Nova Scotia days, were just part of a
system which was sapping his country's strength.
No part nor lot would he have in it. And, rather
than seem to support it, he has spurned brilliant
offers, which would have made him rich and high-
stomached; and has chosen the part, the reward of
which is calumny and annoyance of every description. See how he glories, at last, in the conflict,
and how fully he knows the nature of his foe :—

"No sooner does a man become in any degree formidable to her ['corruption'], than she sets to work
against him in all the relationships of life. In his profession, his trade, his family; amongst his friends, the
companions of his sports, his neighbours, and his servants. She eyes him all round, she feels him all over,
and if he has a vulnerable point, if he has a speck,
however small, she is ready with her stab. How many

hundreds of men have been ruined by her without being hardly able to perceive, much less name, the cause ; and how many thousands, seeing the fate of these hundreds have withdrawn from the struggle, or have been deterred from taking part in it ! "

In the year 1809, Mr. Cobbett was at about the zenith of his fame. Completely emancipated from the aristocratic influence under which he had, several years before, appeared as a political writer in England, his eyes were thoroughly opened to the need of Parliamentary Reform. Early this year his energies had been principally directed on behalf of this popular cause, but he had also dealt hardly with certain notorious scandals. When our history comes to that period, we shall see the various means made use of by his opponents in the endeavour to silence him ; but it is necessary now to refer to that year, because one of those means was the circulation of a pamphlet with the following title :—

" Proceedings of a General Court Martial held at the Horse Guards, on the 24th and 27th of March, 1792, for the trial of Captain Richard Powell, Lieutenant Christopher Seton, and Lieutenant John Hall, of the 54th Regiment of Foot, on several charges preferred against them respectively, by William Cobbett, late Sergeant-Major of

the said regiment; together with several curious letters
which passed between the said William Cobbett and Sir
Charles Gould, Judge-Advocate-General; and various
other documents connected therewith, in the order of
these dates." [London, 1809.]

Copies of the pamphlet were distributed broad-
cast over the country, and in Hampshire, where
Cobbett was then living, carriage people threw
them out to the passers-by as they drove along.
A very great number must have got into circulation; and, as pamphlets go, it is not now a particularly rare one. Of government pamphleteering
we shall have more to say anon; for the present,
we will confine ourselves to Cobbett's full and complete answer as given in an address to the people
of Hampshire, in the " Political Register " for June
17, 1809. Full, complete, and satisfactory it was;
nobody referred to the matter again. Even the
pamphleteering system itself fell into desuetude for
several years. Other and more arbitrary means
were adopted, in the attempt to stifle this voice—to
shut this mouth.

The pamphlet consisted chiefly of a selection of
letters, which passed between the accused officers,
the Judge-Advocate-General, and William Cobbett;
and concluded with an account of the trial. The
three officers appeared perfectly willing to meet

the charges ; and as for the prosecutor there could be no doubt as to the earnestness of his intention,[4] *up to within about a week of the date* first appointed for the court-martial.   That date was the 24th of March ; and, on the court assembling, no prosecutor appeared, the result being a postponement to the 27th.   On that day, the court having re-assembled, the Judge-Advocate-General was himself sworn, and deposed that he had made ineffectual efforts to discover the prosecutor, whilst the landlady at whose house Cobbett had lodged stated that he had removed the previous week.   This witness also produced the three last letters of the Judge-Advocate-General to William Cobbett, unopened ; which letters stated (1) that an important witness for the prosecution was not likely to be well enough to attend, (2) that the day of the trial was fixed, and (3) that the trial was postponed.   The

---

[4] "I have placed myself in London, sir, and have continued here ever since the 26th December last, for no other purpose than the prosecution of this affair" (Letter of 23rd February).

"I must beg leave, sir, *once more* to request that you will be pleased to lay my representation of this matter [*locale* of the court-martial] before the King, and that as soon as possible" (4th March).

"If my accusation is without foundation, the authors of cruelty have not yet devised the tortures I ought to endure" (11th March).

The letter of the 16th March expresses the astonishment of the writer that *the greatest part of the charges were to be left out !*—which throws much light on the subject.

charges were then read, to the effect that the accused had made false musters, mustered persons who were not soldiers, made false returns to the Brigadier-general commanding at New Brunswick, misapplied work-money earned by the non-commissioned officers and men, deducted firewood from the allowance, and disposed of it for their own purposes, disposed of clothing belonging to the men, and obliged them (whilst they were clothed in rags) to accept of an inadequate sum in lieu of the said clothing, signed false certificates respecting the clothing, and defrauded the men of bread. After the "acquittal," a memorandum was submitted to the law officers of the crown, upon the whole case. Their opinion was, that, unless there were proof of conspiracy with others, Cobbett could not be criminally prosecuted ; but that the parties injured by his conduct, which was certainly most highly blamable, might maintain actions upon the case against him.

Such was the offending pamphlet: on the 3rd of June, 1809, a notice appears in the "Political Register," of its publication, evidently under the sanction of Government ; also, that Mr. Cobbett will take the earliest opportunity of giving a full account of the matter. He repudiates positively every insinuation of having acted, at any time of his life, dishonestly or dishonourably ; at the same time, had the whole of the papers connected with this affair been published without misrepresentation he never would have noticed the thing at all, but have left the documents to speak for themselves. A fortnight later a double number of the " Register " contains the full account, with a great deal more in the shape of commentary, touching the topics of the day ;—it occupies the fifth of a series of Letters to the people of Hampshire, which Cobbett was then writing, on the subject of Parliamentary Reform. And it is necessary, in order to do justice to the whole story, to reproduce a great portion of it here.

After repeating the tale of his honourable discharge from the army, he proceeds to say :—

" The object of my thus quitting the army, to which I was, perhaps, more attached than any man that ever lived in the world, was to bring certain officers to justice for having, in various ways, wronged both the public and the soldier. With this object in view, I went straight to London the moment I had obtained my liberty and secured my *personal safety*, which, as you will readily conceive, would not have been the case if I had not first got my discharge. . . . . This project was conceived so early as the year 1787, when an affair happened that first gave an insight into regimental justice. It was shortly this : that the quarter-master, who had the issuing of the men's provisions to them, *kept about a fourth part of it to himself.* This, the old sergeants told me, had been the case for *many years ;* and they were quite astonished and terrified at the idea of my complaining of it. This I did, however ; but the reception I met with convinced me that I must never make another complaint, till I got safe to England, and safe out of the reach of that most curious of courts, a COURT-MARTIAL. From this time forward I began to collect materials for an exposure, upon my return to England. I had ample opportunities for this, being the keeper of all the books, of every sort, in the regiment, and knowing the whole of its affairs better than any other man. But the winter previous to our return to England, I thought it necessary to make extracts from books, lest the books themselves should be destroyed. And here begins the history of the famous court-martial. In order to be able to *prove* that these extracts were correct, it was necessary that I should have a *witness* as to their being *true copies.* This was a very ticklish point. One foolish step here would have sent me down to the ranks with a pair of bloody shoulders. Yet it was necessary to have the witness. I hesitated many months. At one time I had given the thing up. I dreamt twenty times, I daresay, of my papers being discovered, and of my being tried and flogged half to death. At last, however, some fresh act of injustice toward us made me set all danger at defiance. I opened my project to a corporal, whose name was *William Bestland*, who wrote in the office under me, who was a very honest fellow, who

F 2

was very much bound to me for my goodness to him, and
who was, with the sole exception of myself, the only
sober man in the whole regiment. To work we went,
and during a long winter, while the rest were boozing and
snoring, we gutted no small part of the regimental books,
rolls, and other documents. Our way was this : to take
a copy, sign it with our names, and clap the regimental
seal to it, so that we might be able to swear to it when
produced in court. All these papers were put into a
little box, which I myself had made for the purpose.
When we came to Portsmouth there was a talk of search-
ing all the boxes, &c., which gave us great alarm, and
induced us to take out all the papers, put them in a bag,
and trust them to a custom-house officer, who conveyed
them on shore to his own house, whence I removed them
in a few days after.

"Thus prepared, I went to London, and on the 14th
of January, 1792, I wrote to the then Secretary at War,
Sir George Yonge, stating my situation, my business with
him, and my intentions ; enclosing him a letter or petition
from myself to the King, stating the substance of all the
complaints I had to make ; and which letter I requested
Sir George Yonge to lay before the King. I waited from
the 14th to the 24th of January without receiving any
answer at all, and then all I heard was that he wished to
see me at the War-office. At the War-office I was shown
into an antechamber amongst numerous anxious-looking
men, who, every time the door which led to the great
man was opened, turned their eyes that way with a
motion as regular and as uniform as if they had been

drilled to it. These people eyed me from head to foot, and I never shall forget their look, when they saw that I was admitted into paradise, without being detained a single minute in purgatory. Sir George Yonge *heard my story;* and that was apparently all he wanted of me. I was to hear from him again *in a day or two,* and after waiting for *fifteen days,* without hearing from him or any one else upon the subject, I wrote to him again, reminding him that I had from the first told him that I had *no other business in London;* that my stock of money was necessarily scanty; and that to detain me in London was to ruin me. Indeed, I had in the whole world but about 200 guineas, which was a great deal for a person in my situation to have saved. Every week in London, especially as, by way of episode, I had now *married,* took at least a couple of guineas from my stock. I therefore began to be very impatient, and, indeed, also very suspicious that military justice, in England, was pretty nearly akin to military justice in Nova Scotia and New Brunswick. The letter I now wrote was dated on the 10th of February, to which I got an answer on the 15th, though the answer might have been written in a moment. I was, in this answer, informed that it was the intention to try the accused upon only *part of the charges* which I had preferred; and from a new-modelled list of charges sent me by the Judge-advocate, on the 23rd of February, it appeared that, even of those charges that were suffered to remain, *the parts the most material were omitted.* But this was not all. I had all along insisted that, unless the court-martial were held in *London,* I could not think

of appearing in it; because, if held in a garrisoned place
like Portsmouth, the thing must be a mere mockery.   In
spite of this, however, the Judge-advocate's letter of the
23rd of February informed me that the court was to be
held at Portsmouth or Hilsea.   I remonstrated against
this, and demanded that my remonstrance should be laid
before the King, which, on the 29th, the Judge-advocate
promised should be done by himself; but, on the 5th of
March, the Judge-advocate informed me that he had laid
my remonstrance before—*whom*, think you?   *Not the
king*, but *the accused parties*, who, of course, thought the
court ought to assemble at Portsmouth or Hilsea, and
doubtless for the very reasons that led me to object to its
being held there.

" Plainly seeing what was going forward, I, on the 7th
of March, made, in a *letter to Mr. Pitt*, a representation
of the whole case, giving him a history of the obstacles
I had met with, which letter concluded thus: ' I have
now, sir, done all a man can do in such a case.   I
have proceeded regularly, and I may add, respectfully,
from first to last; if I am allowed to serve my country
by prosecuting men who have injured it, I shall do it;
if I am thwarted and pressed down by those whose office
it is to assist and support me, I cannot do it; in either
case, I shall be satisfied with having done my duty, and
shall leave the world to make a comparison between me
and the men whom I have accused.'   This letter (which,
by-the-bye, the public robbers have not published) had
the effect of changing the place of the court-martial,
which was now to be held in London; but, as to my

other great ground of complaint, the leaving of the *regi-mental books unsecured*, it had no effect at all; and it will be recollected that, without those books, there could be, as to most of the weighty charges, no proof adduced without bringing forward *Corporal Bestland*, and the danger of doing that will be presently seen. But now, mark well as to these books: as to this great source of that kind of evidence which was not to be brow-beaten, or stifled by the dangers of the lash. Mark well these facts, and from them judge of what I had to expect in the way of justice. On the 22nd of *January* I wrote to Sir George Yonge, for the express purpose of having the books secured; that is to say, taken out of the hands and put out of the reach of the parties accused. On the 24th of January he told me that HE HAD *taken care to give directions* to have these documents secured. On the 18th of February, in answer to a letter, in which I (upon information received from the regiment) com-plained of the documents not having been secured, he wrote to me—and I have now the letter before me, signed with his own hand—that he would write to the colonel of the regiment about the books, &c.: 'although,' says he, 'I cannot doubt but that the regimental books *have been* properly secured.' This was on the 18th of February, mind; and now it appears, from the docu-ments which the public-robbers have put forth, that the first time any order for securing the books was given was on the *15th of March*, though the Secretary told me he had done it on the *24th of January*, and repeated his assertion in writing on the *18th of February*. There is quite enough in this fact alone, to show the public what sort of a chance I stood of obtaining justice.

Without these written documents nothing of importance could be proved, unless the non-commissioned officers and men of the regiment should happen to get the better of their dread of the lash; and, even then, they could only speak from memory. All, therefore, depended upon those written documents, as to the principal charges. Therefore, as the court-martial was to assemble on the 24th of March, I went down to Portsmouth on the 20th, in order to know for certain what was become of the books; and I found, as indeed I suspected was the case, that they had *never been secured at all;* that they had been left in the hands of the accused from the 14th of January to the very hour of trial; and that, in short, my request as to this point, the positive condition as to this most important matter, had been totally disregarded. There remained, then, nothing to rest upon with *safety* but our extracts, confirmed by the evidence of Bestland, the corporal, who had signed them along with me; and this I had solemnly engaged with him not to have recourse to, unless he was first out of the army; that is to say, out of the reach of the vindictive and bloody lash. He was a very little fellow, not more than about five feet high, and had been set down to be discharged when he went to England; but there was a suspicion of his connexion with me, and therefore they resolved to keep him. It would have been cruel, and even perfidious, to have brought him forward under such circumstances; and, as there was no chance of doing anything without him, I resolved not to appear at the court-martial, unless the discharge of *Bestland* was first granted. Accordingly, on the 20th of March, I wrote from Fratton, a village near Portsmouth, to the Judge-Advocate, stating over again all the obstacles that had been thrown in my way, complaining particularly that the books and documents had been left in the possession of the accused, contrary to my urgent request and to the positive assurances of the Secretary at War, and concluding by demanding the discharge of a man, whom I should name, as the only condition upon which I would attend the court-martial. I requested him to send me an answer by the next day, at night, at my former lodging; and told him,[5] that unless such answer was received, he and those to whom my repeated applications had been made, might do what they pleased with their court-martial; for that I confidently trusted that a few days would place me beyond the scope of their power. No answer came, and as I had learned in the meanwhile that there was a design to prosecute me for *sedition*, that was an additional motive to be quick in my movements. As I was going down to Portsmouth I met several of the sergeants coming up, together with the music-master; and as they had none of them been in America, I wondered what they could be going to London for; but, upon my return, I was told by a *Captain Lane*, who had been in the regiment, that they had been brought up to swear that at an entertainment given to them by me before my departure from the

[5] This accounts for the paragraph in the *London Chronicle;* a thing which is inexplicable till one comes to this sentence.

regiment, I had drunk '*the destruction of the House of Brunswick.*' This was false; but I knew that that was no reason why it should not be *sworn* by such persons, and in such a case. I had talked pretty freely upon the occasion alluded to; but I had neither said nor thought against the King; and, as to the *House of Brunswick*, I hardly knew what it meant. My head was filled with the corruptions and the baseness in the army. I knew nothing at all about politics. Nor would any threat of this sort have induced me to get out of the way for a moment, though it certainly would if I had known my danger, for glorious 'Jacobinical' times were just then beginning. Of this, however, I knew nothing at all. I did not know what the *Suspension of the Habeas Corpus Act* meant. When you have a mind to do a thing, every trifle is an additional motive. Lane, who had enlisted me, and who had always shown great kindness toward me, told me they would send me to Botany Bay; and I now verily believe, that if I had remained, I should have furnished a pretty good example to those who wished to correct military abuses. I did not, however, leave England from this motive. I could not obtain a chance of success, without exposing the back of my poor faithful friend Bestland, which had I not pledged myself not to do, I would not have done. It was useless to appear, unless I could have tolerable fair play; and, besides, it seemed better to leave the whole set to do as they pleased, than to be made a mortified witness of what it was quite evident they had resolved to do.

"Such is the *true* history of this affair, which had the

public-robbers given it as it stood, unmutilated, not a word should I ever have published, by way of defence or explanation."

Cobbett then proceeds to show the hollow and tricky nature of the attack, by summing up the points which tend obviously to show that the whole is a trumped-up charge against his honour and his reputation ; first stating that the five letters from himself, which appear in the pamphlet, were the least important of twenty-seven which he actually wrote, including one to Mr. Pitt, and one, in the shape of a petition, to the King. He then reminds his readers that he would have scarcely put himself to the expense of two or three months' living in London, and to the trouble of writing so many letters and of dancing attendance at the Horse Guards, if he hadn't a good case and were not in earnest about it ; that nine years had elapsed since his return to England, and no process had been taken upon the opinion of the Attorney-General and his colleague ; that his " Life and Adventures of Peter Porcupine " was reprinted in London, in 1796, at the express desire of Mr. Canning, *i. e.* only four years after the incident, and yet nothing had been done to supply the omission (in that publication) of the court-martial story ; that he

had, when dining with Mr. Pitt in August, 1800,
talked freely about Fitzgerald and about the army
"for the express purpose of leading him on to talk
about the court-martial, but it was avoided. In
fact, they all well knew that what I had complained
of was true, and that I had been baffled in my
attempts to obtain justice only because I had
neither money nor friends." That General Carleton (late Governor of Nova Scotia) had visited him
in England, since his return, and that the Duke of
Kent had talked to him in Halifax about the
regiment and its affairs in the year 1800; yet
both these distinguished officers must have known
all about the court-martial, the Governor's name,
in point of fact, having occurred in one of the
"charges." Besides this, there could be little
doubt that the whole facts were not put before Sir
John Scott and Sir John Mitford, or their opinion
would have been very different from what it
was.

Finally, he reminds his readers that he had, in
the year 1805, himself given the cue. Which was
certainly the case, as may be seen by referring to
his writings of that date :—

"In the printed account of my life, there is a small
chasm. When I published that account I was in the

midst of the revilers of England, and particularly of the English army; or, I should have then stated, that the primary cause of my leaving the army, that the circumstance which first disgusted me, and that finally made me resolve to tear myself from a service, to which my whole mind and heart were devoted, was, the abuses, the *shocking* abuses as to money-matters, the *peculation*, in short, which I had witnessed in it, and which I had, in vain, endeavoured to correct. What those abuses were, by whom they were committed, and how, after I quitted the army, I failed in obtaining redress, it would not now, after many of the parties are dead, be proper for me to state; but, if the 'Society of Gentlemen' have, as it is more than probable they have, access to the records of the War Office, and can obtain leave to publish the correspondence upon the subject, the public will then see that I have all my life, and in all situations, been the enemy of peculation. It is, however, incumbent upon me to state, that I have good reason to believe that my failure upon that occasion was in no way to be ascribed to Mr. Pitt, who, as far as a person in so obscure and perfectly friendless a situation as I then was, could judge, was, as to the matter in question, the friend of fair inquiry and of justice."

We may safely dismiss this matter. Should the reader find it worth his while to rake up this old pamphlet, and compare it with Cobbett's "full account," he may find a stray divergence of date or of trifling fact; but nothing more than, as a careless omission, will serve to establish the good faith of the man—a class of evidence which is often as serviceable as a statement clear and unfaltering to the minutest detail. Why the affair went off as it did is obvious to any one who knows the world, and the rules of society, better than Cobbett did : it was a hopeless task, from the very first, to undertake it upon his own responsibility, without professional assistance. A mistake, however, which he seldom corrected through life ; and the consequence being that he as seldom succeeded in gaining a cause : he persisted, to the very last, in being his own advocate—and with the proverbial result.

Let us turn, then, to another incident of this year. An incident which has given the biographer a good deal of trouble ; as it presents an occasion upon which it has seemed difficult to reconcile two statements which, at first sight, seem to vary.

For this purpose, we must again refer to a later date in the history. In the year 1805, Mr. Cobbett made himself very offensive to the Government over the unfortunate difficulties of Lord Melville. The whole contest, between the Government and its opponents, was of the hottest ; and the choicest Billingsgate passed between them. One periodical, inspired by the Pitt and Melville party, made it

its business to assail Cobbett in particular ; and,
on the 27th of July of the above-mentioned year,
the following passage occurred :—

"As Mr. Cobbett can hardly fail to read this review,
I beg leave, through its medium, to ask that worthy
patriot if he knows who was the author, and industrious
circulator through the army, of a pamphlet entitled
The Soldiers' Friend, published about the same time,
but fraught with ten times more mischief than Paine's
'Rights of Man'? A pamphlet calculated to render
soldiers discontented with their situation, and incite them
to mutiny and rebellion ; a pamphlet which, in short, I
have no hesitation in saying, was a considerable source
of the naval mutiny at the Nore."

Now, by the time this effusion appeared in public,
Cobbett had begun to incur the severest displeasure
of his opponents ; he had created mortal enemies
by the development of his warfare upon "corruption." Caricature was at work, keeping pace
with the most virulent attacks on the part of the
ministerial press. For all which he did not care a
pin, but this charge of sedition was more than he
could stand. Perfectly happy (as his letters of
that date will show), both in his domestic pursuits
and in the general public appreciation which he
was then possessing, he enjoyed fair fight ; but
this beginning of dark insinuation roused him ;

and, for the first time since his return to England, he entered upon a proud and energetic boast of the services which he had rendered to his country. The part with which we have at present to do is the answer to the charge of sedition, which is as follows :—

" During the interval of my discharge and of my departure for France, a proposition, preceded by a speech of the Secretary at War, was made in parliament to augment the pay of the army. Some parts of the speech contained matter which a person, with whom I was acquainted, and to whom I had communicated my information upon such subjects, thought worthy of remark in print. Hence arose a little pamphlet, entitled the *Soldiers' Friend.* Of this pamphlet I was not the author; I had nothing to do either with the printing or the publishing of it ; and I never had in my possession, or ordered to be sent to any person, or to any place, three copies of it in my life; and I do not believe that 500 copies, in the whole, ever went from the bookseller's shop ; a fact, however, that may easily be ascertained by application to Mr. Ridgway, who was the publisher of it."

Here, then, is a distinct disavowal : a circumstance that is calculated to worry the impartial biographer, anxious to be fair toward a good (though sometimes ill-advised) man ; the reason for its being a disturbing factor lying in this, that the *Soldiers' Friend* is enumerated, on two distinct occasions during the closing years of Cobbett's life, among the writings by which he had helped to benefit his fellow-men. Let us have his own words (June, 1832) :—

" The very first thing I ever wrote for the press in my life was a little pamphlet entitled the *Soldiers' Friend,* which was written immediately after I quitted the army in 1791, or early in 1792. I gave it in manuscript to Captain Thomas Morrice (the brother of that Captain Morrice who was a great companion of the Prince of Wales); and by him it was taken to Mr. Ridgway, who then lived in King Street, St. James's Square, and Mr. Ridgway (the same who now lives in Piccadilly) published it. I do not know that I ever possessed the pamphlet, except for a week or two, after it was published, &c., &c."

Now these two statements cannot, on a superficial reading, be easily reconciled ; and they form, together, an instance which may be eagerly seized upon, on the part of those who would continue to represent Cobbett as a man who would wilfully utter contradictory things. But, upon examining the matter somewhat more closely, we know, even better than Cobbett himself, something of the actual circumstances. In the first place, the great probability is that Cobbett was not the *originator* of the pamphlet; that this Captain Thomas Morrice, or somebody else (still more interested in awakening the public mind on army-frauds) had instigated him to put his ideas upon paper. The speech of the Secretary-at-War, above referred to, occurs in a debate upon the army estimates, on the 15th February, 1792—a debate in which Mr. Fox, among others, took part; and the item of an additional allowance to the soldiers was that which was the immediate inspiration of the pamphlet; besides being, in all likelihood, productive of some little excitement in military circles generally.[6]

Secondly, it will be observed that the sting of the charge against Cobbett lay in this: that he had been instrumental in spreading sedition in the naval and military services. Now, this was totally false. It *is* a fact that the " Soldiers' Friend " was afterwards circulated largely, and provoked antagonism ; but of this Cobbett knew nothing, and could not know anything, for he had long been safe in Philadelphia, far away from English domestic politics, and much more concerned in earning his bread-and-cheese by hard work, than in spreading

---

[6] Not to interrupt the thread of the narrative, we will append to this Chapter one or two extracts from the " Soldiers' Friend "—a course which will at one and the same time tell the whole story of the grievance ,and introduce us to the first essay of Cobbett's pen.

the principles of the French Revolution. Those who made it their business to circulate clever and spicy pamphlets, saw the merit of this one, and reprinted it for their own objects.

How we come to be satisfied upon this point is this: the pamphlet published by Ridgway (8vo, 6*d.*) was mentioned among "new publications," in the "Scots Magazine" for June, 1792; and reviewed by the "Monthly" and the "Critical" of the same month. Although the "Critical Review" professes to know the person who had been distributing it "on the parade in St. James's Park," this sixpenny pamphlet did not long continue to burden Mr. Ridgway's shelves. It is possible that there is now no copy in existence. But, in the following year, a cheap reprint appeared, without printer's or publisher's name—which had an extensive circulation ; for it was answered by anti-reform tracts, such as "A Few Words to the Soldiers of Great Britain," "The Soldier's and Sailor's Real Friend," &c.

So, the matter seems clearer. Cobbett is in London, preparing for the grand exposure ; he has sympathizers, who durst not, however, show themselves. This Captain Morrice (or somebody) thinks that the speech on the army estimates contains "matter worthy of remark in print." William

Cobbett not only agrees with him (somebody), but he is burning with the desire to set right certain cases of practical injustice, with which he is only too familiar : (of the quarter-master of the regiment defrauding the men of their rice and peas by means of short weights, and so forth,—to the tune of unutterable meannesses.) William Cobbett has the pen of a ready writer, and a grasp of hard facts withal. Hence arises a " little pamphlet :" a little pamphlet, published in respectable octavo form, by a highly respectable house ; addressed to the aristocratic and well-to-do section of society, and published at their very doors. With this printing and publishing W. Cobbett has " nothing to do ;" and he never sees it again after a week or so. But there's some real stuff in it ; and, next year, real stuff is much in vogue !

Those were lively times, in 1792. The extreme "horrors" of the French Revolution had not yet been displayed ; and the news from France, with the new and glorious doctrines of Liberty and Equality, were being eagerly embraced by a large section of the English people. Besides the Society of Free Debate, there were others established in London, which soon caused alarm on the part of the Government ; for their influence and consequence rapidly grew, on account of the frequency

and publicity of their meetings, and the readiness
with which all persons were invited to come and
deliver their sentiments. Of course, ministerial
alarm soon took action. The king's proclamation
appeared in May : new life was put into the magis-
terial office; the trumpery police force of that day
was reorganized ; and prosecutions for libel became frequent. " Not a pamphlet or paper was
published, in which any measure of government
was animadverted on or disapproved of, but proceedings were immediately commenced against the
parties who either wrote, edited, printed, or published it."[7]

So, London is no place for our ex-sergeant, even
if his plans are not already formed. With all his
loyalty, he is beginning to think there must be
something in republicanism. And he will carry
out his notion of going to the United States of
America ; after having visited France, with the object of perfecting himself in the language of that
country :—

" From the moment that I resolved to quit the army,
I also resolved to go to the United States of America,
the fascinating and delusive description of which I had
read in the works of Raynal. To France I went for

7 " Memoirs of John Thelwall," i. 89.

the purpose of learning to speak the French language, having, because it was the language of the military art, studied it by book in America. To see fortified towns was another object; and how natural this was to a young man who had been studying fortification, and who had been laying down Lille and Brisach upon paper, need not be explained to those who have burnt with the desire of beholding in practice that with which they have been enamoured in theory."

As matters stood, then, in March, 1792, there was no longer any occasion for delay; and it appears that he landed in France before the month was out: very much startled and amused, by the way, at seeing written up over a shop-door in Calais,—" *Ici l'on a des Assignats, dès cent francs à un sou.*" He settled at Tilq, a little village near St. Omer, and remained there for about five months. He found the people so unexpectedly kind and hospitable, to a degree that he had never been accustomed to, that all those prejudices, with which Englishmen, at that time, regarded their brave and impulsive neighbours, and which prejudices were fully developed in his own breast—were dispelled in a few weeks. What with his newly-married bliss, and his perfect health, and his zealous reading and study, this must have been the very happiest period of Cobbett's life. He did intend to go to Paris for the winter, but the troublous times prevented that purpose :—

" I perceived the storm gathering : I saw that a war with England was inevitable, and it was not difficult to foresee what would be the fate of Englishmen in that country, where the rulers had laid aside even the appearance of justice and mercy. I wished, however, to see Paris, and had actually hired a coach to go thither. I was even on the way, when I heard at Abbeville that the king was dethroned and his guards murdered. This intelligence made me turn off towards Havre-de-Grâce, whence I embarked for America."

[APPENDIX TO CHAPTER III.]

Extracts from

" The Soldier's Friend ; or, Considerations on the late pretended Augmentation of the Subsistence of the private Soldiers.

"[Motto] 'Laws grind the poor, and rich men rule the law.'— *Goldsmith.*

"Written by a Subaltern.   Price Twopence, or one hundred copies, 10*s*. 6*d*.   1793.

"Amongst the many curious manœuvres of the present administration, I do not recollect one that marks more strongly its character than the late alteration in the pay and establishment of the army.   The augmentation (as they would insinuate it is) of the pay of the British soldiers is represented as arising from a consideration of the wretchedness of their situation ; and the pretended reduction of the foot forces is held out to the public as an act of œconomy.   The people, I am much afraid, are satisfied with this. . . . The situation of the privates in our marching regiments of foot was really so miserable,

that every one endued with the least compassion, must
rejoice to find that a *morsel of bread* has been by any
means added to that scanty meal; and the enormous
load of taxes, that press out the very vitals of the people,
ensures a favourable reception to every reduction, or
pretended reduction, of public expense, let it be ever so
trifling or absurd. . . . .

"'I propose to make a few observations on the alteration that has taken place in the soldiers' pay; in doing
which, although I shall be very concise, I have the
vanity to think I shall discover a little better information
on the subject than the Secretary at War did at his
opening of it in the House of Commons; when he
observed (after having stated the saving that would arise
from the reduction in the infantry) that 'against this
saving he had to mention an increase that had been
made to the pay of the private soldiers to the amount
of 23,000*l.* The situation of the privates had long been
admitted to have been extremely hard. It had in *former
years* been the regulation that a soldier should receive
three shillings a week for his subsistence. It has *of late
years so happened* that he had not had for that purpose
above eighteenpence or two shillings. This was evidently
too little for the bare purpose of existence. By the late
regulation his pay was to be made adequate to the subsistence the common soldier *formerly enjoyed*, an object
which he was confident would meet with the warm
approbation of every man.' . . . .

"As the Secretary observed, 'the situation of the
privates had long been admitted to have been extremely

hard;' but people had not the least notion that it 'had so happened of late years, that the soldier had only eighteenpence or two shillings a week for his subsistence.' Men of humanity thought the soldier's situation hard, but every one thought that he received *three shillings a week* for his subsistence; and why any man unacquainted with the abuses of the army should think otherwise I cannot imagine, seeing that there is an Act of Parliament, a law of the land, that declares it shall be so."

[After reciting the regulations that existed, and which were yearly renewed in each Mutiny Act, he proceeds :—]

"It has *so happened!* and for years too! astonishing! It has *so happened* that an Act of Parliament has been most notoriously and shamefully disobeyed for years, to the extreme misery of thousands of deluded wretches (our countrymen), and to the great detriment of the nation at large; it has *so happened* that not one of the offenders has been brought to justice for this disobedience, even now it is fully discovered; and it has *so happened* that the hand of power has made another dive into the national purse, in order—not to add to what the soldier ought to have received; not to satisfy *his* hunger and thirst; but to gratify the whim or the avarice of his capricious and plundering superiors." ·

[After a good deal more, to the same effect, the writer reverts to the new demand upon the national purse by the Secretary at War :—]

"This is certainly the most curious mode of rectifying abuses that ever was heard of; and it points out in the clearest light the close connexion that exists between the *ruling Faction* in this country and the military officers; and this connexion ever must exist while we suffer ourselves to be governed by a *Faction.* If any other body of men had thus impudently set the laws of the land at defiance,—if *a gang of robbers*, ornamented with red coats and cockades, had plundered their fellow-citizens, what would have been the consequence? They would have been brought to justice, hanging or transportation would have been their fate; but, it seems, the Army is become a *Sanctuary* from the power of the law. Nor shall we be at all surprised at this, if we consider that a standing army is the great instrument of oppression, and that a very numerous one may in a little time be necessary. I am not, therefore, blaming the ministry for this proceeding. I really think they have acted with a great deal of prudence in procuring the 23,000*l.* for their supporters; but (as it was all amongst friends) I think the business might have been opened in a more unequivocal manner; as thus, in the language of truth :—

"'The situation of the privates has long been admitted to be extremely hard. It is a law (which in former years was obeyed) that a soldier shall receive three shillings a week for his subsistence. It has so happened that of late years the officers have thought proper to despise this law, and to give the soldier only eighteenpence or two shillings. This is evidently too little for the bare purpose of existence; and though he has subsisted on it of late years, and might with our good will have done so to the day of judgment, as there now is a necessity to humour the wretch a little, *for reasons best known to ourselves;* we have, by a late regulation, made his pay adequate to what he always ought to have enjoyed : an object that we are confident must meet the warm approbation of our majority in this House. The public burden will, indeed, be increased by this, but it is certainly much better to tax the people to their last farthing than to wound the *honour* of our trusty and well-beloved, the officers of the army, by any odious and *ungentlemanlike* investigation of their conduct.'

"It particularly becomes you, the British Soldier, to look upon this matter in its proper light. The pretended addition to your subsistence is, in fact, no addition at all ; you will now receive no more than you always ought to have received. . . . . If you should have the fortune to become a non-commissioned officer, and were to deduct but a penny from a man unlawfully, you know the consequences would be breaking and flogging, and refunding the money so deducted; but here you see your officers have been guilty of the practice for years, and now it is found out not a hair of one of their heads is touched ; they are even permitted to remain in the practice, and a sum of money is taken from the public to coax you with, now it seems likely that you may be wanted. . . . .

"Soldiers are taught to believe everything they receive *a gift from the Crown.* Cast this notion from you immediately, and know that there is not a farthing you receive but comes out of the *public purse.* What you call your *King's Bounty,* or *Queen's Bounty,* is no bounty from either of them : it is 12*s*. 2*d*. a year of the public money, which no one can withhold from you ; it is allowed you by an Act of Parliament, while you are taught to look upon it as a present from the King or Queen !—I feel an indignation at this I cannot describe— I would have you consider the nature of your situation, I would have you know that you are not the servant of *one man* only ; a British soldier never can be that. You are a servant of the whole nation, of your countrymen, who pay you, and from whom you can have no separate interests. I would have you look upon nothing that you receive as *Favour* or a *Bounty* from Kings, Queens, or Princes ; you receive the wages of your servitude ; it is your property, confirmed to you by Acts of the Legislature of your country, which property your rapacious officers ought never to seize on, without meeting with a punishment due to their infamy."

"FINIS."

CHAPTER IV.

"I LIVED IN PHILADELPHIA."

THE Quaker city may well be the pride of the American nation. Founded by William Penn, shortly after his settlement of Pennsylvania in the year 1682, it has become, after the lapse of two centuries, the most important town in the United States. Second to New York only in the matter of population, it is, at present, the first manufacturing city in the whole country; whilst it has long held supremacy as the centre of literary and philosophical activity. In the centenary year of 1876, Philadelphia possessed no less than 146 daily and weekly newspapers, and twenty public libraries: no bad sign of the state of intellectual advancement of a town containing about seven hundred thousand inhabitants. The population consists largely of members of the Society of Friends, or of their descendants; but there is always a considerable foreign element in the city: the Irish numbering about one-seventh, the Germans one-thirteenth, and the English one-thirtieth. There are at least 400 churches and chapels, and more than 400 public schools; and 100 hospitals and asylums.

The causes of the prosperity of Philadelphia are not difficult to be discovered. It is noticeable, that all flourishing capitals are marked by strong cosmopolitan features, with a background of national characteristic. The characteristic basis of the Pennsylvanian is his Quaker ancestry; and upon this has been grafted, in varying proportions, the religious and political notions, the manners, customs, and national prejudices, of English, Scotch, German, Irish, Welsh, Swedish, and other emigrants, ever since the middle of the last century. The capital of the state took the full-flow of this tide of immigration; further augmented during and after the war of independence, by a number of French people seeking for that peace and security which was denied them in their native land. With all these varying elements, however, the frugal, patient, industrious Quaker spirit has pervaded the place; and reduced all this complexity to some sort of harmony. Of party spirit there has, naturally, been much activity; indeed, at the period of our history, it prevailed more extensively than in almost any other town in the United States ; but the cultivation of knowledge, of the useful arts, and of commercial enterprise, have been the agents in producing the prosperous and beautiful capital of Pennsylvania.

The city of Philadelphia would appear to have been the pole, one hundred years ago, which attracted alike the inquiring traveller and the political fugitive. The Abbé Raynal had collected and published, in 1770, an account of the American colonies,[1] which produced a profound sensation in Europe. It was translated into almost every

---

[1] " Histoire philosophique et politique des établissements et du commerce des Européens dans les deux Indes." The author was assisted by Diderot, and others ; and, at last (about 1780) the work was forbidden in France. Raynal lived to regret the extreme notions which he had advocated, and actually appeared at the bar of the National Assembly (in the month of May, 1791), there, to the surprise and displeasure of his audience, boldly to expostulate with them on their rash and ruinous courses ; the principal charge being that they had too literally followed his principles, and reduced to practice the reveries and abstracted ideas of a philosopher, without having previously adapted and accommodated them to men, times, and circumstances ! Raynal exercised a great deal of influence upon his generation, and may be considered as having contributed largely to the uprooting of institutions which resulted from the French Revolution ; and this singular piece of moral courage was displayed at an advanced period of his life, when he had little to fear from any possible violence ; the usual consequence, in those days, of reaction in opinion.

European language. The literary characteristics of the book were great animation and plausibility; and, although it excited many strictures, from the political facts being largely ixed up with rhetorical allusions to the wrongs and errors of past generations, the work was, for a time, exceedingly popular, and furnished a basis for much of the cotemporary information on America. The unfortunate Jean Pierre Brissot, who was at Philadelphia in or about the year 1788, declared that Raynal had exaggerated everything; and Cobbett always qualified any allusion to the Abbé's writings by some expression or other, to a similar effect. Brissot adds, however, his own impressions of the city, which were high enough, both with reference to the beauty of its situation and of its public buildings, and to the prosperity of its inhabitants.

An English traveller,[2] who visited the States in 1795-6, gave some curious particulars of the condition of society in Philadelphia at that period. Quakers appeared to number about one quarter of the whole population. The average Philadelphian was represented as being deficient in hospitality and politeness towards strangers :—

---

[2] Isaac Weld. See his "Travels through the States of North America, and the Provinces of Upper and Lower Canada, during the years 1795, 1796, and 1797" (2 vols., London, 1800).

" Amongst the uppermost circles in Philadelphia, pride, haughtiness, and ostentation are conspicuous. . . . In the manners of the people in general, there is a coldness and reserve, as if they were suspicious of some designs against them, which chills to the very heart those who come to visit them.   In their private societies a *tristesse* is apparent, near which mirth and gaiety can never approach.   It is no unusual thing, in the genteelest houses, to see a large party of from twenty to thirty persons assembled, and seated round a room, without partaking of any other amusement than what arises from the conversation, most frequently in whispers, that passes between the two persons who are seated next to each other.   The party meets between six and seven in the evening ; tea is served with much form ; and at ten, by which time most of the company are wearied with having so long remained stationary, they return to their own homes.   Still, however, they are not strangers to music, cards, dancing, &c."

Until about 1779 no public amusements were suffered in the city ; but, after a few years later, Philadelphia would seem to have got a little gayer,[1] at least in the winter time—when the Congress and the State Assembly were sitting, and President Washington made his annual stay of some weeks.   The President's birthday became a special

---

[1] According to Brissot, even the Quakers were getting less strict, some of them being inclined to lapse into luxury, and have carpets !

anniversary, when all the citizens (except Quakers) would make a point of paying him a visit. Concerts and public assemblies were held, and two or three theatres, even, were started. The great political revolution, in point of fact, produced a social one of quite as definite a character, even in prim Philadelphia. As concerning the manners of the lower classes, Weld records a sad deficiency: they would return impertinent answers to questions couched in the most civil terms, and would insult a person bearing the appearance of a gentleman, on purpose to show how highly they estimated the principles of liberty and equality. Hostlers and servants always appeared to be "doubtful whether they ought to do anything for you or not;" civility was not to be purchased with money; it seemed incompatible with freedom, and with the ideas which would convince a stranger that he was really in a land of liberty.

Now, Mr. William Cobbett, late of his Majesty's 54th Regiment, had heard of this new country. His reading, hitherto, had been purely literary; but, plunged into the world of London—a novice in politics—he imbibes the then popular notions of republicanism, and is an enthusiastic admirer of the new ideas. The eloquent pages of Tom Paine,

—unanswerable in themselves, yet, at that day, rigorously proscribed,—help to intoxicate ; and, boiling with indignation (as he says) at the abuses he had witnessed, he has, indeed, become a republican. That is, a theoretical republican : for, when he soon comes to see all sides of republicanism, he reverts to his intrinsic love for the constitution under which he was born.

And to this new land of liberty he will go.

He landed in Philadelphia in October, 1792, and, for a short time, took up his residence at Wilmington, a little port[4] on a creek of the Delaware, about twenty-eight miles below Philadelphia. Here Cobbett found the very thing to give him a start in life ; for the place was swarming with French emigrants, who wanted, above all things, to learn the English language. After a little time it appears that he found Philadelphia itself a better field for his energies ; and, accordingly, having removed thither, he soon had as many pupils as he could attend to. This occupation was the occasion, also, which produced the " English Grammar for Frenchmen : "—

"When I afterwards came to teach the English language to French people in Philadelphia, I found that

---

[4] Now a flourishing town, with several newspapers, and extensive manufactures.

none of the grammars, then to be had, were of much use to me. I found them so defective, that I wrote down instructions and gave them to my scholars in manuscript. At the end of a few months, this became too trouble-some; and these manuscript instructions assumed the shape of a grammar in print, the copyright of which I sold to Thomas Bradford,[6] a bookseller in Philadelphia, for 100 dollars (or 22*l.* 11*s.* 6*d.*); which grammar, under the title of *Maître d'Anglais,* is now in general use all over Europe."

Cobbett seems to have held a rather qualified opinion upon this French grammar: for he else-where says it was "a very hasty production," and that it was so defective that he was almost ashamed to look into it [1829]; but that it had the great merit of "*clearness,* and of making the learner see the *reason* of the rules." Yet the book still holds

---

[6] Thomas Bradford, a leading Philadelphian of the period, was one of the members of a family that exercised a good deal of influence in the city for a long course of years. He died in 1838, at the advanced age of ninety-four. His father was Colonel William Bradford, a hero of the Revolutionary War, and his great grand-father William Bradford, one of the fellow-emigrants of Penn. This founder of the family was the first printer in Pennsylvania, and he lived to see some of his descendants amongst the most useful and esteemed citizens of Philadelphia. The Bradfords, during an entire century (1719—1819), published and conducted a newspaper in the city. Thomas Bradford was among the founders of the American Philosophical Society. His son, Thomas, became a judge of the United States.

its own; and it has been repeatedly reprinted in France, Belgium, &c.[6]

Besides the teaching of English to the emigrants, there was some translating done for the booksellers.

[6] The actual title, at first, was " Le Tuteur Anglais, ou grammaire regulière de la langue Anglaise, en deux parties, &c. (à Philadelphie, chez Thomas Bradford, 1795)."

The 35th Edition (Paris, 1861 : Baudry) has the following remarks in the preface, after alluding to the original success of the work : " La clarté de sa méthode l'a fait accueillir en France avec un plus vif empressement encore qu'en Amerique ; ce qui s'explique parfaitement, car cette grammaire étant à l'usage des Français, il fallait que son mérite fût bien réel pour obtenir dans un pays étranger un succès qui n'a fait que grandir depuis. Sa supériorité incontestable sur les autres ouvrages du même genre ne peut donc faire doute, et ce qui le prouve, c'est que le public et la plupart des professeurs les plus en renommée parmi ceux qui ont conservé leur libre arbitre n'ont cessé de se servir de cette grammaire."

A republication of this grammar was undertaken by Mons. L. H. Scipion, Comte Du Roure, who made large additions, with critical emendations, to Cobbett's book (5th Edit. Paris, 1816). This gentleman adds his testimony to the general estimation in which the work was held, both in America and Europe, and says, " Ce qui distingue avantageusement le travail de M. Cobbett, c'est qu'il *raisonne* souvent, et oblige, plus souvent encore, le lecteur à raisonner." But he must needs give currency to a report which he had heard, that Cobbett was not the real author of the *Maître d'Anglais :*—" Plusieurs personnes, bien dignes de foi, m'ont assuré qu'il était tres-eloigné, surtout en 1795, de posséder suffisamment la langue Française pour pouvoir écrire dans cette langue ; et que d'ailleurs M. Cobbett, très-célèbre écrivain politique sans doute, n'avait pas fait dans sa jeunesse toutes les études classiques que la composition d'une Grammaire rend indispensables. *Peut-être ai-je été mal informé*" ! A little bit of national pique, let us suppose. Of course we know more about Mons. Cobbett's classical studies. And Mons. Du Roure got a little wiser on that point, if he read the No. of the " Political Register " for Feb. 21, 1818.

The first of any importance, and which Cobbett alludes to somewhere as his "*coup d'essai* in the authoring way," was the work of Von Martens on the "Law of Nations;" at that date a book of considerable authority :—

"Soon after I was married, I translated, for a book-seller in Philadelphia, a book on the Law of Nations. A member of Congress had given the original to the book-seller, wishing for him to publish a translation. The book was the work of a Mr. Martens, a German jurist, though it was written in French. I called it *Martens's Law of Nations*. . . . I translated it for a quarter of a dollar (thirteenpence halfpenny) a page ; and, as my chief business was to go out in the city to teach French people English, I made it a rule to earn a dollar while my wife was getting the breakfast in the morning, and another dollar after I came home at night, be the hour what it might ; and I have earned many a dollar in this way, sitting writing in the same room where my wife and only child were in bed and asleep."

Another task of similar character was the translation of "A Topographical and Political Description of the Spanish part of St. Domingo," the author of which was Moreau de St. Méry,[7]

---

[7] Médéric Louis Elie Moreau de St. Méry, a Frenchman of good family. He had passed a somewhat distinguished career as a legislator, in his native country, until the period of the Revolution;

one of the more distinguished of the French
emigrants. This worthy man's shop, at No. 84,
South Front Street, was probably a favourite
resort of the *literati*, as he was a person of considerable attainments, and a member of the Philosophical Society of Philadelphia ; whilst the bulk
of his expatriated fellow-countrymen consisted,
without doubt, of a cultivated class of men. Louis
Philippe and his brothers were there. Talleyrand
was there for a time,[*] and Cobbett recalls the fact,

when he had to flee from Robespierre. Having safely reached the
United States with his family, he became a merchant's clerk for a
short time, and eventually opened a bookseller's shop, to which
was afterwards added a printing office. He wrote and published
several works in Philadelphia, and returned to France in 1799.
Died 1819, ætat. sixty-nine.

[*] The residence of Talleyrand in America is an obscure period in
his history. We may learn more of it when the long-expected
memoirs are published. The first part of his exile was spent in the
neighbourhood of New York, and time hung heavily on his hands,
for his pecuniary resources were scanty ; and, indeed, this period
was afterwards one of the most painful memories of his life. There
does not appear any foundation for the suspicion that Talleyrand
was a spy in the pay of the French Government, although it is probable enough that he kept his eyes open on his own account. At
last he determined (as he wrote to Madame Genlis) to try and
retrieve his fortunes with mercantile speculations ; and in this he
was successful. Towards the close of 1795, he sent a petition for
the revocation of his banishment, which was ultimately granted,
and he returned to France in the course of the following year.
(*Vide* " Biographie Universelle ;" also Touchard-Lafosse : " Hist.
Polit. de Talleyrand.")

A singular contribution to Talleyrand's history occurs in " Men and
Times of the Revolution," by Elkanah Watson (New York, 1856, pp.

many years after, of having met him in St. Méry's house.

Several of Cobbett's best anecdotes of Philadelphian life are associated with Frenchmen ; here is one :—

" A Frenchman, who had been driven from St. Domingo to Philadelphia, by the Wilberforces of France, went to church along with me one Sunday. He had never been in a Protestant place of worship before.

387, 388). It will serve to refute the notion that he had any particular mission. "In the years 1794 and 1795, I resided in the northern suburbs of Albany, known as the Colonie. Monsr. Le Contaulx, formerly of Paris, a very amiable man, was my opposite neighbour. His residence was the resort of the French emigrants. During that period, Count Latour Dupin, a distinguished French noble, made a hair-breadth escape from Bordeaux with his elegant and accomplished wife, the daughter of Count Dillon. They were concealed in that city for six terrible weeks, during the sanguinary atrocities of Tallien, and arrived at Boston with two trunks of fine towels, containing several hundred in each, the only property they had been able to save from the wreck of an immense estate. . . . . They purchased a little farm upon an eminence nearly opposite Troy. Here they were joined by Talleyrand, who had arrived about the same time in Albany, also an exile and in want. I became intimate with them. . . . . They avowed their poverty, and resided together on the little farm, suffering severe privations, bringing to Albany the surplus produce of their land, and habitually stopping, with their butter and eggs, at my door. They yielded with a good grace to their humiliating condition. In the year following, I was surrounded in my office by a group of distinguished Frenchmen ; the Count, Talleyrand, Volney, the philosophical writer and traveller, Mons. Pharoux, . . . and Desjardins, a former Chamberlain of Louis XVI." This intercourse at length terminated, through the avowed dislike of the *émigrés* to American institutions, habits, and customs.

Upon looking round him, and seeing everybody *comfortably seated*, while a couple of good stoves were keeping the place as warm as a slack oven, he exclaimed, ' *Pardi! on se sert Dieu bien à son aise ici !* ' "

It need not be imagined, however, that he had no American friends. On the contrary, as we shall see in the sequel, he made some friendships that lasted through life.

CHAPTER V.

"HEARING MY COUNTRY ATTACKED, I BECAME
HER DEFENDER THROUGH THICK AND THIN."

NEARLY two years had elapsed, before Cobbett's
life was disturbed by any greater excitement than
would be furnished by his daily pursuits as a
teacher of the French language. Even in Philadelphia, where party spirit was strong, and anti-
pathy to England was particularly manifest, a
busy, hard-working man, with his bread to earn,
and who had no natural taste for politics, had no
need to interfere—and Cobbett would not have
interfered, probably, had not the occasion been
brought about almost by accident. The little
republicanism which had leavened his mind, whilst
in London, had disappeared, when he came to see
more of human nature in his new country; and the
municipal contests, and the flaring speeches and
writings, which excited less industrious minds, had

no charm for him. "Newspapers," he says, "were a luxury for which I had little relish, and which, if I had been ever so fond of, I had not time to enjoy."

But a circumstance occurred, about the middle of the year 1794, which aroused Cobbett's native spirit ; and offered, at the same time, an opportunity for its exercise :—

"One of my scholars, who was a person that we in England should call a coffee-house politician, chose, for once, to read his newspaper by way of lesson ; and, it happened to be the very paper which contained the addresses presented to Dr. Priestley at New York, to-gether with his replies. My scholar, who was a sort of republican, or at best, but half a monarchist, appeared delighted with the invectives against England, to which he was very much disposed to add. Those Englishmen who have been abroad, particularly if they have had time to make a comparison between the country they are in and that which they have left, well know how difficult it is, upon occasions such as I have been describing, to refrain from expressing their indignation and resentment ; and there is not, I trust, much reason to suppose, that I should, in this respect, experience less difficulty than another.

"The dispute was as warm as might reasonably be expected between a Frenchman, uncommonly violent even for a Frenchman, and an Englishman not re-

markable for *sang-froid;* and, the result was, a declared
resolution, on my part, to write and publish a pamphlet
in defence of my country, which pamphlet he pledged
himself to answer ; his pledge was forfeited ; it is known
that mine was not. Thus, sir [he is addressing Mr.
Pitt], it was, that I became a writer on politics. 'Happy
for you,' you will say, 'if you had continued at your verbs
and your nouns.' Perhaps it would : but the fact absorbs
the reflection ; whether it was for my good, or otherwise,
I entered on the career of political writing ; and, without
adverting to the circumstances under which others have
entered on it, I think it will not be believed that the pen was
ever taken up from a motive more pure and laudable. I
could have no hope of gain from the proposed publication itself, but, on the contrary, was pretty certain to
incur a loss ; no hope of remuneration, for not only had
I never seen any agent of the British government in
America, but was not acquainted with any one British
subject in the country. I was actuated, perhaps, by no
very exalted notions of either loyalty or patriotism ; the
act was not much an act of refined reasoning, or of
reflection ; it arose merely from *feeling*, but it was that
sort of feeling, that jealousy for the honour of my native
country, which I am sure you will allow to have been
highly meritorious, especially when you reflect on the
circumstances of the times and the place in which I ventured before the public.

" Great praise, and still more, great success, are sure to
operate, with young and zealous men, as an encouragement
to further exertion. Both were, in this case, far beyond my

hopes, and still farther beyond the intrinsic merits of my performance. The praise was, in fact, given to the boldness of the man who, after the American press had, for twenty years, been closed against every publication relative to England, in which England and her king were not censured and vilified, dared not only to defend but to eulogize and exalt them ; and, the success was to be ascribed to that affection for England, and that just hatred of France, which, in spite of all the misrepresentations that had been so long circulated, were still alive in the bosoms of all the better part of the people ; who openly to express their sentiments, only wanted the occasion and the example which were now afforded them."

JOSEPH PRIESTLEY was one of the most estimable of men. Among those who have thrust back the barriers of Ignorance, he holds no mean place, whether as a student of natural philosophy, or as a Christian teacher. But he belongs to a period when the Pioneer had to suffer for his opinions.

Born in 1733, he early evinced the qualities of a thorough student, mastered several European and Eastern languages, spent his spare cash in scientific instruments, and entered the ministry as an inflexible opponent of the cruel notions of " eternal wrath." He was a man rather inclined to take always the heterodox side of things, as one who had discovered that most popular doctrines, in politics and religion, were founded on baseless traditions. Priestley's contributions to science brought him within the fold of the Royal Society; and he was pursuing his studies at the same time that he had charge of an important dissenting congregation at Birmingham, when the French Revolution broke out, in 1789. By this time he was known as an ardent and honest controversialist, and had numerous warm friendships among the advanced Liberals of London and Paris; and his position at Birmingham was becoming hazardous, on account of the denunciations he underwent on the part of the orthodox in Church and State. Matters came to a crisis in the summer of 1791; when, a feast being held for the purpose of celebrating the fall of the Bastille, a mob assembled, highly strung with loyalty; which, after disturbing the diners, broke the windows of the hotel, proceeded to demolish Priestley's and another meeting-house, his dwelling, and the houses of several other influential dissenters. In short, there was a genuine riot, for which the county had to pay.

And Dr. Priestley had to leave Birmingham. Nor did three years of London life, with the fierce controversies of the day, serve to console him. Having succeeded his friend, the celebrated Dr. Richard Price, as pastor of a meeting at Hackney, he fought alternately with French sceptics and with English " divines ;" but age was creeping upon him ; his beloved scientific pursuits were being neglected ; and he looked wistfully to the new land of liberty and toleration. His domestic hearth was a happy one, and he could at least take that with him wherever he went. So, in the spring of 1794, he set sail for America.

His departure, however, was the signal for a good deal of affectionate demonstration. Addresses were presented to him, and he left his native shores with the good wishes and the regrets of thousands. But, flattering as this was, it was nothing to the reception Priestley experienced on his arrival at New York. He found himself welcomed to "a country worthy of him ;" to a land where reason had "successfully triumphed over the artificial distinctions of European policy and bigotry ;" by those who had "beheld with the keenest sensibility the unparalleled persecutions" which had attended him in his native country.

So, the Philadelphia newspapers of June, 1794, published these addresses—the most noted of which were from the Tammany Society of New York, the Democratic Society of the same, the Republican Natives of Great Britain and Ireland resident in the City of New York, the Medical

Society of New York, and the American Philosophical Society of Philadelphia. The Philadelphia newspapers, ready for all sorts of fiery attack upon England, printed these addresses in full, along with Dr. Priestley's grateful replies. One of Mr. Cobbett's intelligent pupils, in his studious zeal, produces such a newspaper, that his English exercises may be presented in the English of the day. As one of his own omelettes, he will have his English served up fresh ; no musty Addison nor dry Delolme for him ; no stale oligarchical stuff, ready for hatching into villainy and oppression ; but the sweet, new-laid principles of liberty, equality, and fraternity. Which principles, as exemplified in their latest fruits, Monsieur le Maître d'Anglais abhors, with all his heart and soul.

Accordingly, there forthwith appeared an anonymous pamphlet, under the title of "Observations on Priestley's Emigration ;" consisting of a review of the circumstances which had driven the Doctor from Birmingham, and eventually from England ; and a running commentary upon the republican addresses which had been presented to him. The whole tenour of the tract, however, consisted in its expressed horror of the ruin and desolation which the theorists had brought upon France, and in pointing out what would be (in the mind of the writer) the logical result of the new ideas being disseminated in England. Priestley's emigration, in point of fact, was made the peg on which to hang an anti-revolution tirade. Certain sound principles, however, were enunciated: an extract or two will serve to show this, and, by the felicitous terms in which they are conveyed, to display the wonderful command which Cobbett had already acquired over his native tongue.

"System-mongers are an unreasonable species of mortals; time, place, climate, nature itself, must give way. They must have the same governments in every quarter of the globe; when, perhaps, there are not two countries which can possibly admit of the same form of government at the same time. A thousand hidden causes, a thousand circumstances and unforeseen events, conspire to the forming of a government. It is always done by little and little. When completed, it presents nothing like a system; nothing like a thing composed, and written in a book. It is curious to hear people cite the American government as the summit of human perfection, while they decry the English; when it is absolutely nothing more than the government which the kings of England established here, with such little modifications as were necessary on account of the state of society and local circumstances. If, then, the Doctor is come here for a change of government and laws, he is the most disappointed of mortals. He will have the mortification to find in his '*asylum*' the same laws as those from which he has fled, the same upright manner of administering them, the same punishment of the oppressor, and the same protection of the oppressed. In the courts of justice he will every day see precedents quoted from the English law-books ; and (which to him may appear wonderful) we may venture to predict, that it will be very long before they will be supplanted by the bloody records of the revolutionary tribunal."

"Even supposing his intended plan of improvement had been the best in the world, instead of the worst, the people of England had certainly a right to reject it. He claims as an indubitable right, the right of thinking for *others*, and yet he will not permit the people of England to think for *themselves*. . . . If the English choose to remain slaves, bigots, and idolaters, as the Doctor calls them, that was no business of his; he had nothing to do with them. He should have let them alone; and, perhaps in due time, the abuses of their government would have come to that 'natural termination,' which he trusts, 'will guard against future abuses.' But no, said the Doctor, I will reform you—I will enlighten you—I will make you free.—You shall not, say the people.—But I will ! says the Doctor. By ——, say the people, you shall not ! '*And when Ahithophel saw that his counsel was not followed, he saddled his ass, and arose, and gat him home to his house, to his city, and put his household in order, and hanged himself, and died, and was buried in the sepulchre of his father.*'"

"I am one of those who wish to believe that foreigners

come to this country from choice, and not from necessity.
. . . . The most numerous, as well as the most
useful, are mechanics. Perhaps a cobbler, with his
hammer and awls, is a more valuable acquisition than a
dozen philosophi-theologi-politi-cal empirics, with all
their boasted apparatus."

Mr. Thomas Bradford was again his publisher.
The circumstance is fully related in the American
autobiography :—

"When the ' Observations ' on the Emigration of this
'martyr to the cause of liberty' were ready for the
press, I did not, at first, offer them to Mr. Bradford. I
knew him to retain a rooted hatred against Great
Britain, and concluded, that his principles would prevent him from being instrumental in the publication of
anything that tended to unveil one of its most bitter
enemies. I therefore addressed myself to Mr. Carey.[1]
This was, to make use of a culinary figure, jumping out

[1] Matthew Carey, an Irishman, born in Dublin, 1760. At a
very early age he was prosecuted for a "libel" on the Government,
and retired to Paris for a time, where he made the acquaintance of
Franklin and Lafayette. He emigrated to Philadelphia in 1784,
and in the following year started the *Pennsylvania Herald*. In
1793 he commenced the bookselling and printing business, which
he continued prosperously for thirty years. Carey was a public-
spirited citizen of Philadelphia for more than half a century. At
his death, in his eightieth year, his remains were followed to the
grave by thousands who recollected with gratitude his philanthropic
labours. Carey's family is still represented among the leading
Philadelphians.

of the frying-pan into the fire. Mr. Carey received me as booksellers generally receive authors (I mean authors whom they hope to get but little by) : he looked at the title from top to bottom, and then at me from head to foot.—'*No, my lad,*' says he, 'I don't think it will suit."—*My lad!* God in heaven forgive me! I believe that, at that moment, I wished for another yellow fever to strike the city ; not to destroy the inhabitants, but to furnish me too with *the subject of a pamphlet,* that might make me rich. Mr. Carey has sold hundreds of the 'Observations' since that time, and therefore I dare say he highly approved of them, when he came to a perusal. At any rate, I must not forget to say, that he behaved honourably in the business ; for, he promised not to make known the author, and he certainly kept his word, or the discovery would not have been reserved for the month of June, 1796. This circumstance, considering Mr. Carey's politics, is greatly to his honour, and has almost wiped from my memory that contumelious ' my lad.'

"From Mr. Carey I went to Mr. Bradford, and left the pamphlet for his perusal. The next day I went to him to know his determination. He hesitated, wanted to know if I could not make it a little *more popular,* adding that, unless I could, he feared that the publishing of it would endanger *his windows.* 'More popular,' I could not make it. I never was of an accommodating disposition in my life. The only alteration I would consent to was in the title. I had given the pamphlet the double title of ' The Tartuffe Detected ; or, Observa-

tions,' &c. The former was suppressed, though, had I
not been pretty certain that every press in the city was
as little free as that to which I was sending it, the
'Tartuffe Detected' should have remained; for the
person on whom it was bestowed merited it much better
than the character so named by Molière.

"These difficulties, and these fears of the bookseller,
at once opened my eyes with respect to the boasted
liberty of the press. Because the laws of this country
proclaim to the world, that every man may write and
publish freely, and because I saw the newspapers filled
with vaunts on the subject, I was fool enough to imagine
that the press was really free for every one. I had not
the least idea, that a man's windows were in danger of
being broken, if he published anything that was *not
popular.* I did, indeed, see the words *liberty* and
equality, the *rights of man*, the *crimes of kings*, and such
like, in most of the booksellers' windows; but I did
not know that they were put there to save the glass,
as a free republican Frenchman puts a cockade tricolor
in his hat to save his head. I was ignorant of all these
arcana of the liberty of the press.

*   *   *   *   *

"The work that it was feared would draw down
punishment on the publisher, did not contain one un-
truth, one anarchical, indecent, immoral, or irreligious
expression; and yet the bookseller feared for his
windows! For what? Because it was not *popular
enough.* A bookseller in a *despotic* state fears to publish a work that is 'too popular,' and one in a free state

fears to publish a work that is not 'popular enough.' I leave it to the learned philosophers of the 'Age of Reason' to determine in which of these states there is the most liberty of the press; for, I must acknowledge, the point is too nice for me: fear is fear, whether inspired by a Sovereign Lord the King, or by a Sovereign People.

"The terms on which Mr. Bradford took the 'Observations,' were what booksellers call *publishing it together*. I beg the reader, if he foresees the possibility of his becoming an author, to recollect this phrase well. Publishing it together is thus managed: the bookseller takes the work, prints it, and defrays all expenses of paper, binding, &c. and the profits, if any, are divided between him and the author.—Long after the 'Observations' were sold off, Mr. Bradford rendered me an account (undoubtedly a very just one) of the sales. According to this account, my share of the profits (my share only) amounted to the enormous sum of *one shilling and sevenpence half-penny*, currency of the State of Pennsylvania (or, about elevenpence three farthings sterling), quite entirely clear of all deductions whatsoever!

"Now, bulky as this sum appears in words at length, I presume, that when 1*s.* 7½*d.* is reduced to figures, no one will suppose it sufficient to put a coat upon my back. If my poor back were not too broad to be clothed with such a sum as this, God knows how I should bear all that has been, and is, and is to be, laid on it by the unmerciful democrats. Why! 1*s.* 7½*d.* would not cover the back of a Lilliputian; no, not even in rags, as they sell here."

The allusion to the *coat* was occasioned by a report, which Cobbett thought fit to notice, that Mr. Bradford had provided him with the means of procuring one. Whether the "Observations" proved remunerative or not, it is certain that the tract was immediately reprinted in London, by Stockdale, and noticed in the magazines; and we will presently refer to the comments which were raised in England by the new politician.

Meanwhile the pamphlet was read, and became notorious; and its author had discovered where his strength lay. He would prepare another onslaught upon the anti-federalists.

In order, however, that we may understand the position which Cobbett soon came to occupy as a politician, it will be necessary to take a glimpse of the leading questions which were agitating the public mind of America. The chief cities of the United States, receiving, as they did, the overflowings of European ebullition, had also their own internal squabbles, and were become so many centres of revolutionary intrigue; and the perils and the strife thus engendered opened the field of political adventure to many an aspiring mind. It was a period of terrible personal animosities, both in Europe and America: men's friendships, and men's reputations, never had a harder lot, in the face of differences of opinion.

The Revolution, which culminated in the Declaration of Independence in the year 1776, did not, in all respects, ultimately suit the tastes of the whole American people. A numerous section, after the immediate cause of the quarrel with the mother country had been despatched, remained "loyal;" and would have been well pleased to see re-union with England. Others, again, satisfied with Independence, were yet desirous that the Constitution should be as near as possible on a monarchical plan, with a basis of government centralized at the capital. A still larger class,— daily augmented, too, by the arrival of English, Irish, and French refugees,—were for republicanism pure and simple.

France had given support to the infant republic, from the first; having recognized "Independence" in 1778, and, from that date, continued to give aid in the shape of food supplies and war material, during the progess of the conflict. The treaty of peace being concluded with Great Britain, in the year 1783, and the States settling down to consider their future, it was soon discovered that the Constitution, which had first been hastily framed, was inadequate for the purposes of good government ; there was no power to compel individual states, where unanimity, or, at least, general consent, was desirable.[2]   A new Constitution was therefore promulgated, by which absolute power was lodged in a central Federal Congress of the States.   From that date the two prominent political parties came into existence : the one, known as the Federalist, strongly in favour of centralization ; the other, the anti-Federalist or Democratic party, which was for independent state sovereignty, and which was too deeply republican in its nature not to fear the risks, which centralized power would entail upon the new-born liberties of the nation.   The leading partisans on the former side were Washington, John Adams, Alexander Hamilton, and John Jay ; whilst Thomas Jefferson and James Madison were the most eminent among the Democratic leaders. It must be noted, however, that the statesmen of both parties were unanimous on the point of re-publicanism *per se :* their aim was one object, about

---

[2] As Cobbett himself very correctly says, "The war once ended, and the object of that war obtained, ... the Congress became an inefficient body, and each State, having carefully retained its independent sovereignty, looked to its particular regulations, and its separate interests, which were often (not to say always) opposed to the regulations and the   terests of all the other States.— " P. P. Works," i. 38.

which there could be no further question ; their differences consisted in the consideration of the best means of attaining it.

Mr. Jefferson had been minister to France ; and returned to America in 1790, to take a part in the administration. He has left upon record his experience, upon resuming his place in society, of the reaction against extreme republicanism which had already taken place ;[3] other testimony, of similar bearing, could be adduced, but it is hardly necessary

[3] " Being fresh from the French Revolution, while in its first and pure stage, and consequently whetted up in my own republican principles, I found a state of things, in the general society of the place (New York), which I could not have supposed possible. Being a stranger there, I was feasted from table to table, at large set dinners, the parties generally from twenty to thirty. The Revolution I had left, and that we had just gone through in the recent change of our own Government, being the common topics of conversation, I was astonished to find the general prevalence of monarchical sentiments, insomuch that in maintaining those of republicanism, I had always the whole company on my hands, never scarcely finding among them a single co-advocate in that argument, unless some old member of Congress happened to be present. The furthest that any one would go, in support of the Republican features of our new Government, would be to say, 'The present Constitution is well as a beginning, and may be allowed a fair trial ; but it is, in fact, only a stepping-stone to something better.' Among their writers, Denny, the Editor of the *Portfolio*, who was a kind of oracle with them, and styled the Addison of America, openly avowed his preference of monarchy over all other forms of government, prided himself on the avowal, and maintained it by argument freely and without reserve, in his publications."—T. J. to Wm. Short, Jan. 8, 1825 : Jefferson's "Writings," vii. 390

for our purpose, considering the amount of support which Cobbett received during the whole period of his residence in America. There seems to have been, in point of fact, a Federal majority from the very first,—and, when the European war broke out, early in 1793, this section of the nation sympathized, generally speaking, with the English. A strong anti-British feeling prevailed, however, among the Democrats, which was displayed in the most fiery and intemperate language,[4] and found particular vent in a hearty enthusiasm for the French cause. The first outbreak of the French revolution was hailed with joy by the extreme republicans; and, at last, when Mr. Pitt came to think that England was called upon to declare war against France, in defence of the old European doctrines, this hatred of England was naturally intensified. Washington's proclamation of neu-

---

[4] "In the year 1794, or 5, a Mr. Rutledge, who was a judge in South Carolina, made a speech, in which he besought his country to join itself with the Republic of France in a mortal war against England. 'She will,' said he, 'never forgive us for our success against her, and for our having established a free constitution. Let us, therefore, while she is down, seize her by the throat, strangle her, deliver the world of her tyranny, and thus confer on mankind the greatest of blessings.' As nearly as I can recollect them, these were his very words. I am sure that I have the ideas correct. I and many more cried aloud against the barbarity of such sentiments. They were condemned in speeches and pamphlets innumerable."— "Political Register," xxvi. 422.

trality was in vain, to check the ardour of the pen-and-ink warriors ; and the constant arrival of proscribed persons was just so much fuel added to the flames. Another outbreak of war, between England and America, was even apprehended ; and would have taken place, but for the moderate counsels which prevailed in the minds of Washington and his advisers.

At this juncture, there arrived as ambassador to the United States, one GENEST,[5] a man eminently fitted for the useful task of stirring up strife ; and it is, indeed, difficult to believe that the man was not selected with this object in view. Of the strongest republican principles, he thoroughly scorned the traditions of diplomacy ; and landed at Charleston [April 1793] more with the air of a newly-appointed provincial governor than with that of envoy from a friendly nation. Several weeks elapsed before he presented his credentials to Washington : meanwhile, he was actually engaged in superintending the fitting-out of priva-

---

[5] Edmond Charles Genest, born 1765, died 1834. He possessed remarkable abilities from his youth, and early entered the diplomatic service. After four years in Russia as *Chargé d'Affaires*, he was sent to America, as related in the text ; and, having been eventually superseded, he elected to remain and become naturalized. His life was thenceforth occupied in promoting improvements in agriculture and in the arts and sciences. (Vide " Biog. Universelle," also Drake's " American Biography.")

teers! And on his arrival at Philadelphia there were festivities and congratulations, and speeches, to be attended to, before he could condescend to wait upon the President. His subsequent conduct was all of a piece with this; till, the President having found it necessary to repudiate a French vice-consul on account of his gross infractions of neutrality, Genest's high-toned appeal upon the matter obliged Washington, at last, to consider the question of demanding his recall. This was effected in the following year.[6]

But all this did not happen without largely affecting the temper of the American people. Although Washington generously distinguished between the conduct of the minister and "the friendly spirit of the nation which sent him;" although, as Jefferson records, the Government were "determined to see, in these proceedings, but the character of the individual, and not to believe that they were by instructions from his employers," yet it was undoubtedly a new spur to the active spirit of democracy. The Philadelphia politicians, especially, raved and stormed over the iniquities of Britain and the virtues of France.

[6] For full details of this curious episode, see Jefferson, "Writings," iv., pp. 32—46; Cobbett, "P. P. Works," x. 101, *et seq.*; also the "Annual Register," for 1793-94.

A more serious trouble to the American Government arose, soon after the war between England and France had continued some time. As, when the young Republic was fighting for its life, they had been assisted by the French, so they now shipped large aids, chiefly in the shape of provisions, to the French ports. These cargoes were unquestionably contraband; and the British Government, holding that view, ordered that all American vessels be detained,—those laden with corn to be seized,—and a reasonable price to be paid for the cargoes and freights. Later on, another order was issued, directed against American cargoes which consisted of provisions and stores for the French colonies. All this naturally irritated the Americans; they considered it simply an infraction of their independence; and they were not disposed tamely to yield to a power which, in the eyes of many, was not unlikely to dream of future reconquest.

Some alarm was also aroused by the conduct of the British troops in Canada, who retook possession of certain frontier forts, which had been ceded to America at the treaty of peace. At the same time, public attention was directed to a conference held between Lord Dorchester, the Governor of Canada, and several Indian tribes; on which occasion language was held by the

Governor, which seemed to carry with it a willing-
ness on the part of England to proceed to
hostilities, upon a given contingency.

Fortunately, however, the disposition of the
American Administration was such, that the fury
of the Democrats was powerless to disturb its
equanimity; and the only serious step, which the
Government was induced to take, was to lay an
embargo upon the British shipping in American
ports, for the space of thirty days.[7] It was
necessary, however, to come to an understanding ;
accordingly, an envoy, in the person of Mr. Jay,
repaired to England with full powers, in the hope
that existing difficulties might be removed, and a
proper feeling of amity be secured, between the
two nations.

Mr. Jay's mission was eminently successful, as
regarded the two Governments ; but the Treaty in
which it resulted only served to make the breach
wider, that existed between the Democrats and
their opponents. His return to America was
signalized by an unexampled storm of invective
and abuse ; and Jay had, in fact, to retire from
public life.[8] The principle that the flag does not

---

[7] Vide " Annual Register," 1794, for the interesting state papers
on these topics.

[8] Mr. Jay was a genuine patriot. He was moderate in politics,

cover the merchandise was the feature which gave
the greatest offence ; but the real objections were
sentimental, and were, in fact, brewing as soon as
Jay's appointment as envoy became known.[9] The
treaty was the work of the Washington administration, the members of which were known to be
favourably disposed towards England ; and it was
considered likely to injure the relations existing
between America and France. Its opponents
maintained, from the first, that the disposition of
Great Britain being naturally hostile to the United
States, there could be no prospect of real reci-
procity ; and, when the document arrived, their
first thought was that its ratification would give
umbrage to the French. That, if the United States
could convert the evil disposition of England into
one of amity and peace, the projected treaty would

but no trimmer. After his retirement he devoted himself to questions of social improvement, especially the abolition of slavery.

[9] For a complete analysis of the opposition views on the British
Treaty, *vide* " Life of A. J. Dallas," pp. 160 *et seq*. As a specimen of the mad and vindictive feelings then current, see a letter to
the editor of the New York *Argus*, signed " An Individual," and
dated Jan. 17, 1796, in which he informs the editor that the
Treaty meets with his entire disapprobation ; and continues, " I
have come to a solemn resolution, that I will not hereafter import,
sell, or consume any goods, wares, or merchandise, the produce or
manufacture of Great Britain and her dependencies. I leave others
to act as they please, but this is my firm determination with respect
to myself whilst the said Treaty continues in force."

be too high a price to pay for the change; and if there must be war with either Great Britain or France, it were "more politic for the state, and more congenial with the sentiments of the people, to engage the former," as France would give aid "with all the energy of her triumphant arms;" whilst, in the case of a war with France, the Americans could neither count upon the affections, nor rely upon the power, of Great Britain.

But what served, much more, to augment the numbers and vehemence of the Radical party, and to foment bad feeling between the two countries, was the constant stream of refugees from the United Kingdom. Mr. Pitt's repressive measures were in full force; and the year 1794 witnessed some of the most glaring instances of tyranny that had been displayed in England since the days of James the Second. Frequent trials for " sedition " only served to inflame and to energize the spirit of free inquiry; and men boldly talked of revolution. Some suffered imprisonment, many more managed to escape; and of those who escaped, many found a free asylum in Pennsylvania. Some of these men were of good education and great natural ability; and all were inspired with the hopes of the day: an imminent deliverance of mankind, generally, from all kinds of despotism whatsoever.

So, this is how it was in Philadelphia, in these
lively times. The most enlightened and philosophical city in the United States was, at the
same time, the hot-bed of democracy: the home of
all that was aspiring in the human heart and mind.
Thus, we can understand something of the feelings
which animate the breast of Mr. William Cobbett,
ardent Loyalist. He knows little of theoretical
politics ; his short experience of republicanism has
only, at present, served to show him that man is
little better off as the subject of a sovereign people,
than as a subject of a sovereign king ; provided that
similar constitutional principles prevail. His recollections of Tom Paine's animated book, and his former enthusiasm for republicanism, are—as in the
minds of thousands of his cotemporaries—crushed
and buried beneath the torrent of blood and tears
which has been shed in France. A natural reaction
has set in : his native land, with all her faults,
comes back to his memory as a land of average comfort and well-being ; and the thought is uppermost
that, perish " liberty and equality," if all their
results are to consist in a murdered king, and in
the home of his childhood desolated by the blood-
thirsty apostles of progress.

One of these emigrants was Mr. James Thom-
son Callender. His reading of English history

had caused his mind to dwell, somewhat heavily, upon the underhand means which ministers and parties had used, to carry their points, during the last century. Abuses in Church and State : this is the sort of *pabulum* for the public taste, and Mr. Callender, accordingly, undertakes to put them all into a popular form, under the title of "The Political Progress of Britain."[1] The result is, that

---

[1] " The Political Progress of Britain ; or, An Impartial History of Abuses in the Government of the British Empire, in Europe, Asia, and America. From the Revolution in 1688 to the present time : the whole tending to prove the ruinous Consequences of the popular System of Taxation, War, and Conquest." It was a little too violent for its purpose ; and, although it contained a good deal of truth, the tract was malevolent and unpatriotic, and the author deserved to be prosecuted (from a ministerial point of view).

The preface to the American edition is worth reading, as telling some of the story of the times :—" Advertisement.—The first edition of 'The Political Progress of Britain' was published at Edinburgh and London, in autumn, 1792. The sale was lively, and the prospect of future success flattering. The plan was, to give an impartial history of the abuses in government, in a series of pamphlets. But, while the author was preparing for the press a second number, along with a new edition of the first, he was, on the 2nd of January, 1793, apprehended, and with some difficulty made his escape. Two booksellers, who acted as his editors, were prosecuted, and, after a very arbitrary trial, they were condemned, the one to three months, and the other to six months of imprisonment. A revolution will take place in Scotland before the lapse of ten years at farthest, and most likely much sooner. The Scots nation will then certainly think itself bound, by every tie of wisdom, of gratitude, and of justice, to make reparation to these two honest men for the tyranny which they have encountered in the cause of truth. In Britain, authors and editors of pamphlets have long con-he is a fugitive before many weeks are over his head, and any further attacks which he has to make, upon the government of Mr. Pitt and his predecessors, must be offered from the other side of the Atlantic. The pamphlet, republished in Philadelphia, comes under the eye of our neophyte politician, and Mr. Cobbett sniffs war. The "Political progress" presented just the sort of topic which would serve as provocation : here was another villain maligning his country, and the wretch must be made an example of.

Accordingly, on the 8th of January, 1795, Mr. Thomas Bradford has for sale, "A Bone to Gnaw for the Democrats;" consisting of a review of Callender's book, followed by a still more daring

---

ducted the van of every revolution. They compose a kind of forlorn hope on the skirts of battle ; and though they may often want experience, or influence, to marshal the main body, they yet enjoy the honour and the danger of the first rank, in storming the ramparts of oppression.

" The verdict of a packed jury did not alter the opinions of those who had approved of the publications. Five times its original price hath, since its suppression, been offered in Edinburgh for a copy. At London, a new edition was printed by Ridgway and Symonds, two booksellers, confined in Newgate for publishing political writings. They sell the pamphlet, and others of the same tendency, openly in prison. It is next to impossible for despotism to overwhelm the divine art of printing," &c., &c.

Mr. Callender eventually became a newspaper editor at Richmond, Va., and distinguished himself as an uncompromising opponent of the Federalist administrations.

attack upon the democratic press and upon the numerous clubs connected with the party.

The "Bone to Gnaw" was a distinct advance upon the "Observations." The writer had evidently begun to discuss, and to wrangle. And the discovery that he had the power to wield a very vigorous pen soon brought the inclination to use it. There is a good deal of coarseness, as we should look at it now-a-days, but that was the temper of the times. The pamphlet raised up a host of enemies, whilst the number of Cobbett's admirers proportionately increased ; and readers were found, both in England and America, to give their warmest approbation.

But, among others, was "one Smith, a malignant democrat," who had started an "American Monthly Review." In reviewing "A Bone to Gnaw," he endeavoured to weaken the writer's nerve by attacking his grammar and composition. To very little purpose, except to bring Mr. Cobbett up, smiling, with a rejoinder. For, in February, was published "A Kick for a Bite," consisting principally of a humorous lesson in the art of criticism, addressed to the editor of the *Review ;* and in March, Part II. of "A Bone to Gnaw for the Democrats."

It was about this date, January or February,

1795, when some newspaper correspondent likened
the new federalist writer to a porcupine. The idea
was instantly adopted; and Cobbett announces
himself to the editor of the "American Monthly
Review," as "PETER PORCUPINE, at your service."
Thus arose one of the most famous of pseudonyms.[2]
It was a long while before the bearer of it was generally known, *i.e.* beyond a very small circle of
acquaintances; yet it appears that the "British
Critic," as early as Dec. 1795, had discovered the
owner of the name. But the publication of a name,
pseudonymous or otherwise, furnished as it were a
handle for opponents; one insisted on calling him
"Mr. Hedgehog," another styled him "the pork-
patriot," and so on. Beyond the play upon words,
however, and fresh showers of Billingsgate upon
the British name, there was very little talent in
these early attacks upon Mr. Cobbett. One of
them, which has survived, is excessively tame,
although the writer undertakes to wring Porcupine's nose, and humble his vanity and pre-
sumption; and proceeds to insinuate, that he
conceals himself through fear of the horsewhip;
and that he is neither more nor less than an

---

[2] It cannot be said that the title of "Porcupine" was altogether
appropriate. The vulgar notion (derived from Pliny) that this
harmless animal had the power of shooting its quills at an adversary
was probably the origin of the appellation.

obscure pedagogue, whose moral rectitude would not bear the test of scrutiny beyond the Atlantic."[2]

" A Bone to Gnaw, Part II.," is taken up by a denunciation of the Society of United Irishmen, a democratic club in Dublin, which had published an account of its proceedings ; and of the acts of the French Convention at Lyons, where unheard-of cruelties had just been perpetrated.   The following bit of humour conveys so many ideas, illustrative of the prevailing topics of controversy, that it is worth while reproducing here :—

"It would have been unpardonable in a society like that of the *United Irishmen*, if, among their numerous addresses, none was to be found to the firebrand philo-

---

[2] " A Rub from Snub ; or, a Cursory Analytical Epistle ; addressed to Peter Porcupine, author of the Bone to Gnaw, Kick for a Bite, &c., &c.   Containing Glad Tidings for the Democrats, and a word of comfort to Mrs. S. Rowson, wherein the said Porcupine's moral, political, critical, and literary character is fully illustrated." (Philadelphia, 1795.)   Here is a little specimen of the style :— " Nature must have had the hysterics when you were born ; mastiffs howled, and owls sang anthems to congratulate you into existence, and your jaws must have been furnished with indissoluble tusks expressive of the disposition that was inspired within you."

Mrs. Rowson was an English emigrant, who had arrived in Philadelphia in 1793, and soon blazed forth as an actress and novelist, and enjoyed great popularity.   One of her novels is still reprinted.   Cobbett had made a review of the " roma-drama-poetic works of Mrs. S. Rowson " the object of some humour in " A Kick for a Bite."

sopher, Priestley. 'Farewell,' say they, in their conso-
latory address to him,—'farewell, great and good man!
Your change of place will give room for the matchless
activity of your genius; and you will take a sublime
pleasure in bestowing on Britain the benefit of your
future discoveries.' Every honest man ought to wish that
this were true; for the doctor has already made some
discoveries of the utmost importance to future chemical
emigrants, if he could be prevailed on to publish them.
He might let his brethren into the secret of buying land
(or rather *rock*) at a dollar an acre, and selling it again
at ninepence-halfpenny. This is a sort of anti-chemistry,
by which copper is extracted from silver; and the process by which it is accomplished must certainly be a
desideratum in the learned world. The doctor might
also favour curious foreigners with the feats of those
American magi, vulgarly called land-surveyors, whose
potent art levels the mountain with the valley, makes the
rough way smooth, the crooked straight; whose creative
pencil calls into being nodding woods and verdant lawns;
and, like the rod of Moses, makes rivulets gush from
the solid rock.

" 'Farewell,' continue the *United Irishmen*, 'farewell,
great and good man; but, before you go, we beseech a
portion of your parting prayer' (down upon your marrow-
bones, reader) 'for Archibald Hamilton Rowan, Muir,
Palmer, Margarot, and Gerald, who are now, like you,
preparing to cross the bleak ocean. Farewell! soon
will you embrace your sons on the American shore,
Washington will take you by the hand, and the *shade*

of Franklin look down, with calm delight on the first
statesman of the age, extending his protection to its first
philosopher.' Here is certainly some mistake in the
close of this farewell. What do they mean by the shade
of Franklin looking *down*? To look *down* on a person
one must be in an elevated situation; and I fancy it is
pretty generally believed, by those who understand the
geography of the invisible world, that Franklin's *shade*,
as it is termed, has taken a different route, &c."

Meanwhile, the ferment of the public mind over
the British Treaty was now so intensified, that the
people were becoming frantic with rage. Jay was
hung in effigy, and the democratic press poured
forth upon his head an untiring volley of misrepresentation and abuse. In Virginia, there was an
open threat of secession, in case of the treaty being
ratified. At Boston, there were riots. The treaty
reached America in March, but was not presented
to the Senate till early in June; but its articles
got wind, in some way or other, and were
fully discussed by the press and the radical
clubs long before being entertained by the Legislature.

An opportunity soon occurred, for Mr. Cobbett
to produce another apology for Anti-Gallic principles. A pamphlet appeared, in the course of the
summer, under the title of "The Letters of

Franklin," dealing with the treaty question, in a strongly dissuasive manner.[4]

In August, therefore, Mr. Bradford had another work, at the hands of the now-celebrated Peter Porcupine, entitled, "A Little Plain English, addressed to the People of the United States, on the Treaty, &c., in answer to 'The Letters of Franklin.'" This is, in some respects, one of the best of Cobbett's writings. It is almost purely argumentative, and there is a sobriety of tone, and a seriousness about its logic, which contrast well with the humour, and even buffoonery, in which he had previously indulged. There was less to joke about. His opponents (and especially this "Franklin") were becoming illogical in their rage. Mr. Madison wanted to force all the nations of Europe, and especially Great Britain, into the acceptance of a commercial treaty; and this one, alas! was positively being carried through in a friendly spirit. England was noted for her perfidy

---

[4] It does not appear to be known who was the author of these anonymous "letters." Cobbett charged A. J. Dallas with the authorship; and they certainly have the same stamp as Dallas's "Features of the English Treaty." But it must be left to conjecture. Cobbett gives his reason for selecting the "Letters" to write down, out of all "the volumes, or rather *bales*," that had already appeared, because these seemed to him the fairest sample of the opinions and language of the opposers of the treaty. They had originally appeared in the *Aurora* newspaper.

and double-dealing, and they therefore could not make a treaty with her ; but, as Mr. Cobbett pointed out, her bad character was rather a reason for binding her hands, and controlling her over-reaching ways. And, as to the magnanimity of the French Republic, and its desire to "protect" its sister, it was clear that little could be hoped for on that score, seeing that she was losing part of her own colonies and making war upon the remainder ; besides that it was notorious that French privateering was quite as bad as English, as far as it could go, in its depredations on American commerce. In reality, Cobbett's aim was to deter the Americans from a French alliance, as "Franklin's" desire was to secure it. And "Franklin," so ridiculous as to urge the impeachment of the President, for not having courted the French, and for having sent "the slave, the coward, the traitor" Jay (of all men) as envoy to Great Britain, is fairly, but mercilessly exposed.

"A Little Plain English" soon appeared in London, being reprinted by Rivington, and was instantly welcomed with the applause it deserved. It was considered to prove, to every impartial mind, that the engagement entered into between the two countries was honourable to both. The eloquent and sparkling language, in which his ideas were conveyed, raised the author into the first rank of English writers. And, on account of his loyal sentiments, with their anti-revolutionary bias, Mr. Cobbett was declared, by people at home, to have rendered inestimable services to his native land.

The British Treaty was, however, in far greater peril than could be averted by the soundest arguments or the warmest loyalty. Whilst the treaty was being discussed throughout the States, an incident occurred which eventually laid bare the real source of the danger which threatened the amicable negotiations; that danger proved to be French intrigue.

The incident alluded to was one of that class which furnish the sensational parts of a melodrama, where a fortunate chance renders nugatory the craftiest of plans, and buries your villain beneath the ruin of his own devices. One Captain Goddard (the hero of the piece, and, of course, a British Tar) has the ill-luck to fall into the hands of a French privateer. The latter, proceeding homeward from the American shores, and in charge of despatches from Fauchet, the French envoy at Philadelphia, is herself obliged, in turn, to strike her colours to a British frigate, almost within sight of home. Her captain, pursuant to instructions, goes below to secure Fauchet's despatches; and, as the frigate's boat approaches, commits the precious documents to the waves. But there's a British Tar aboard, who, with instinctive readiness understanding the situation, plunges into the sea, and secures the packet, is picked up by the boat, and checkmates " Mossoo." And Captain Goddard, as he stands dripping on the deck, little knows what a prize has fallen to his turn!

For, these intercepted despatches contained highly-compromising matter. A certain member of Washington's administration, EDMUND RAN-DOLPH,[5] Secretary of State, was a thorough-paced Radical, and an opponent of the President's policy. Up to the end of July, or the beginning of August, 1795, he had led the opposition to the treaty; and, although the Senate and the people had become not only reconciled to its provisions, but desirous that the affair should be settled, Washington still felt unable to conclude it, on account of the dis-sensions in his Cabinet. But, on the 14th of August, Randolph being absent from the council, the treaty was ratified. The surprise of the latter was great, when he heard of this sudden delibera-

[5] Edmund Randolph, sometime governor of Virginia, and a very eminent lawyer of his day. He supported the Revolution, and was disinherited by his father for deserting the royal cause. He was Secretary of State 1794-5. Born 1753, died 1813.

tion ; and, on learning the cause, his only resource
was to resign his appointment, and to go home and
consider his future. For it actually appeared, that
one of the French Minister's letters thus intercepted described an interview with Randolph, in
which the latter, and two or three other persons,
expected pecuniary assistance in return for their
support of French ascendancy. So, when the
English Embassy produced these precious documents, just received from London, and urged the
immediate ratification of the treaty, there was only
one course for Washington to pursue, viz. to accede
to the request. Mr. Randolph was in sufficient
disgrace ; but he was foolish enough to make it
widely known, by devoting more than a hundred
pages of octavo to full details of the circumstances
which led to his abrupt departure from office.[6]
These pages were given to the public about the
middle of December ; and among that eager
public was Mr. William Cobbett,—who saw his
opportunity.

So, on the 1st of January, 1796, is announced

[6] "A Vindication of Mr. Randolph's Resignation." (Philadelphia, S. H. Smith, 1795.) Mr. Smith advertises afterwards
(*Aurora* of Feb. 17, 1796) that a copyright had been taken out for
the "Vindication," so that as many entire copies might be diffused
as possible ; also to cover the cost of printing. Also, he now gives
permission to all the printers in the United States to republish it if
they like.

"A New Year's Gift to the Democrats ; or, Observations on a Pamphlet, entitled, 'A Vindication
of Mr. Randolph's Resignation,' by Peter Porcupine ;" which turns out to be a very smart piece
of writing, calculated to disturb the equanimity of
every French sympathizer in the States.

The preface to "A New Year's Gift," &c. is
worth giving in full :—

"The Democrats and I have long been in the friendly
habit of making presents to each other; and, this being
a season of the year when an interchange of civilities
of this kind is more particularly looked for, I was just
turning about me for a subject that might serve as some
little mark of my attention, when the vindication of
Mr. Randolph's resignation made its long-looked-for
appearance.

"If the reader knows anything of the Democrats, he
will allow that this vindication is most eminently calculated to furnish me with the means of making them a
grateful offering : and I was the more anxious to be
prompt in the performance of this duty of etiquette, as,
from their present formidable situation, it was to be
feared, that they might have the will as well as the
power to turn their vengeance against me, in case of the
slightest neglect.

"When we take a view of their affairs for a year
past, it is impossible not to perceive that they are
wonderfully improved. They have had address sufficient to stir up the mob to burn the greatest part of the

Federal senators in effigy; they have dared publickly and vilely to traduce the President of the United States; their own President has been elected a member of the legislature of Pennsylvania; the legislature of Virginia has declared in their favour; and a fresh importation of thieves and traitors from Ireland is daily expected to arrive. These are great and solid advantages, and when we add to them the '*precious confessions*,' which they may, by the help of '*some thousands of dollars*,' be able to draw from their new and communicative brother, we cannot help regarding their club as the rising sun of this country.

"To this great luminary, then, I kneel; not to ask a boon, but to offer one; and such a one as I hope will be acceptable, as its great object is to commemorate actions flowing from the purest principles of democracy."

As for the pamphlet itself, it was in Porcupine's best style; running through the items, *seriatim*, to which Randolph had inconsiderately given needless publicity. Mr. Bradford himself admired it, and showed it gleefully to his leading customers; several of whom stated that it had been intended to answer Randolph's "Vindication," but that it was now unnecessary, seeing that Peter Porcupine was in the field; also that the officers of government were exceedingly delighted with his publications.

CHAPTER VI.

"PETER PORCUPINE, AT YOUR SERVICE!"

MR. THOMAS BRADFORD'S Political Book Store, No. 8, South Front Street, is furnished with all the latest publications. The works of Paine, Volney, Godwin and others, fill his shelves, and those of the new Federal light enliven his counter. He is doing a roaring trade ; senators look in and gossip, and laugh over Porcupine ; members from the House of Representatives come in and flatter the writer, and want to be blessed with a sight of him—" one wanted to treat me to a supper, another wanted to shake hands with me, and a third wanted to embrace me."

But Mr. Cobbett is getting too independent. On the next proposal to publish, he actually wants to have a voice in the matter, over some detail ; and, early in 1796, their engagements are sundered.

The plan for opening the new year was a commentary on the debates in Congress, under the title of " The Prospect from the Congress Gallery." The first number appeared at the end of January. The circumstances under which Cobbett broke off with his publisher are thus given in the American autobiography (published in the ensuing August):

" My concerns with Mr. Bradford closed with " The Prospect from the Congress Gallery ;" and, as our separation has given rise to conjectures and reports, I shall trouble the reader with an explanation of the matter. I proposed making a mere collection of the debates, with here and there a note by way of remarks. It was not my intention to publish it in numbers, but at the end of the session, in one volume; but Mr. Bradford, fearing a want of success in this form, determined on publishing in numbers. This was without my approbation, as was also a subscription that was opened for the support of the work. When about half a Number was finished, I was informed that many gentlemen had expressed their desire, that the work might contain a good deal of original matter, and few debates. In consequence of this, I was requested to alter my plan; I said I would, but that I would by no means undertake to continue the work.

" The first Number, as it was called (but not by me) was published, and its success led Mr. Bradford to press for a continuation. His son offered me, I believe, a hundred dollars a Number, in place of eighteen ; and, I should have accepted his offer, had it not been for a word that escaped him during the conversation. He observed, that their customers would be much disappointed, for that, his *father had promised* a continuation, and *that it should be made very interesting*. This slip of the tongue opened my eyes at once. What! a bookseller undertake to promise that I should write, and that I should write to please his customers too! No; if all his *customers*, if all the Congress with the President at their head, had come and solicited me; nay, had my salvation depended on a compliance, I would not have written another line.

" I was fully employed at this time, having a translation on my hands for Mr. Moreau de St. Méry, as well as another work which took up a great deal of my time; so that, I believe, I should not have published the *Censor* had it not been to convince the *customers* of Mr. Bradford, that I was not in his pay; that I was not the puppet and he the showman. That, whatever merits or demerits my writings might have, no part of them fell to his share."

The " Prospect " was pretty successful; and it was resolved to continue it occasionally. The next number was not published, however, till the end of March ; and the title was changed to " The Political Censor." But we now find on the title-page the name of Benjamin Davies, at No. 68, High Street —so it appears that the dissatisfaction with Mr. Bradford had some meaning in it. Between the first and second numbers of the " Censor," Peter

Porcupine produced a little book on French "horrors," which had a great sale both in America and England, under the name of "The Bloody Buoy, thrown out as a Warning to the Political Pilots of all Nations: or, a faithful Relation of a Multitude of Acts of Horrid Barbarity, such as the Eye never witnessed, the Tongue expressed, or the Imagination conceived, until the Commencement of the French Revolution," &c. This was published at Davies' Book-store, and its announcement in the papers was probably the first intimation that Mr. Bradford had of the impending loss of Porcupine's custom.

The later transactions between Cobbett and Bradford are thus disposed of in the auto-biography:—

"After the 'Observations,' Mr. Bradford and I published together no longer. When a pamphlet was ready for the press, we made a bargain for it, and I took his note of hand, payable in one, two, or three months. That the public may know exactly what gains I have derived from the publications that issued from Mr. Bradford's, I here subjoin a list of them, and the sums received in payment.

	Dollars.	Cents.
Observations	0	21
Bone to Gnaw, 1st part . .	125	0
Kick for a Bite	20	0

	Dollars.	Cents.
Bone to Gnaw, 2nd part . .	40	0
Plain English	100	0
New Year's Gift . . .	100	0
Prospect	18	0
Total	403	21

"The best way of giving the reader an idea of the generosity of my bookseller is, to tell him, that upon my going into business for myself, I offered to purchase the copyrights of these pamphlets at the same price that I had sold them at. Mr. Bradford refusing to sell, is a clear proof that they were worth more than he gave me, even after they had passed through several editions. Let it not be said, then, that he put a coat upon my back."

Upon Mr. Bradford finding that "The Political Censor" was to be carried on without his assistance and patronage, he wrote to Cobbett requesting him to fulfil the contract, which, he alleged, existed between them by the sale of the first "Prospect," and threatened an "applycation" to the laws of his country, &c. Mr. Cobbett, remarking on this, says,—

"It is something truly singular, that Mr. Bradford should threaten me with a prosecution for not writing, just at the moment that others threatened me with a prosecution for writing. It seemed a little difficult to set both at open defiance, yet this was done, by continuing to write, and by employing another bookseller. Indeed, these booksellers in general are a cruel race. They imagine that the soul and body of every author that falls into their hands is their exclusive property. They have adopted the birdcatcher's maxim: 'A bird that can sing, and won't sing, ought to be made sing.' Whenever their devils are out of employment the drudging goblin of an author must sharpen up his pen, and never think of repose till he is relieved by the arriva of a more profitable job. Then the wretch may remain as undisturbed as a sleep-mouse in winter, while the stupid dolt, whom he has clad and fattened, receives the applause."

An influential and respectable citizen of Philadelphia, at this period, was Benjamin Franklin Bache;[1] a strong Democrat, and particularly

---

[1] His father, Richard Bache, was a zealous revolutionist who had emigrated from Settle, in Yorkshire, and settled in America as a merchant. He married Sarah Franklin, and succeeded her distinguished father as Postmaster-General of the United States. Died at Settle, Penn., in 1811. Sarah Franklin Bache was long remembered for her patriotic services during the revolutionary war. Their son, Benjamin Franklin Bache, accompanied his grandfather to Paris, gained a knowledge of printing at Didot's, and returned to America in 1785. Five years later, he started the *General Advertizer*, subsequently called the *Aurora*, which paper exercised considerable influence in opposition to the administration of Washington and Adams. Born 1769, died 1798, of the fever which was then devastating the city.

zealous on behalf of French opinions. He conducted a daily newspaper, the *Aurora,* and kept
a political book-store. The *Aurora* was one of the
ablest and most influential journals on the
American Continent ; besides being, in its general
appearance, a newspaper which put to shame even
the London ones of that day. And the Editor and
publisher of the *Aurora,* in his capacity of chief-
whipper-in to the Democrats of Pennsylvania,
among other matters, thought proper to allow
his paper to become the vehicle for abusing Peter
Porcupine. This newspaper, having escaped the
usual fate of ephemeral publications, will furnish
us with the means of judging exactly what Peter's
opponents thought of him.

As a specimen of the opposing factions, however,
we will, at present, only refer to two New York
papers.

Minerva, Jan. 15, 1796.

" PETER PORCUPINE has
given an excellent key to
Mr. Randolph's Vindica-
tion. Never was a present
better timed, than his New
Year's Gift to the Demo-
crats. Every man who has
read the Vindication, should

Argus, Jan. 18, 1796.

"An impartial corres-
pondent desires us to say,
that of all the vulgar catch-
pennies that ever he saw
in print, the late one of
PHINEAS PORCUPINE bears
off the bell! This Porcupine
or Hedgehog, after having

read Peter's explanations and comments upon it, especially all *Whigs*, to whom the *Argus* recommends the perusal of the Vindication. We recommend Peter's gift to the Democratic Society, and trust that, at their next meeting, they will publish resolutions expressing their approbation of the work, as they have lately done with respect to the president's answer to the French minister."

fled (on account of his vile treachery to this his native country) for mere bread, became a garreteer writer for the refugees in London, and a clerk to an Old Bailey solicitor there; and it was through the interest of those refugees that this Hedgehog was returned upon us, in the character he now sustains! His views manifestly are to get himself tarred and feathered, that he may go back howling to England, for further promotion; but, from this hint, it is hoped that he will be disappointed by the democratic Philadelphians."

Mr. Cobbett's design of opening a shop of his own was, probably, formed very early in this year, 1796, and it may be set down as one result of the discovery that Bradford was making capital out of him. The plan appears to have been delayed for some months, and it was not until July that it was carried out. Meanwhile, several numbers of the " Censor " appeared, at the shop of Mr. Davies, and obtained considerable popularity. The original idea was a review of the political transactions of the past month; with an "account of every democratic trick, whether of native growth, or imported from abroad." All of which meant, a defence of Great Britain with vigorous Federal partisanship.[2] Here is one extract from the first number, which will illustrate one of the leading topics that occupied the public mind. It must be recollected that the French Government were now more anxious than ever to court American alliance, they having been specially exasperated at the happy result of the treaty negotiations with England. They accordingly instructed Adet, their envoy, to begin the new year by presenting the national colours to the United States. Washington received the attention very graciously, and informed the minister that the colours would be deposited with the archives of the States. But he also considered it right "to exhibit to the two houses of Congress, these evidences of the continued friendship of the French republic." This was accordingly done, on the 5th of January; and here is Porcupine's account of the proceedings :—

[2] "The *Censor*, a work by Peter Porcupine, administers his monthly correction to our disorganizers. The author is said to be an Englishman who has kept a school in this city."—Letter from C. Goodrich to Oliver Wolcott, printed in "Memoirs of the Administrations of Washington and Adams," by O. W.

" I was rather late in my attendance in Congress this day; a circumstance the more distressing, as I found not only the gallery, but even the passage also, full of spectators. . . . Every person within the walls of this House seemed to be waiting for the development of some great and important mystery. The members were paired off, laying their heads together, whispering and listening with great eagerness; while the Speaker, seated with his chin supported between his right finger and thumb, and his eyes rivetted to the floor, appeared lost, buried alive, as it were, in profundity of thought. Never did wisdom appear more lovely in my eyes. . . . The seriousness of the members of the House naturally produced the most anxious expectation in the minds of the good citizens in my quarter. A thousand ridiculous inquiries were made, in the twinkling of an eye, which were answered by a thousand still more ridiculous conjectures. One said that a law was going to be read to oblige the Virginians to free their slaves and pay their just debts; but another swore that was impossible. A third declared a second embargo was to be laid; and a fourth observed that it was to hinder the cruel English from carrying off our poor horses, to eat them in the West Indies. . . . To tell the reader the truth of my opinion, I was afraid that some new confiscating or sequestrating project was on foot; and when Mr. Dayton, the Speaker, awoke from his reverie, and began to speak,—'Lord have mercy,' said I, 'upon the poor British creditors.' My fears on this account were soon dissipated. The Speaker told us that this message was of the most *solemn* and *serious* nature, and he therefore requested both the

members of the House and the strangers in the gallery
to observe the profoundest silence.

" The reader will easily imagine that a warning like
this increased the torture of suspense. It was now that
we felt the value of the hearing faculty. I observed my
neighbours brushing aside their matted and untutored
locks, that nothing might impede the entrance of the
glad tidings. We were, as the poet says, 'all eye, all
ear.' But there was a little man down below, whose
anxiety seemed to surpass that of all the rest. He crept
to within a very few paces of the leeward side of the
chair, and, turning himself sideways, lifted up the left
corner of his wig, placing the auricular orifice open and
extended, in a direct line with the Speaker's mouth, so
that not a single breath of the precious sounds could
possibly escape him. His longing countenance seemed
to say, in the language of his countryman, Macbeth :—
'Speak ! Speak ! had I three ears, by heaven I'd hear
thee.' . . . .

" All at once, as if by the power of magic, the doors
flew open, 'grating on their hinges harsh thunder,' and
the President's secretary was introduced with an American
officer bearing a flag, which I took to be a representation
of the day of judgment. It had a *thunderbolt* in the
centre, with a *cock* perched upon it ! the emblems of
Almighty vengeance and of watchfulness. At two of the
corners the *globe* was represented in a flame. The staff
was covered with black velvet, sad colour of death, and
crowned with a Parisian pike,—fatal instrument, on
which the bleeding and ghastly heads, nay, even the

palpitating hearts of men, women, and children, have so often been presented to the view of the polite and humane inhabitants of that capital.

"Curiosity now gave way to another passion, that of fear. For my part, I am not ashamed to confess, that I never was in such trepidation since I first saw the light of day. Nor were my companions in a more enviable state. I looked round, and beheld the affrighted group huddled up together, like a brood of chickens waiting the mortal grip of the voracious kite. In this general picture of consternation one object attracted particular notice. It was a democrat, who was so fully persuaded that the flag was the harbinger of fate, that he began to anticipate the torments of the world to come. Never did I before behold such dreadful symptoms of a guilty conscience. He was as white as paper, his knees knocked together, his teeth chattered, he wrung his hands, and rolled his eyes, but durst not lift them towards heaven. His voice was like the yell of the inhabitants of the infernal regions. 'Oh, Franklin Bache! Franklin Bache! Oh! that infernal atheistical calendar!' This was all we could get from him; but this was enough to assure me that he was one of those unhappy wretches, who had been led astray by the profligate correspondents of Mr. Bache, and by the atheistical decadery calendar; which that gentleman has, with so much unholy zeal, endeavoured to introduce amongst us, in place of the Christian one we, as yet, make use of.

"My attention was called off from this terrific picture of despair by a voice from beneath. A tall spare man,

dressed all in black from head to foot . . . . was beginning, in a hollow voice, to read (as I expected) the
decrees of fate, but to my agreeable surprise I found it
was a decree of the National Convention : it was in the
following words, &c."

It was soon after this date that Cobbett made
the acquaintance of Monsieur Talleyrand.   The
notion that the latter was a spy, was at once
formed in Cobbett's mind ; and he long continued
to have that idea, on the ground that Talleyrand
was received with open arms, very soon after his
return to France, by the very men who had proscribed him.   There is no real basis for the suspicion
(which, indeed, has been entertained in other
quarters), but Mr. Cobbett gives very colourable
reasons for his belief :—

" First he set up as a *merchant and dealer* at New
York, till he had acquired what knowledge he thought
was to be come at among persons engaged in mercantile
affairs ; then he assumed the character of a *gentleman*, at
the same time removing to Philadelphia, where he got
access to persons of the first rank,—all those who were
connected with, or in the confidence of, the Government.
Some months after his arrival in this city, he left a
message with a friend of his, requesting me to meet him
at that friend's house.   Several days passed away before
the meeting took place.   I had no business to call me

that way, and therefore I did not go. At last this modern Judas and I got seated by the same fireside. I expected that he wanted to expostulate with me on the severe treatment he had met with at my hands. I had called him an apostate, a hypocrite, and every other name of which he was deserving; I therefore leave the reader to imagine my astonishment, when I heard him begin with complimenting me on my *wit* and *learning.* He praised several of my pamphlets, the 'New Year's Gift' in particular, and still spoke of them as mine. I did not acknowledge myself the author, of course; but yet he would insist that I was; or, at any rate, they reflected, he said, *infinite honour* on the author, let him be who he might. Having carried this species of flattery as far as he judged it safe, he asked me, with a vast deal of apparent seriousness, whether I had received my education at *Oxford* or at *Cambridge!* Hitherto I had kept my countenance pretty well; but this abominable stretch of hypocrisy, and the placid mien and silver accent with which it was pronounced, would have forced a laugh from a quaker in the midst of meeting. I don't recollect what reply I made him, but this I recollect well, I gave him to understand that I was no trout, and consequently was not to be caught by tickling.

"This information led him to something more solid. He began to talk about *business.* I was no *flour merchant,*[*] but I taught English; and, as luck would have it, this was the very commodity that Bishop Perigord

---

[*] Certain mysterious flour-contractors are heard of in Randolph's "Vindication," and Porcupine used the term afterwards to signify persons who could take French money.

wanted. If I had taught Thornton's or Webster's language,[4] or sold sand or ashes, or pepper-pot, it would have been just the same to him. He knew the English language as well as I did; but he wanted to have dealings with me in some way or other.

"I knew that, notwithstanding his being proscribed at Paris, he was extremely intimate with Adet; and this circumstance led me to suspect his real business in the United States. I therefore did not care to take him as a scholar. I told him that being engaged in a translation for the press, I could not possibly quit home. This difficulty the lame fiend hopped over in a moment. He would very gladly come to my house. I cannot say but it would have been a great satisfaction to me to have seen the *ci-devant* Bishop of Autun, the guardian of the holy oil that anointed the heads of the descendants of St. Louis, come trudging through the dirt to receive a lesson from me; but, on the other hand, I did not want a French spy to take a survey either of my desk or my house. My price for teaching was six dollars a month;

---

[4] Thornton's language—this is an allusion to a prize dissertation on written and printed language, by one Wm. Thornton, M.D. It was published in Philadelphia in 1793, and introduced some new symbols. Cobbett's objection to it was, that it was an attempt to make an *American* language, as an improvement on English. For the curious in such matters, the title of the Essay is "Cadmus; or, a Treatise on the Elements of Written Language," &c.

Noah Webster, long before the great Dictionary made him famous, had written "Dissertations on the English Language" (1789), which included an Essay on Spelling Reform, a capital advantage of which reform would be the "making a difference between English and American orthography." (*Vide* Allibone; also Duyckinck's "Cyclo. Amer. Lit.")

he offered me *twenty*, but I refused; and before I left him, I gave him clearly to understand that I was not to be purchased."

Preparations were now being made for opening the bookselling business; and after midsummer the house was ready. The shop was opened on the 11th of July, and Mr. Cobbett took advantage of the opportunity thus furnished to make a grand demonstration. The account of this new start in life is better told in his own words:—

" Till I took this house I had remained almost entirely unknown as a writer. A few persons did indeed know that I was the person who had assumed the name of Peter Porcupine; but the fact was by no means a matter of notoriety. The moment, however, that I had taken the lease of a large house, the transaction became a topic of public conversation, and the eyes of the Democrats and the French, who still lorded it over the city, and who owed me a mutual grudge, were fixed upon me.

" I thought my situation somewhat perilous. Such truths as I had published, no man had dared to utter in the United States since the rebellion. I knew that these truths had mortally offended the leading men amongst the Democrats, who could, at any time, muster a mob quite sufficient to destroy my house, and to murder me. I had not a friend to whom I could look with any reasonable hope of receiving efficient support; and as to the law, I had seen too much of republican justice to expect anything but persecution from that quarter. In short, there were in Philadelphia about ten thousand persons, all of whom would have rejoiced to see me murdered; and there might probably be two thousand who would have been very sorry for it; but not above fifty of whom would have stirred an inch to save me.

"I saw the danger, but also saw that I must at once set all danger at defiance, or live in everlasting subjection to the prejudices and caprice of the democratical mob. I resolved on the former, and as my shop was to open on a Monday morning, I employed myself all day on Sunday in preparing an exhibition that I thought would put the courage and the power of my enemies to the test. I put up in my windows, which were very large, all the portraits that I had in my possession of kings, queens, princes, and nobles. I had all the English ministry, several of the bishops and judges, the most famous admirals, and, in short, every picture that I thought likely to excite rage in the enemies of Great Britain.

"Early on the Monday morning I took down my shutters. Such a sight had not been seen in Philadelphia for twenty years. Never since the beginning of the rebellion had any one dared to hoist at his window the portrait of George the Third. . . . .

"I had put up a representation of Lord Howe's victory in a leaf of the 'European Magazine;' but a bookseller with whom I was acquainted, and who came to see how I stood it, whispered me, while the rabble were gazing and growling at my door, that he had two large repre-

sentations of the same action. They were about four feet
long and two wide : the things which are hawked about
and sold at the farm-houses in England. . . . . The
letters were large ; the mob, ten or twenty deep, could
read, and they did read aloud too, 'LORD HOWE'S
DECISIVE VICTORY OVER THE FRENCH FLEET;' and,
therefore, though the price was augmented from sixpence
to two dollars each, I purchased them, and put one up at
the window. . . . . The other I sold to two Englishmen,
who were amongst the numbers that went to America
about the years 1794 and 1795, misled by the representations of Paine and others, and being, as they frankly
acknowledged to me, enemies of their country when they
left it. They had mixed amongst the crowd, had taken
the part of their country, and had proposed to maintain
their words with their fists. After the quarrel had in
some degree subsided, they, partly, perhaps, by way of
defiance, came into the shop to purchase each of them a
picture of Lord Howe and his victory. Finding that
I had but one for sale, they would have purchased that ;
but as it amounted to more money than both of them
were possessed of, they went and, in their phrase, which
I shall never forgot, *kicked their master,*—that is to say,
got money in advance upon their labour. . . . . Having
thus obtained the two dollars, each of them took an end
of the print in his hand, displayed it, and thus carried it
away through the mob, who, though they still cursed,
could not help giving signs of admiration."

The result of all this was just what was to be

expected.   Threats of personal violence, with
plenty of abuse in the newspapers, at once ensued.
On the 16th of July, Cobbett's landlord, John
Oldden, received a threatening letter, to the effect
that that "daring scoundrell," his tenant, was
about to be punished; and with a view of preventing Mr. Oldden's feeling the blow designed for
Porcupine, his correspondent addresses him; as,
when the time of retribution arrives, "it may not
be convenient to discriminate between the innocent
and the guilty," and his property may suffer.   As
a friend, therefore, he advises him to save his property by either compelling Mr. Porcupine to leave
his house, or at all events oblige him "to cease
exposing his abominable productions or any of his
courtly prints at his window for sale."   On the
same day, a correspondent of the *Aurora* informs
the readers of that paper that the "hireling writer
of the British Government" has just refused to pay
his taxes, and was behaving very saucily; until the
tax-collector began to bully him, and call him a
d——d rascal, and threaten to break every bone
in his skin.   At which display of spirit, Peter was
cooled, &c.

In vain all this.   Before the week is out, all
this is brought before the Philadelphia public.   A
pamphlet appears on the 22nd, entitled "The

Scare-Crow; being an infamous letter, &c., with remarks on the same," in which Mr. Cobbett makes fun of the affair, has another fling at the French and the Democrats, and announces that his taxes are paid up to January, 1797.

The charge of being in British pay had now been cropping up for some time, and it was necessary to take some notice of it, if only for the sake of British credit. At length, a very abusive paragraph having appeared in the *Aurora* about this time, presuming to identify the agent who was supplying Peter with the gold of Pitt, the matter became imperative. Accordingly, Cobbett took the opportunity of publishing the history of his life;[5]—a thing which he says he had determined to do, whenever a fair occasion offered.

The communication to the *Aurora* newspaper stated, among other things, that Porcupine had been "obliged to abscond from his darling old England to avoid being turned off into the other world before his time;" that his usual occupation at home was that of a "garret-scribbler" (excepting a little "night-business" occasionally, to supply unavoidable contingencies); and that he had to take

[5] This is the short autobiography from which some of the preceding information as to Cobbett's early life has been derived:— "The Life and Adventures of Peter Porcupine." [Philadelphia, 1796.]

French leave for France; that he was obliged as suddenly to leave that Republic, and figured some time in America as a pedagogue; "but as this employment scarcely furnished him salt to his porridge, he having been literally without hardly bread to eat, and not a second shirt to his back, he resumed his old occupation of scribbling, having little chance of success in the *other employments* which drove him to this country." He is a fugitive felon; but his sudden change of condition shows that secret-service money has been liberally employed; "for his zeal to make atonement to his mother country seems proportioned to the magnitude of his offence, and the guineas advanced." And so on.

The first announcement of "The Life and Adventures of Peter Porcupine" appears in the *Gazette of the United States*[6] of the 9th August; and its publication was the signal for a fresh outburst of spleen on the part of Peter's opponents. And no wonder; for, as a mixture of artlessness and cool impudence, the "Life and Adventures" has seldom been equalled. Gaily daring, he begs his opponents to come on, and fire away at his reputa-

---

[6] A Federalist evening paper, edited by John Fenno. This newspaper was not so distinctively political as the *Aurora*; it dealt much more with mercantile affairs.

tion "till their old pens are worn to the stump," and expresses his extreme sorrow that lies and threats will be all in vain, for he is "one of those whose obstinacy increases with opposition." In point of fact, Peter was just now somewhat intoxicated with success. The applause of friends, and of that large class in every community that is ready to worship successful impudence—along with the virulence of his opponents, and the consciousness of honourable and patriotic motives— had their natural results in the mind of an ardent and earnest man who has recently emerged from obscurity, and who has suddenly learnt how easy it is to become famous—in a country, too, where a spade might be called a spade without fear of an Attorney-General—in a land where existed (at that period) the only semblance of liberty in the whole world.

And, as it turned out, years after, this daring "scoundrell" was the only man found worthy— because the only one with pluck enough—to do good work when he got face to face with his country's enemies at home.

Mr. Cobbett's reply to the charge of being in the pay of the British Government was easy enough :—

" It is hard to prove a negative ; it is what no man is expected to do ; yet I think I can prove that the accusation of my being in British pay is not supported by one single fact, or the least shadow of probability.

" When a foreign Government hires a writer, it takes care that his labours shall be distributed, whether the readers are all willing to pay for them or not. This we daily see verified in the distribution of certain blasphemous gazettes, which, though kicked from the door with disdain, fly in at the window. Now, has this ever been the case with the works of Peter Porcupine ? Were they ever thrusted upon people in spite of their remonstrances? Can Mr. Bradford say that thousands of these pamphlets have ever been paid for by any agent of Great Britain ? Can he say that I have ever distributed any of them ? No ; he can say no such thing. They had, at first, to encounter every difficulty, and they have made their way supported by public approbation, and by that alone. Mr. Bradford, if he is candid enough to repeat what he told me, will say that the British Consul, when he purchased half a dozen of them, insisted upon having them *at the wholesale price !* Did this look like a desire to encourage them ? Besides, those who know anything of Mr. Bradford will never believe that he would have lent his aid to a British agent's publications ; for, of all the Americans I have yet conversed with, he seems to entertain the greatest degree of rancour against that nation.

" I have every reason to believe that the British Consul was far from approving of some at least of my publications. I happened to be in a bookseller's shop,

unseen by him, when he had the goodness to say that
I was a '*wild fellow.*' On which I shall only observe,
that when the king bestows on me about five hundred
pounds sterling a year, perhaps I may become a *tame
fellow*, and hear my master, my countrymen, my friends,
and my parents, belied and execrated, without saying one
single word in their defence.

" Had the Minister of Great Britain employed me to
write, can it be supposed that he would not furnish me
with the means of living well, without becoming the
retailer of my own works ? Can it be supposed that he
would have suffered me ever to have appeared on the
scene ? It must be a very poor king that he serves, if he
could not afford me more than I can get by keeping a
book-shop. An ambassador from a king of the gipsies
could not have acted a meaner part. What ! where was
all the 'gold of Pitt' ? That gold which tempted, according to the Democrats, an American envoy to sell his
country and two-thirds of the Senate to ratify the bargain—that gold which, according to the Convention of
France, has made one half of that nation cut the throats
of the other half—that potent gold could not keep Peter
Porcupine from standing behind a counter to sell a pen-
knife or a quire of paper.

" Must it not be evident, too, that the keeping of a
shop would take up a great part of my time—time that
was hardly worth paying for at all, if it was not of higher
value than the profits on a few pamphlets ? Every one
knows that the 'Censor' has been delayed on account of
my entering into business ; would the Minister of Great

Britain have suffered this, had I been in his pay? No; I repeat that it is downright stupidity to suppose that he would ever have suffered me to appear at all, had he even felt in the least interested in the fate of my works, or the effect they might produce. He must be sensible that, seeing the unconquerable prejudices existing in this country, my being known to be an Englishman would operate weightily against whatever I might advance. I saw this very plainly myself; but, as I had a living to get, and as I had determined on this line of business, such a consideration was not to awe me into idleness, or make me forego any other advantages that I had reason to hope I should enjoy.

" The notion of my being in British pay arose from my having now and then taken upon me to attempt a defence of the character of that nation, and of the intentions of its Government towards the United States. But have I ever teazed my readers with this, except when the subject necessarily demanded it? And if I have given way to my indignation when a hypocritical political divine attempted to degrade my country, or when its vile calumniators called it ' an insular Bastile,' what have I done more than every good man in my place would have done? What have I done more than my duty—than obeyed the feelings of my heart? When a man hears his country reviled, does it require that he should be paid for speaking in its defence?

" Besides, had my works been intended to introduce British influence, they would have assumed a more conciliating tone. The author would have flattered the people of this country, even in their excesses ; he would have endeavoured to gain over the enemies of Britain by smooth and soothing language ; he would ' have stooped to conquer ;' he would not, as I have done, have rendered them hatred for hatred, and scorn for scorn.

" My writings, the first pamphlet excepted, have had no other object than that of keeping alive an attachment to the Constitution of the United States and the inestimable man who is at the head of the Government, and to paint in their true colours those who are the enemies of both; to warn the people, of all ranks and descriptions, of the danger of admitting among them the anarchical and blasphemous principles of the French revolutionists—principles as opposite to those of liberty as hell is to heaven. If, therefore, I have written at the instance of a British agent, that agent must most certainly deserve the thanks of all the real friends of America. But, say some of the half Democrats, what right have you to meddle with the defence of our Government at all ?— The same right that you have to exact my obedience to it, and my contributions towards its support."

It does not appear that Porcupine had the battle entirely on his own hands. Mr. Fenno's *Gazette* occasionally ventured into the arena ; and the presidential following was still strong, even in democratic Philadelphia. Still, Peter seems to have borne the brunt of it for a few months, before others dared to follow. That others did, after a time, he expressly states. But the position he occupied, in the public mind, for a short period in 1796, is almost unexampled. Scarcely a week passed, in the months of August and September, without some new attack upon him, on the part of the *Aurora* newspaper;[7] and there is one day

[7] The reader will be entertained, no doubt, by a specimen or two :—

> " An outcast e'en in hell, and order'd thence,
> The skulking Peter hides," &c.

" Mr. Bache,—You will excuse me for expressing my regret on seeing a character who styles himself Peter Porcupine so often noticed in your paper. What have the people of the United States to do with this man? . . . . What importance can a British sergeant-major acquire in this country by traducing the heroes and counsellors of our late revolution? . . . . His pamphlets are a libel upon common decency and common sense. . . . . Is such a man worthy of being noticed in your paper, Mr. Bache? The best and only way would be to treat him with a silent contempt."

" Anecdote of Peter Porcupine.—The British renegado was met one day by a French gentleman, who asked him if he was not Peter Porcupine. The question disordered the nerves of this assassin exceedingly, and with trembling accent he declared he was not. The French gentleman told him he doubted him; however, said he, ' I will whip you, and you whip Peter Porcupine ;' and he horsewhipped him severely. This must have been trifling as to its effect upon Peter's back, who had been used to a cat-o'-nine-tails when he served in the ranks in the British army, and before he deserted, &c."

" Such a contemptible wretch as Peter Porcupine, who never gave any specimen of *his* philosophy, but in bearing with Christian patience a severe whipping at the public post, &c."

" The infamous Peter Porcupine, whose life has been one continued series of disgraceful crimes."

But the most outrageous piece of " sarcasm " was this: the *Aurora* of Sept. 13th inserted a pretended communication from Cobbett, in

in September upon which that great "public instructor" had two anti-Porcupine paragraphs, and several advertisements of such productions as these:

the following terms :—" Whereas it has been falsely asserted in the *Aurora* that I had suffered the lash for certain misdemeanours, I beg leave, through the same channel, to deny the assertion, and to invite those who may still be tempted to place confidence in the calumnies of my enemies to favour me with a visit at any time between nine in the morning and one in the afternoon, or from three to six in the evening, when I shall be able to afford them *ocular demonstration* that the charge is unfounded, and to prove Mr. Bache's correspondent *a liar.*—(Signed) P. Porcupine." The next evening, in Fenno's *Gazette*, appears the following, evidently to show merely that Cobbett has seen the above, and affects contempt for it :—" Mr. Fenno,—I see that poor Richard's grandchild published a notice yesterday morning, signed Peter Porcupine. Pray, sir, inform your readers that this wayward splinter from old lightning-rod never published an advertisement for me, and never will.—I am, &c., Peter Porcupine." Mr. Bache, however, thinks he has started too good a joke, and proceeds, in his paper of the 16th, to inform his readers that "Peter Porcupine's levée yesterday and the day before, it is said, was more crowded than that of the President's generally is. All his visitors, however, are not satisfied with the proofs he has exhibited of his never having been scourged *à la militaire;* some indeed appear to be fully convinced that his skin is absolutely whole. Some pretend to have perceived on his back slight transversal marks, which they think resemble old scars ; but he assures that, if any such are to be observed, they must have been the effects of the trifling flagellation he received in this city from the Frenchman. His considering that accident as a trifle strengthens the belief that he speaks from experience and by comparison. Others of his visitors cannot see the marks observed by the first ; but, in the stubborn spirit of determined unbelievers, declare that they have heard of a chemical preparation which, by persevering application, will remove the largest scars, and they maliciously surmise that Peter Porcupine must be in possession of the secret."

"A Pill for Porcupine; being a specific for an obstinate itching, which that hireling has long contracted for lying and calumny, containing a vindication of the American, French, and Irish characters, against his scurrilities."

"Porcupine, a print; to be had at Moreau de St. Méry's book-store."

"The Blue Shop, or Impartial and Humourous Observations on the Life and Adventures of Peter Porcupine; with the real motives which gave rise to his abuse of our distinguished patriotic characters; together with a full and fair view of his late Scare-Crow.   ☞ This is interesting to all parties."

"The Impostor Detected, or a review of some of the writings of Peter Porcupine.   By Timothy Tickletoby.

> "'He is a monster of such horrid mien,
>   As to be hated needs but to be seen.'—*Pope.*"

"This day is published, price one quarter of a dollar, embellished with a curious frontispiece,—

"The Adventures of Peter Porcupine, or the Villain Unmasked; being the Memoirs of a notorious Rogue lately in the British Army, and *ci-devant* member of an extensive *light-fingered* association in England. Containing a narrative of the most extraordinary and unexampled depravity of conduct perhaps ever exhibited to the world, in a letter to a young gentleman in New York.

> "'These things are strange, but not more strange than true.'

To which is added a postscript to Peter Porcupine,

being remarks on a pamphlet lately published by him,
entitled his 'Life and Adventures.' By Daniel Detector.

" ' I'll tell the bold-faced villain that he lies.'

" ☞ As this pamphlet was *hurried* through the
press, several mistakes were unavoidable : particularly,
in the first three hundred which were sold, the word
England instead of France appeared in the first line of
the paragraph beginning in the forty-fifth page."

Mr. Bradford was the publisher (if not the
author) of one of these, viz., "The Impostor
Detected ;" and it seems that Cobbett had, when
"The Bone to Gnaw, part ii." appeared, written a
letter to the editor of the *Aurora* (as an indirect
puff), running down the pamphlet. But Mr.
Bradford omitted to state that the bookseller had
instigated the author. Cobbett, however, acknow-
ledges the fact, in the "Political Censor" for
September ; and, after duly spitting Mr. Bradford
for the breach of confidence, proceeds to justify
the "puff indirect" by appealing to precedents,
instancing Addison and Pope as persons who had
done that sort of thing.

Here is a bit on the Porcupine side, from Mr.
Fenno's *Gazette* :—

"The enemies of the President of the United States,
and of the Federal Government, pretend to be affronted

that a man born in England should presume to say a
civil thing of the character of George Washington. The
consistency of this will appear when the public are
assured that very few of the abusive scribblers who
slander his reputation have one drop of American blood
in their veins."

Which of course brings up the *Aurora*, the
editor of which is desirous of assuring the public
that his contributors are all native Americans.

But this is, perhaps, enough for our purpose, in
showing the acrimonious feelings which existed at
the period. Suffice it to say that any person who
defended George Washington was certain of getting
the foulest abuse from his opponents ; whilst the
idea of a discharged British non-commissioned
officer entering the lists was not to be borne. As
one correspondent of the democratic newspaper
said, "While I am a friend to the unlimited freedom of the press, when exercised by *an American*,
I am an implacable foe to its prostitution to a
foreigner, and would at any time assist in hunting
out of society any meddling foreigner who should
dare to interfere in our politics." These writers,
however, did not allow their principles to govern
them so far, that they could deny themselves the
duty of interfering in foreign politics, especially
those of England. Rounds of abuse follow, from

day to day, upon everything that is not revolutionary and anti-monarchical. As for Mr. Pitt's new notion of uniting Ireland with Great Britain, a more "atrocious and diabolical project" never entered the mind of man.

Peter Porcupine, however, stands all this with calm audacity. The advertisements of his new business appear in the *Gazette of the United States;* and he announces,—among "New Drawing Books from the Best Masters," Watson's "Apology for the Bible," &c.,—"The Blue Shop," "The Impostor Detected;" besides a full supply of all "the Grub-street pamphlets vomited forth from the lungs of filth and falsehood against Peter Porcupine." And this game was carried on, more or less, for a month or two longer; but its very violence was fatal to its continuance, and the combatants seemed to get weary of throwing so much dirt at each other. At the end of September, the "Political Censor," No. 5, was devoted, partly, to a review of some of the anonymous pamphlets [8] against

---

[8] For the use of any possible bibliographer, it may be well to name other squibs which appeared, besides those already enumerated :—

"The History of a Porcupine."

"The Little Innocent Porcupine Hornet's Nest."

"The Last Confession and Dying Speech of Peter Porcupine, with an Account of his Dissection."

"A Roaster ; or, A Check to Political Blasphemy : intended as

Porcupine, and to a brisk rejoinder to the misrepresentations of Bradford and his son, relative
to his pecuniary transactions with Cobbett. The
number concluded as follows :—

" I now take leave of the Bradfords, and of all those
who have written against me. People's opinions must
now be made up concerning them and me. Those who
still believe the lies that have been vomited forth against
me are either too stupid or too perverse to merit further
attention. I will, therefore, never write another word

a Brief Reply to Peter Porcupine, alias Billy Cobbler. By Sim
Sansculotte."
    " The Political Massacre ; or, Unexpected Observations on the
Writings of our present Scribblers. By James Quicksilver, Author
of the ' Blue Shop.' "
    " British Honour and Humanity ; or, American Patience, as
exemplified in the Modest Publications, and Universal Applause, of
Mr. William Cobbett, &c., &c. By a Friend to Regular Govern-
ment."
    On the other side we find,—
    " Tit for Tat ; or, A Purge for a Pill. Being an Answer to a
scurrilous pamphlet lately published, entitled ' A Pill for Porcupine,' &c."
    There was also a temperate answer to "The Bloody Buoy :"—
" Reflections on French Atheism and on English Christianity. By
William Richards, A.M., Member of the Pennsylvania Society for
Promoting the Abolition of Slavery."
    Besides the straight hits above-mentioned, Mr. Cobbett complains
(*Porcupine's Gazette*, 7th March, 1797) of an attack on Christianity
which had been published some months before, entitled "Christianity contrasted with Deism. By Peter Porcupine ;" the thing
being no work of his, and his assumed name being placed on the
title-page, either to discredit his own performances, or for the more
innocent purpose of promoting the sale of the work.

in reply to anything that is published about myself. Bark away, hell-hounds, till you are suffocated in your own foam ! Your labours are preserved, bound up together in a piece of bear-skin with the hair on, and nailed up to a post in my shop, where whoever pleases may read them gratis."

Besides, other matters wanted attention: the French Embassy was again becoming a disturbing factor, and Washington had announced that he should retire from public life at the approaching close of his second term of office.

CHAPTER VII.

"AT LAST GOT THE BETTER OF ALL DIFFIDENCE IN MY OWN CAPACITY."

THE popular clamour against the Government of Great Britain was now at its height. The very name of England was such a by-word, that even immigrants learnt to evade a direct confession that that was their native land,—unless it so happened that the vengeful Pitt, by the advice and verdict of twelve good men and true, had been the cause of expatriation. The marble statue of Chatham had been hanged and afterwards beheaded, and the effigies of King George II. had been solemnly desecrated. The name of George III. was seldom heard in Philadelphia without being graced by some contumelious epithet.

But there were not wanting signs, at the close of the year 1796, that the tide was turning in favour of reconciliation with the old country. The insolence of each successive French envoy was becoming too apparent—too ridiculous—for any but the blindest partisans to overlook; and the present representative of the French Convention, Adet, having announced that the Directory were highly incensed at the ratification of the British treaty, many reflecting Americans began to consider that "fraternity" was one of those good things of which they might have, on occasion, too much. The best of it was, that French privateering did quite as much harm as English, whilst the American prize-courts persisted in dealing fairly and impartially with all cases brought to their knowledge, irrespective of nationality.

A certain estrangement naturally grew between the two republics, and the high-toned conduct of Adet—more like that of a spoiled child than anything worthy of his dignified office—was highly characteristic of the then rulers of the French nation. The American administration was first startled by reading, in the newspaper, a note from the French Convention which had not yet been submitted to the Secretary of State—a document which, indeed, it was in their discretion to publish at all. The ground of complaint being the new position of English and American merchant-vessels flowing from the new treaty, the answer of the Secretary of State was by no means conciliatory.

After a few days' consideration, therefore, Mons. Adet informed the American Government (and the public by means of an advertisement [1] in the *Aurora!*) that he "suspends himself from his functions" as minister-plenipotentiary of the French Republic. This measure, he subsequently adds, is "not to be considered in the light of a rupture, but as a mark of the sense of injury" felt by the Convention. . . . "which is to last until they can obtain satisfaction."

Now, a jealousy of British supremacy, and a watchful eye upon the dealings of that perfidious nation, were a very proper state of consciousness for a patriotic Frenchman; but the attempt to enforce, time after time, French dictation, was quite another thing. And when, a few months after, the fact came out that three American envoys to Paris were refused the usual diplomatic courtesies, because they refused to pledge the present of a large sum of money to the impecunious Directory, it is no wonder that coolness and indifference began to spread, on the part of Americans generally, toward the sister Republic.[2]   In

[1] An act justly stigmatized by Oliver Wolcott as "the grossest insult ever offered to a nation not yet subjugated."—"Memoirs, &c.," i. 380.

[2] In July, 1797, the French treaties then existing were solemnly repudiated by Act of Congress.

the course of two or three years, contrariwise, England began to occupy that place in the hearts of the American people from which she had been excluded for a quarter of a century.

There were many circumstances which contributed to heal the differences between the two countries; but the failure of French intrigue, and the steady consistency of the Federalist statesmen, were the leading factors. It is clear that Washington had great suspicion of the motives of France, and was anxious to control the tendency of many of his fellow-citizens to be led away by the delusive fancies of that regenerated country. His farewell address to the people of the United States (one of the noblest papers of the kind ever penned) counsels them to steer clear of permanent alliances with other nations, especially with those of Europe, as their interests could have but a remote relation one with another. He adds,—

"Foreign influence is one of the most baneful foes of republican government. . . . Excessive partiality for one foreign nation, and excessive dislike of another, cause those whom they actuate to see danger only on one side, and serve to veil and even to second the arts of influence on the other. Real patriots, who may resist the intrigues of the favourite, are liable to become suspected and odious, while its tools and dupes usurp the applause and confidence of the people to surrender their interests." [3]

So, from this period, the Federal press began to gain upon its opponents, and one of its acknowledged leaders was Mr. William Cobbett.

The "Political Censor" was continued to the eighth number, being published monthly, excepting when interrupted by a pamphlet with some distinctive aim.   One of these latter was a collection of Adet's notes and proclamations above alluded to, under the title of "The Diplomatic Blunderbuss." The "Censor," besides a running commentary on the debates in Congress, was occupied by violent attacks on Tom Paine (including a reproduction of George Chalmers's biography of that worthy), and upon the French sympathizers ; one whole number being devoted to "Remarks on the Blunderbuss."

But the tardy publication of a monthly protest against his opponents was not enough for the now full-fledged powers of Peter Porcupine. He feels his feet : he knows his strength.   Friends and admirers are flocking to his shop, urging him to the fray.

[3] For this and other interesting State papers the student **may** consult the *Annual Register*, where they are printed in full.

The political part of the daily press which possessed the best literary talent was, in Philadelphia, mainly on the side of the Democrats ; whilst many Englishmen were there, disinclined to be known as such, and none daring (except this "daring scoundrell") to utter a word in public in defence of his native country. There must, therefore, be a daily Federal paper, of most distinctive principles, established in the camp.

Accordingly, an announcement appears, in Mr. Fenno's *Gazette* of the 1st of February, 1797, as follows :—

"Proposals by William Cobbett, opposite Christ Church, Philadelphia, for publishing a newspaper, to be entitled,—

"PORCUPINE'S GAZETTE AND DAILY ADVERTISER.

"Methinks I hear the reader exclaim : 'What ! have we not gazettes enough already? Yes, and far too many; but those that we have are, in general, conducted in such a manner that their great number, instead of rendering mine unnecessary, is the only cause that calls for its establishment.

"The gazettes in this country have done it more real injury than all its enemies ever did, or can do. They mislead the people at home, and misrepresent them abroad. It was these vehicles of sedition and discord that encouraged the counties in the west to rebel; it was they that gave rise to the depredations of Britain, by exciting the people to such acts of violence against that nation as left no room to doubt that we were determined on war; and it was they, when an accommodation had been happily effected, that stirred up an opposition to it such as has seldom been witnessed, and which was overcome by mere chance. These gazettes it was that, by misrepresenting the dispositions of the people, encouraged the French to proceed from one degree of insolence to another, till at last their minister braves the President in his chair, and a bullying commander comes and tells us that his only business is to seize our vessels, in violation of a treaty, in virtue of which alone he claims a right to enter our ports : and it is these gazettes that now have the impudence to defend what their falsehood and malice have produced.

" I shall be told that the people are to blame; that they are not obliged to read these abominable publications. But they *do* read them ; and thousands who read them read nothing else. To suppress them is impossible; they will vomit forth their poison; it is a privilege of their natures that no law can abridge, and therefore the only mode left is to counteract its effects.

"This must be done, too, in their own way. Books, or periodical publications in the form of books, may be of some service, but are by no means a match for their flying folios. A falsehood that remains uncontradicted for a month begins to be looked upon as a truth, and when the detection at last makes its appearance, it is often as useless as that of the doctor who finds his patient expired. The only method of opposition, then, is to meet them on their own ground; to set foot to foot; dispute every inch and every hair's breadth; fight them at their own weapons, and return them two blows for one.

"A gazette of this stamp is what I have long wished to see, but I have wished and expected it in vain. Indignation at the supineness of others has at last got the better of all diffidence in my own capacity, and has determined me to encounter the task. People have heard one side long enough; they shall now hear the other."

Then follow the conditions of publication, subscription, &c. Sufficient support was given to the project to enable the publisher to issue the first number on the 5th of March; indeed, there were more than one thousand subscribers' names on his books by that date.

John Adams had just succeeded to the Presidential chair, and Mr. Cobbett determined that his paper should be the means by which all the assistance in his power might be rendered to the new administration. It was to be a rallying-point for the friends of Government. The editor's introductory address announced that he was not going to be a mere newsmonger; although he certainly expected, from the encouragement he had received, to be behind no other in the early possession of

intelligence, whether home or foreign. It was to
be an unmistakably partisan paper, and to be at
the service of all correspondents who were disposed
to assist him.

Porcupine's Gazette had a course of nearly three
years. It was consistent in its principles from
beginning to end of its career, but it was violent
toward its adversaries—too violent, in point of
fact, for many of Peter's friends; and there were
some, indeed, who believed him to be really hostile
to American politics altogether—many considered
him a dangerous ally; and, in those days of
terrible political animosity, a friend might be
turned into a foe at a moment's notice.

In truth, Mr. Cobbett's determination was to
take the side of England, whatever happened, in
all the international questions which were at that
time constantly arising; and he meant to make
his paper the vehicle of his passionate feelings on
such topics. According to his own account, often
repeated in after-years, he was mainly instrumental
in preventing America from joining France in the
war then raging; and it is probable that he really
had a very considerable share in restoring the
bonds of good feeling between America and England. The proof of this lies, to a great extent, in
the evidences of opposition which have survived.

It was, indeed, far into the nineteenth century, before the democratic newspaper-writers of America ceased to defame the "pensioned" British corporal.[4]

It is not necessary, however, to dwell any longer upon the stormy events of that era. Suffice it to say that even Americans themselves recommend

[4] One of the most violent of Cobbett's adversaries was no less a person than Matthew Carey. The latter was at this time a hot-headed young Irishman, and *would not* have his toes trodden upon. He seems to have taken particular offence at the story of his having refused to publish Cobbett's first pamphlet ; and afterwards, when J. W. Fenno had included his name among a list of the United Irishmen, and Cobbett had reproduced it with sarcastic reference to the "O'Careys," he burst out into a fearful display of ill-temper. His Billingsgate was terrible. He produced "The Porcupiniad : a Hudibrastic Poem," and "A Plumb Pudding for the Humane, Chaste, Valiant, Enlightened Peter Porcupine." The latter is embellished with a vignette, exhibiting a porcupine suspended from a street lamp-post ; and it would be impossible to exceed the virulence of its style or the vileness of its language, whilst, in truth, Cobbett had endeavoured to avoid falling foul of Carey. But time healed all this. Thirty years later, Cobbett and Carey were corresponding in their old age as if there had never been anything of the sort.

Another opponent was William Duane, also an Irishman of some talent, who had succeeded Bache as editor of the *Aurora.* And there are some curious effusions among the poems of Philip Freneau, a man whose writings breathe the most virulent hatred, not only against Great Britain, but against the Washington and Adams administrations.

The poet of the other side was William Cliffton, who died at an early age in 1799. He was a warm admirer of Cobbett, and a hearty Federalist. When Gifford's "Baviad and Mæviad " was republished in America, he composed, at Cobbett's request, an Epistle Dedicatory, addressed to Mr. Gifford.

the study of Cobbett's writings, in order to understand the history of parties.

Amid all this exciting warfare, Mr. Cobbett's
life in Philadelphia was full of amenities of one
kind or other.   He did not like the Americans :
their republican insolence was too much for him ;
but among the families of the older settlers he
found much excellence of character.   " A part of
the people of the United States," he says, " always
appeared to me to be among the best of mankind.
Scrupulously upright, hospitable, kind and generous to excess, and most nobly steady in their
friendships."   But the riff-raff, composing many of
the newer emigrants, disgusted him with republicanism ; and he would meet their violence with
manifold vigour.   The coarseness which too often
disgraced his writings in later life—after his temper had been soured by outrageous tyranny—is to
be traced back to this period, when threats of
being murdered, or tarred-and-feathered, poured
in upon him ; and when slander after slander was
invented, and which did not even spare his wife,
in order to induce him to give up British advocacy.

Some of the friendships he made in America
lasted till death.   His landlord, Oldden (already

mentioned), wanted him to take the house off his hands as a free gift. James Paul, another Quaker and a farmer, gave a name to Cobbett's second son. Several men followed him to England, and had some share in his future fortunes. And, as time went on, the members of the British Embassy were not ashamed to honour him with their acquaintance. As early as 1798, Mr. Liston,[5] who was then envoy, informed Cobbett that the Government at home were fully sensible of the obligations which the country owed him—that they were prepared to advance his interests, or those of his relatives. To all such offers he persisted in a firm and honourable refusal—a conduct which naturally served to produce feelings of respect and admiration on their part. Lord Henry Stuart, another member of the Embassy, was likewise a great supporter of Cobbett, besides having certain sporting sympathies, which were revived in after-years. Business relations were also commencing with several London booksellers.

Several good anecdotes might be reproduced here, to illustrate the manner of Cobbett's life in

[5] "A gentleman for whom I entertained a very high respect, and whose conduct constantly evinced that he was not merely a receiver of the public money, but one who had the interest and honour of his king and country deeply at heart."—*Political Register*, viii. 548.

Pennsylvania. He was always ready to recall, in his later years, the incidents of that period, when he would point a moral or adorn a tale. Here, for example, is a "shooting" story :—

"I was once acquainted with a *famous shooter*, whose name was William Ewing. He was a barrister of Philadelphia, but became far more renowned by his gun than by his law cases. We spent scores of days together a-shooting, and were extremely well matched—I having excellent dogs, and caring little about my reputation as a shot—his dogs being good for nothing, and he caring more about his reputation as a shot than as a lawyer. The fact which I am going to relate, respecting this gentleman, ought to be a warning to young men how they become enamoured of this species of vanity. We had gone about ten miles from our home to shoot where partridges were said to be very plentiful. We found them so. In the course of a November day, he had, just before dark, shot, and sent to the farm-house, or kept in his bag, *ninety-nine partridges*. He made some few double shots, and he might have a *miss* or two, for he sometimes shot when out of my sight, on account of the woods. However, he said that he killed at every shot; and, as he had counted the birds, when we went to dinner at the farm-house and when he cleaned his gun, he, just before sunset, knew that he had killed ninety-nine partridges, every one upon the wing, and a great part of them in woods very thickly set with largish trees. It was a grand achievement; but, unfortunately, he wanted to make it *a hundred.* The sun was setting, and in that country darkness comes almost at once; it is more like the going out of a candle than that of a fire ; and I wanted to be off, as we had a very bad road to go; and as he, being under petticoat government—to which he most loyally and dutifully submitted—was compelled to get home that night, taking me with him, the vehicle (horse and gig) being mine. I therefore pressed him to come away. . . . No, he would kill the *hundredth* bird! In vain did I talk of the bad road and its many dangers for want of moon. The poor partridges, which we had scattered about, were *calling* all around us ; and, just at this moment, up got one under his feet, in a field in which the wheat was three or four inches high. He shot, and *missed.* 'That's it,' said he, running as if to pick up the bird. 'What!' said I, 'you don't think you killed, do you?' 'Why, there is the bird now, not only alive, but *calling*, in that wood,'—which was about a hundred yards distance. He, in that *form of words* usually employed in such cases, asserted that he shot the bird and saw it fall; and I, in much about the same form of words, asserted that he had missed; and that I, with my own eyes, saw the bird fly into the wood. This was too much! To miss once out of a hundred times! To lose such a chance of immortality! He was a good-humoured man; I liked him very much; and I could not help feeling for him when he said, 'Well, sir, I killed the bird and if you choose to go away and take your dog away, so as to prevent me from finding it, you must do it ; the dog is yours, to be sure.' 'The dog,' said I, in a very mild tone, 'why, Ewing, there is the spot, and could we not see it upon this smooth green surface if it were there?' However, he began to *look about*, and I called the dog, and affected to join him in the search. Pity for his weakness got the better of my dread of the bad road. After walking backward and forward many times upon about twenty yards square, with our eyes to the ground, looking for what both of us knew was not there, I had passed him (he going one way and I the other), and I happened to be turning round just after I had passed him, when I saw him, putting his hand behind him, *take a partridge out of his bag and let it fall upon the ground!* I felt no temptation to detect him, but turned away my head, and kept looking about. Presently he, having returned to the spot where the bird was, called out to me, in a most triumphant tone, 'Here, here! Come here!' I went up to him, and he, pointing with his finger down to the bird, and looking hard in my face at the same time, said, 'There, Cobbett; I hope that will be a warning to you never to be obstinate again!' 'Well,' said I, 'come along;' and away we went as merry as larks. When we got to Brown's, he told them the story; triumphed over me most clamorously; and, though he often repeated the story to my face, I never had the heart to let him know that I knew of the imposition, which puerile vanity had induced so sensible and honourable a man to be mean enough to practise."

One of Mr. Cobbett's warmest adherents, in Philadelphia, was the Rev. James Abercrombie, minister of the American Episcopal Church, and incumbent of Christ Church, opposite which was situated Porcupine's shop. He was a man held in great esteem as a preacher, and as a teacher of the young.[6] But he got into disgrace with the Democrats, who called him "one of Peter Porcupine's news-boys." A correspondence was kept up between Cobbett and the doctor, for some time after the return of the former to London. It must be noted, by the way, that, soon after Porcupine had set up the defiant British standard, there were not wanting many to support him ;[7] but, as he says, they kept suitably in the rear. A complaint of the *Aurora* newspaper speaks for itself, as to the power and number of its opponents :—"The British faction, composed of apostate Whigs, old Tories, toad-eaters of Government, British riders and runners, speculators, stock-jobbers, bank-directors, mushroom merchants, &c., &c." There is no doubt, however, that Mr. Cobbett's boast, of being the forlorn hope to less adventurous spirits, was true enough ; and that his admiring fellow-countrymen, both at home and in America, considered that his undaunted British advocacy merited

---

[6] Dr. Abercrombie died in 1841, at a very advanced age.

[7] "By the month of August, 1797, the *Gazette* had more than 2500 subscribers.

the highest encomiums and rewards. What they did say in England may be reserved to another chapter.

Meanwhile, we must now consider the circumstances which ultimately led to Mr. Cobbett's return home. He persisted, from the first, in being looked upon as an alien ; rightly thinking that the taking out letters of naturalization would impair his right to defend his native country. But the intention to return to England was, at this time, very distant from his mind.

CHAPTER VIII.

"WHEN I LEFT THEM, I CERTAINLY DID SHAKE THE DUST OFF MY SHOES."

As a champion of the liberty of the press, Mr. Cobbett holds a place among the very foremost; and, indeed, a minor object of the biographer, in this history, is to establish his claim to that place. But it may still remain open to question how far that liberty is to go : perhaps it will always vary, according to each particular judge and jury,[1] as to what is "liberty" and what is "libel." It is certain that the two cases in which Cobbett was involved, while a newspaper-writer in America, were decided without much consideration of their real merits. One went in his favour, the other against him; and both the prosecutions were undertaken, instigated

---

[1] "Is he a man I choose to punish?—I make it a libel. Is he a man I choose not to punish?—I make it a non-libel."—*Bentham : Works*, v. 281.

by political rancour. We have got the better of this sort of thing, at last, in England ; but only after much shame. And we are not perfect yet.

Mr. Cobbett's career of " crime," during these tumultuous days in Philadelphia, consisted in his being a genuine satirist. In this respect he was unapproachable by any of his scribbling brethren ; and there lay the fundamental reasons for the hatred of those who were amongst his opponents. He had imported into the arena of political con-troversy the squibbing propensities of his great master, Jonathan Swift ; and, armed with the results of his laborious study of grammar and logic, it was useless for any one to expect successfully to contend with him on his own ground. The weapons, therefore, to which they resorted were lies and filth of most abominable character. The phlegmatic, practical, native Pennsylvanian could sit and laugh over Porcupine's hard hits, for they did not, as a rule, touch him. But the hot-blooded importations since the Revolution—soured with the mortified feelings occasioned by unwilling expa-triation—rendered more and more violent by the intoxicating influence of French principles, and, to some extent, made reckless by the exigencies of change, were a different class. The vocabulary of personal abuse formed their resource. It is not very surprising, then, to find after a time some disposition, on the part of Cobbett, to yield to a similar indulgence in coarse language. Upon the whole, however, a perusal of his American writings does not justify the calumnious epithets which have been bestowed upon them. All true humourists, from Rabelais downwards, have suffered a similar penalty. The knave, even more than the fool, both fears and hates your lampooner, and can only resort to base imputations in the expectation that a part of his slime must stick. We, in these later days, will take to heart the maxim of Montesquieu : *To judge justly of men, we must overlook the prejudices of their times.* We know Mr. Cobbett to have been an earnest, honest, highspirited man, whose whole life, both public and private, was governed by principles of conduct which were far in advance of his times ; an uncorrupt politician, who may be placed by the side of Andrew Marvel ; a husband and a parent, whose example cannot be excelled ; in a day when most public writers had their price, and when the bonds of family ties were exceptionally loose.

The Chief Justice of the State of Pennsylvania, at this date, was one Thomas M'Kean : a violent democrat, and a somewhat unscrupulous character.

Every democratic state, in the early stages of its history, is much like a simmering pot; and it is not improbable that Mr. M'Kean belonged to that portion of its contents which floats on the surface. Cobbett's account of him is so bad, and the freedom with which he denounced him to his face was so uncompromising, that the historian would naturally hesitate to make any needless reference to the chronic feud which existed between them. At the period of the Revolution M'Kean had distinguished himself by cruelty to all political opponents, and particularly to any Quakers who ran foul of him.[2] Besides being hated for his partiality, he is alleged to have been a notorious drunkard; he had been horsewhipped by a fellow-citizen; and it was stated that a number of members of the bar had signed a memorial to the effect that "so great a drunkard was he that, after dinner, person and property were not safe in Pennsylvania." According to Oliver Wolcott, a leading member of the Washington and Adams

---

[2] There is one incident of the Revolutionary War (for the catastrophe of which M'Kean is held responsible) which arouses the old Adam in the breast of the Pennsylvanian Quaker to this very day. John Roberts and Abraham Carlisle, two very worthy members of the Society of Friends, were arraigned, condemned, and hanged, ostensibly for having given assistance and comfort to the British troops when occupying Philadelphia—a perfectly groundless charge. The thing was done to "save the country," *à la Française.*

administrations, Peter Porcupine's exposure of
M'Kean was not by any means undeserved ; and
that he openly supported the seditious clubs
which were ever seeking to undermine the Federal
Constitution.[3] It is certain that Cobbett spared no
pains to remind the public of the little defects in
M'Kean's character. The Chief Justice, therefore,
made it his business to attend closely to the say-
ings and doings of Peter Porcupine.

He was not long in finding an opportunity which
might serve to bring the latter within his power. The
Chevalier D'Yrujo, envoy from Spain, had written
a dictatorial letter to Pickering, Secretary of State,
after the pattern of the French, and tending, likewise,
to reduce the independence of the United States
to a mere shadow. Mr. Cobbett at once undertakes
to keep a vigilant eye upon the affair ; and his
Gazette gleams forth with such paragraphs as this :

" We hear that DON SANS-CULOTTA DE CARMAGNOLA
MINOR[4] is preparing another *Diplomatic Blunderbuss*.
Forewarned, forearmed ;—but, whether armed or not,
it is to be hoped that nothing discharged from that most
contemptible quarter will ever scare the people of
America."

At length, the editor receives two or three com-

---

[3] *Vide* Wolcott's " Memoirs, &c.," i. 231, ii. 388, &c.
[4] " Dansons la *Carmagnole*" was one of the French revolutionary
songs.

munications, which he prints : being strong appeals against foreign interference, and reflecting too plainly upon the persons who were causing the liability to that danger. That danger, however, is not so great, in the eyes of Chief Justice M'Kean, as the danger of allowing Britishers to interfere in American politics. Accordingly, the printer and publisher of *Porcupine's Gazette* is served with a bill of indictment; charging him with defaming His Catholic Majesty the King of Spain, his envoy, and the Spanish nation, with the object of alienating their affections and regard from the Government and citizens of the United States.

The heat of the judge's resentment was, perhaps, intensified by the feelings of a father-in-law ; for his daughter, one of the belles of Philadelphia, had espoused the distinguished Chevalier. It was several months before the case was brought to trial ; but, at length, at the November sessions (1797) the bill of indictment was presented to the Grand Jury, and Chief Justice M'Kean proceeded with his charge. He began with a "definition of the several crimes which generally fall under the cognizance of such a court, as treason, rape, forgery, murder, &c., &c. But these his honour touched slightly upon. He brushed them over as light and trifling offences, or, rather, he blew them aside as the chaff of the criminal code, in order to come at the more solid and substantial sin of LIBELLING," and proceeded to attack the defendant with the greatest bitterness. It was in vain, however. The Grand Jury threw out the bill, to the judge's great discomfiture.

Mr. Cobbett, with his usual alacrity and fearlessness, at once proceeded to draw up a statement of the whole affair, and produced a pamphlet under the title of the " The Republican Judge ; or the American Liberty of the Press, as exhibited, explained, and exposed, in the base and partial prosecution of William Cobbett, for a Pretended Libel against the King of Spain and his Ambassador." On reading the judge's charge, it is difficult to believe how an honest man could have selected the comparatively mild effusions of *Porcupine's Gazette* for prosecution ; seeing that his own partisans had used with impunity the vilest epithets toward the "The Father of his country ;" one paper, indeed, charged Washington with murder. Here is one passage from M'Kean's speech, for example: " Libelling has become a national crime, and distinguishes us not only from all the states around us, but from the whole civilized world. Our satire has been nothing but ribaldry and Billingsgate ; the contest has been, who could

call names in the greatest variety of phrases ; who
could mangle the greatest number of characters ;
or who could excel in the magnitude or virulence
of their lies," &c., &c. And Mr. Cobbett showed
pretty plainly, by a judicious selection of recent
anti-federal blackguardisms,[3] what was the real
nature of the fight. For himself, he writes in his
best manner, as the following will show :—

" As to my writing, I never did slander any one, if the
promulgation of useful truths be not slander. Innocence
and virtue I have often endeavoured to defend, but I
never defamed either. I have, indeed, stripped the close-
drawn veil of hypocrisy ; I have ridiculed the follies,
and lashed the vices of thousands ; and have done it
sometimes, perhaps, with a rude and violent hand. But
these are not the days for gentleness and mercy. Such
as is the temper of the foe, such must be that of his
opponent. Seeing myself published for a rogue, and my

---

[3] Both Mifflin, the Governor of Pennsylvania, and M'Kean himself, had many a time committed themselves to the foulest asper-
sions against Britain, as well as their own country, on occasion,
"after the cloth was removed." But Mr. Bache, whether at a
civic feast, or in the columns of the *Aurora*, was a real professor of
venom. Britain is a " perfidious nation ;" its people are "bloody
savage islanders ;" the Government " a mixture of tyranny, profli-
gacy, brutality, and corruption ;" and he would heartily rejoice if
the Royal family "were all decently guillotined." And concerning
Spain, for several years preceding the new amicable arrangements,
we read of the " slaves of Madrid," the "most cowardly of the
human race ;" the " ignorant soldiery of the infamous tyrant of
Castile ! " &c.

wife for a * * * * *; being persecuted with such infamous, such base and hellish calumny in the philanthropic city of Philadelphia, merely for asserting the
truths respecting others, was not calculated, I assure
you, to sweeten my temper, and turn my ink into honey-
dew.

"My attachment to order and good government, nothing
but the impudence of Jacobinism could deny. The
object, not only of all my own publications, but also of
all those which I have introduced or encouraged, from
the first moment that I appeared on the public scene to
the present day, has been to lend some aid in stemming
the torrent of anarchy and confusion; to undeceive the
misguided, by tearing the mask from the artful and
ferocious villains, who, owing to the infatuation of the
poor, and the supineness of the rich, have made such a
fearful progress in the destruction of all that is amiable,
and good, and sacred among men. To the Government
of this country, in particular, it has been my constant
study to yield all the support in my power. When either
that Government, or the worthy men who administer it,
have been traduced and vilified, I have stood forward in
their defence; and that, too, in times when even its
friends were some of them locked up in silence, and
others giving way to the audacious violence of its foes.
Not that I am so foolishly vain as to attribute to my
illiterate pen a thousandth part of the merit that my
friends are inclined to allow it."

There was, however, another string to the bow,

in the hand of Mr. Cobbett's enemies—which bow, being handled with dexterity and resolution, eventually sent its weapon home.

It would appear, from an insight into the local and personal history of these stormy times, that a man's reputation depended entirely upon the nature of his political leanings. There was not a single public character, then living, who did not suffer the penalties of partisanship. In all professions, the man who emerged ever so slightly from obscurity found himself, on one side or another, involved in a stupendous party conflict—a conflict in which no feelings were spared by his opponents, and no fulsome praise left out by his friends. His faults exposed, his weaknesses magnified, and his best actions distorted—he, in turn, heaped upon his adversaries similar contumely. To take by itself (if it were possible) the general sum of abuse, one would conclude that society was a collection of base ruffians, aiming at mutual extermination ; on the other hand, ignoring all that opponents said, it would be easy to prove that everybody was a truly disinterested patriot. And Americans have such a strong tendency to eulogize the departed, that, strange to say, the grave no sooner closes over one of their statesmen or politicians, and his part in the struggle for place and

power is no more, than his name is at once
purged.

There is no doubt at all, that many unscrupulous
men were in the front, at the time in which we are
now interested—many who, having once made
their influence felt, were enabled with the assistance of fortune and audacity to hold their own;
in spite of public exposure, their vigour and native
abilities made them necessary to their party.[6] This
was the class of men that Cobbett loved to fight—
a class unknown in the land whence he came: indeed, unknown to the world of men which he had
himself created; for it must be noted that Mr.
Cobbett had a very limited acquaintance with
human nature in its depths. The reading and
study, which he had gone through some years
before, were all of too abstract a character to make
a man of the world (as it is called). Mankind from
books he knew well, an ideal Mankind, which the
self-educated are especially liable to conjure up,
and by means of its gigantic and perfect form, to
hide that subtle, wayward, self-absorbed creature of
many motives, called MAN. In this superficiality,

---

[6] There was one William Blount, for example, who was expelled
the Senate, on account of intrigue, or downright treachery, went
home to Tennessee, was received with acclamations, and re-elected
Governor of the State !

as regards the hidden springs of human action, and the consequent inability to transfer himself, mentally, into the standpoint of his antagonist, lies the key to Cobbett's frequent failure, just when a little considerate yielding to the feelings of that antagonist would have produced conviction. There were certain rough notions of perfectibility about his conceptions of Humanity which did not admit of the smallest incline toward what he thought to be wrong. In short, he was a Soldier, from beginning to end ; and as a soldier he lived, and worked, and wrote, and fought, with his face to the enemy ; —which enemy must needs be dealt with uncompromisingly, if it meant fighting at all.

The city of Philadelphia, with all its native and acquired advantages, at last got an unenviable distinction, toward the close of the last century, as a plague-spot. As in all such capitals, increasing almost too rapidly, the population crowded together in limited space ; and the dissolute and the very poor, as those classes always do under similar circumstances, began to be a detriment to the health of the city. Sluggish drainage and indifferent water-supply did their fell work. Nearly half of the children born in the city died under two years of age, with stomach or bowel complaints.

At last, in 1793, the yellow fever, which had not visited the city for thirty-one years, reappeared, and carried off 4000 inhabitants in the course of about three months.

And with the yellow fever came the doctors, of course; who, amongst themselves, roused one of those curious disputes for which the history of medical science is somewhat famous. A yellow-fever literature sprang up; statistics were brandished about; wonderful and novel remedies were suggested; and one of the more ingenious of the doctors came to the front in the person of Benjamin Rush.

Dr. Rush is one of the highly-eulogized. His benevolence was unexampled, and he was "honoured and esteemed, both at home and abroad. It was his constant object to popularize and render attractive the principles of medicine."[7]

---

[7] *Duyckinck,* i. 294. See also "An Eulogium upon Benjamin Rush, M.D.," by David Ramsay, M.D. (Philadelphia, 1813), for some particulars of his life and career. He died in April, 1813, aged sixty-nine. Several members of his family attained distinction, the most notable being his son Richard, who was ambassador to London in 1821, and who filled that office with great dignity and credit. His "Recollections of a Residence at the Court of London" has been several times reprinted. Dr. Rush and his systems had much opposition to contend with, in England as well as in America; *vide, inter alia,* a pamphlet by Dr. William Rowley, a London physician, who calls him the celebrated professor of singu-

He gave away his Sunday fees in charity;—and had a more intimate acquaintance with the human pulse than any man living!

After several attempts to master the yellow fever, of which violent purging formed the leading idea, Dr. Rush hit upon the plan of copious bleeding ; and so successful was it (according to his own account) that ninety-nine out of every hundred of the cases he treated recovered! The other doctors said that Rush's treatment was certain death. And so on.

The yellow fever went away for that time, but returned in 1797 with similar fatal results. Phlebotomy became again the rage, and the doctors still disagreed. Dr. William Currie implored his fellow-citizens to "open their eyes." A Scotch physician, passing through Philadelphia, wrote a long letter to *Porcupine's Gazette*, in which he argued strongly against this artificial hemorrhage, and declared that the physicians of the city had sunk from a position of eminence to "a condition bordering on contempt."

But Dr. Rush had other merits, for he was a zealous republican, and a member of the Democratic Society of Philadelphia. He had supported

larities, &c. : "Treatise on Putrid, Malignant, Infectious Fevers " (London, 1804).

Independence from before the Revolution, and was now one of that set of politicians who opposed Federalism; and, having thus incurred the displeasure of the British Corporal, that eminent writer resolved to have a fling at the doctor—a matter which was not so difficult, seeing that Rush had already inspired some amount of ridicule on the part of his fellow-citizens. Cobbett's reading enabled him at once to find a parallel to the zealous phlebotomist. "Gil Blas" had already furnished him with many a happy stroke of humour, and, now that a rash bleeder was to be taken to task, where could be found anything so appropriate as the character of *Dr. Sangrado*, who would draw from a patient several porringers of blood in one day, who would bleed in a dropsy, who thought bleeding the proper means for supplying the want of perspiration, and who stood alone in his strange opinions? The picture was complete; and when to this jest was added the epithet of "quack," besides an insinuation that Dr. Rush killed and tortured with purgatives more patients than he cured, the latter found it necessary to speak out, lest his fame and practice should be irretrievably damaged.

Besides Cobbett, another editor made himself obnoxious to Dr. Rush. This was Mr. J. W.

Fenno, who had succeeded his father in the proprietorship of the *Gazette of the United States*, and
who was firing away against bleeding in much the
same spirit as Peter Porcupine. Also, "many
gentlemen of Philadelphia (not physicians) expressed to me their dread of the practice and their
indignation at the arts that were made use of to
render it prevalent. They thought, and not without reason, that it was lawful, just, and fair to
employ a newspaper in decrying what other newspapers had been employed to extol. In fact, I
wanted very little persuasion, to induce me to
combat the commendations of a practice which I
had always looked upon as a scourge to the city in
which I lived; but this practice and the wild
opinions of the inventor and his followers really
appeared to me to be too preposterous, too
glaringly absurd, to merit serious animadversion;
while, therefore, I admitted the sober refutations
of those medical gentlemen who thought Rush
worth their notice, I confined myself to squibs,
puns, epigrams, and quotations from 'Gil Blas.'
In this *petite guerre* I had an excellent auxiliary in
Mr. Fenno, Jun. Never was a paper war carried
on with greater activity and perseverance, or
crowned with more complete success."

So, in October, 1797, the fever being at its worst,

Dr. Rush makes the following communication to the *Philadelphia Gazette :—*

" Mr. Brown,—Having brought actions against John Fenno, junior, and William Cobbett, for their publications against me in their papers, I request you not to insert anything in your paper which may be offered, in answer to those publications, or in defence of my character.

"BENJ. RUSH."

Well, this was " libel," certainly. A man who was compelled to ask his friends to desist from repartee must be suffering either in his sensibilities or in his income ; and whatever justification there may have been, it is always held that a charge of libel can be entertained in such cases.

The suit against Fenno was never heard of more. Mr. Fenno was an American, although a political opponent. Not so, however, with Peter Porcupine's case ; for there were others behind Dr. Rush who wanted some old scores paid off. But the trial was put off from time to time, until two years had elapsed.

"At last, on the 13th December, 1799, it was resolved to bring it to an issue. The moment I saw the jury-list, ' Ah,' said I to a friend that happened to be with me,

' the action of Rush is to be tried this time.'—We looked over the list again and again, and, after the most mature consideration, we could find but seven men out of the forty-eight whom we thought fit to be trusted on the trial ; but, as I had the power of rejecting no more than twelve, there were left, of course, twenty-nine whom I disapproved of; and, as every one of these seven was struck off by Rush, there remained not a single man on the jury in whose integrity I had the slightest confidence."

Meanwhile, Peter Porcupine had been for some time considering a plan for removal from Philadelphia. The Chief Justice M'Kean was a candidate for governorship of the State, and Cobbett openly stated his determination not to remain, in the case of his election, any longer a resident of Pennsylvania. The event proved that the Democratic element was the stronger, for M'Kean was elected by a small majority over his Federal opponent. Accordingly, *Porcupine's Gazette* having been discontinued at the end of October, Mr. Cobbett made preparations for transferring his business to New York. It would almost appear that advantage was wilfully taken of his temporary absence from Philadelphia to bring the cause to an issue; "it was known that my books, furniture, &c., &c., were already sent off to New York, but I remained in the neighbourhood of the city (where I was seen every day) in order to be present at the trial, if it should come on. On the 7th of December there was no prospect of the cause being brought to trial ; on the 8th, therefore, I came off for New York, where my affairs required my presence. On the 11th, my correspondent wrote me that the cause was put off to another court ; but the very next day it was all at once resolved to bring it to trial immediately." He attributes this sudden decision to the advertisement in the newspapers, signifying his arrival in New York, and his resolution not to revive his *Gazette*.

Mr. Cobbett's leading counsel was EDWARD TILGHMAN, a gentleman who had acquired distinction at the bar, and whose name is still remembered with honour. He had been recently a candidate for representing the state in Congress, but was beaten by John Swanwick, Democrat. Mr. Tilghman took up Cobbett's side *con amore ;* but there is no record of his speech.[a] *Claypoole's Advertiser* goes so far as to say that "the pleadings on both sides were lengthy, ingenious, and eloquent," but does not reproduce them. Mr.

---

[a] It was usual at that time for the offices of attorney and counsel to be united in one person. The practice is not even now discontinued ; and there must be some advantages connected therewith which would recommend it in England.

Harper, however, another counsel for the defendant, is stated by Brown's *Gazette* to have spoken as though he had a bad cause in hand, and "appeared resolved not to defend it at the sacrifice of his honour and character as a gentleman." The judge's summing-up has not, likewise, gone into oblivion ; for Mr. Cobbett took pains to preserve it, and it appears among his reprinted American publications.

The judge (Shippen) dwelt strongly upon the imputation of personal malice, which had been advanced by the prosecution, and urged that no attempt had ever been made to combat the doctor's arguments with regard to the system he had pursued with his fever-patients. To call the plaintiff a quack and ·an empiric—to charge him with intemperate bleeding, and the injudicious administration of mercurial purgatives, and with "puffing himself off," besides calling him the Samson of medicine, for he had "slain his thousands"—was slander, and a pernicious abuse of the liberty of the press. He concluded with reminding the jury that offences of this kind had, for some time past, too much abounded in the city, and it was high time to restrain them ; and, to suppress so great an evil, it would not only be proper to give compensatory, but exemplary damages! Which the jury did, to the tune of five thousand dollars, and to the dismay of the defendant.

The court was crowded with the plaintiff's friends, and the announcement of the verdict was received with great applause. Outside there was also much rejoicing, although the newspaper-men heard the news with mingled feelings. They professed to "derive pleasure and satisfaction" therefrom, and behaved very tenderly to each other for several days. Mr. Duane's paper, the *Aurora*, which had been fifty times as bad as *Porcupine's Gazette*, was subdued and silent; its old opponent, the *Philadelphia Gazette* ironically observed that "not a single sally of wit or sprightliness, and, what is more surprising, not many lies or much impudence, have appeared in it since this memorable verdict was given. . . . No wonder Master Duane looks pale, &c., &c." But the same paper was somewhat rash to continue in the following strain, referring to Dr. Priestley :—

"The *repose-seeking* philosopher of Northumberland [Pennsylvania] will hardly exult at the late verdict. He, too, may be the subject of future litigation; and, although his grey hairs should rise in frightful hostility with the infamy of his pen, justice insulted, violated justice, may alight upon the head of the venerable Jacobin."

In a week or so, however, the papers recovered their tone; Brown's *Gazette* reviled Governor M'Kean; the *Aurora* abused the British Embassy; whilst Mr. Woodward, of 17, Chesnut Street, advertised a full report of the trial, price 2s. 9½d.

As for the benevolent plaintiff, he obtained immediate execution; for the Sheriff was disposing of Mr. Cobbett's goods nine days after the verdict was given.[9] And Mr. Cobbett himself made further advertisement that he would, in a few days, recommence his bookselling business, at New York, "with an assortment which his late importations from London have rendered even more extensive and elegant than that which he usually kept in Philadelphia."

The oddest thing of all was, that George Washington departed this life during the time the trial was proceeding, having been bled and purged to

---

[9] Advertisement from the *Aurora* of Dec. 24 :—"Philadelphia, Dec. 20, 1799.—By virtue of a writ of Fieri Facias to me directed, will be sold by public vendue, on Tuesday, the 24th of Dec. inst., at one o'clock in the afternoon, at the house lately occupied by William Cobbett, editor of *Porcupine's Gazette*, &c. A quantity of books, types and type-boxes, two printing-presses, sundry books in sheets; also 1 mahogany desk, 1 dining do., 1 octagon card-table, 1 walnut book-case, 8 pictures, 14 windsor chairs, sundry pine-tables and old chairs, 2 writing-desks, and printing-stands. Also a smoke-jack and spit, one ten-plate stove and pipes, &c. Seized and taken in execution as the property of said Cobbett, and sold by Jonathan Penrose, Sheriff."

death on the Rush system! According to the medical certificate, published in the *New York Daily Advertiser* of the 30th of December, several doses of tartar emetic were administered, and upwards of forty ounces of blood drawn, between Friday night and Saturday night, the 13th and 14th of that month! The reputed cause of his death was inflammatory sore throat.

Several letters are extant, written by Cobbett to his counsel, which the biographer is enabled to present to the reader.[1] The first is dated from Bustleton, a small place (at that date), a few miles out of Philadelphia, where Cobbett had for some time past occasionally dwelt, when business would let him get out into the fields to ruralize.

WM. C. to EDWARD TILGHMAN (*Dec.* 9, 1799).

"Sir,—I am this moment setting off for New York. In case of a decision against me, in both or in either of the cases,[2] you and the other gentlemen will please to remove the causes into the High Court of Errors and Appeal, where I think I shall stand a better chance of justice. If Quack Rush should obtain a verdict for any sum less

---

[1] Through the courtesy of Mr. William M. Tilghman, a grandson of the great lawyer.

[2] "Both of the cases:" there is no trace of anything to explain this.

than *four hundred dollars*, you tell me, that sum must immediately be paid,—and you will please, sir, to apply in that case to Mr. John Morgan, No. 3, So. Front Street, who will provide the money without delay. If security be wanted, the same gentleman will be my security; he is worth more than ten times the sum, and will cheerfully pay attention to anything you request of him in my name. The other gentleman, of whom I spoke to you, I could not see, and, as I was obliged to leave town, another friend was necessary to be applied to. All you will have to do will be to give Mr. Morgan timely notice, and explicit instructions, and he will fail in nothing that you may desire him to perform for my service.

"I am perfectly well assured that, by leaving my causes in such hands, I have taken all the precaution that can be taken; but if he should finally prevail against me, I shall not be much disappointed; and, let the matter go how it will, I will most honourably discharge every demand my counsellors shall make, and I shall for ever retain a due sense of the obligations I am under to them.—I am, &c."

The following is dated New York, and was written, apparently, as soon as the news of the verdict came :—

Wm. C. to Edward Tilghman (*Dec.* 18, 1799).

"Sir,—If anything, done by a Philadelphia Court and Jury, could astonish me, the decision in Rush's case cer-

tainly would. It is, however, in vain to complain . . . .
My friend North will tell you that I at once resolved *not
to flee* from the worst. It was, doubtless, your anxiety
for my welfare that led you to advise me to this step, and,
therefore, I sincerely thank you for it, more especially as
it was, on your part, a striking proof of disinterestedness ;
but, sir, it would never do. No, the republicans may
rob me, and probably they will, of everything but my
honour, but that is, in these degenerate times, too scarce
a commodity to be sold for 5000 dollars. In a sovereign
citizen, flight from a writ might be very becoming ; but
in me, who have the honour to be an Englishman, and
the greater honour to be a subject of George the Third,
it would be esteemed a most cowardly and disgraceful
act. It would indicate a consciousness of guilt ; it would
blast the fair reputation which I have hitherto preserved,
and which it is my duty to transmit untarnished to my
children.

"North tells me that you say they will come here and
seize my body. Blessed be God, the villains cannot
seize my soul. Let them come. Imprisonment in such
a cause has no horrors for me. Were I to be put to
death, I should only share the fate of ROBERTS and
CARLISLE.

"It cannot be many days, ere every man of sense will
be convinced that I am not mulcted in this shameful
manner for being a *libeller*, but for being an *alien*, an
Englishman, a *royalist*, and for having had the ' *audacity*,'
as it is termed, to come into a republican country and
swear that I still retained my allegiance to the sovereign,

whose paternal arm protected me in my infancy, and
nursed me to manhood. This is my great crime ; and
that an attempt to ruin me has been made for this, and
for this alone, I shall not fail to prove to the conviction
of every impartial mind.

" In the meantime, sir, I earnestly request that you
will be pleased to forward me (under cover to Mr.
Thomas Roberts, No. 134, Pearl Street, New York) the
following papers duly authenticated :—

" 1. A transcript of the declaration.

" 2. A copy of the petition and affidavit, presented for
the purpose of removing the cause into the Federal Court,
with the decision of the Court hereon.

" 3. A transcript of the judgment, as soon as
recorded.

" 4. A minute of the motion (which North says you
will make) for a new trial, with the decision hereon.

" 5. A list of the jury.

" From the account I have received from my friend
North, I think myself under great obligations to you for
your exertions in my behalf. I wish I could say the
same with respect to the conduct of Mr. Harper.—I am,
&c."

WM. C. to E. TILGHMAN (30*th Dec.*).

" Sir,—I wrote you some time ago, but have as yet
received no answer, which I impute to the time which it
requires to get the papers. I now take the liberty to
trouble you for advice on the following points :—

" 1. Morgan was in advance to me in a much greater

sum than all the property in his hands amounts to. Cannot he dispose of that property before the Court meets?

"2. By now selling my debts (in Pennsylvania) to some one here, cannot the person whom I sell them to have them collected there, without being subject to any annoyance?

"3. Having an article of considerable value in Pennsylvania, suppose I sell it to some one here, cannot this person go and claim it and bring it away (if he finds it not already attached) without accounting for it to any one?

"I mean not to budge an inch, but to stand and face everything that can be done against me; and the more injustice that is committed against me, the better I shall like it; but I want to hamper them as much as possible, in order to obtain as many facts against them as I can get.

"They have not brought Fenno's affair to trial, you see! But he is not an Englishman; he is a citizen; he has not avowed his allegiance to King George.

"I hear that the rascally sovereign people hissed you while you were pleading on my behalf; you, undoubtedly, understood this as a very high compliment, and trust that the day will yet come when you will have no need to be afraid of such base miscreants.

"Be assured that, though I may be embarrassed a little for a few months (by being obliged to be prepared for the worst), I will not fail to discharge to the full every demand you may have against me. My business here is very flourishing, and my reception, in every respect, forms a striking contrast with what I experienced at Philadelphia. In hopes of hearing from you soon,—I remain, &c."

E. TILGHMAN to WM. C.

"I have yours of yesterday. My answer to your other letter is in the post-office, and was written immediately on the receipt of it.

" 1. Mr. Morgan may pay himself out of any partnership property, for whatever he is in advance to you in consequence of such partnership. Other property of yours in his possession, and not appropriated by you to the payment of him, is liable to attachment, unless he turns it into money and carries it to his own credit before an attachment comes.

" 2. A *bonâ-fide* sale for a full consideration of your debts in Pennsylvania to a person in New York will certainly be good. Such person may compel your debtors to pay the money to him, unless an attachment has been laid in the hands of the debtor previously to such sale.

" 3. What has been said (2) applies to the third query. It is to be understood that the sale must be a real one, for a full value, and not with intention to defeat a creditor of his debt. A court and jury will judge what was the intention.

" I do not believe I was hissed by the gods. Such gods I have never either feared or worshipped, from my youth upwards, nor shall my grey hairs be disgraced by either. There was a clap when the verdict was given. It was rather a faint one, and the court declared its disapprobation of it.—I am, &c."

Mr. Cobbett was not ruined by the verdict. The enforced sale of the few effects left in Philadelphia fetched a trifling sum; and was the cause of unnecessary annoyance, in that a large quantity of newly-printed matter, in sheets, was thus disposed of at a sacrifice. But the damages[3] were discharged by voluntary subscription.

" The decision was, in America, regarded as unjust; and, that I was regarded as a person most grossly injured, was fully proved by the offer that was made me at New York, to pay the damages in my stead. This offer I did not accept of, a similar offer having been before made by some of my own countrymen in Canada and the United States, of which offer I had accepted."

The expenses of the trial, however, were some three thousand dollars more; and this liability hampered his efforts for a time. But Mr. Cobbett seems, at the end of the year, to have begun to think of revisiting England, at least for a time. The following (unpublished) letter is evidently written in haste, in reply to one from London :—

[3] According to Duyckinck, Dr. Rush is said to have distributed the 5000 dollars amongst the poor (i. 294).

"Wm. C., New York,
to John Wright, Bookseller, Piccadilly (Jan. 4, 1800).

" Dear Sir,—I have but two moments to tell you of a very infamous affair. You heard, about two years ago, of a villainous quack, by the name of Rush, having sued me for scandal. The trial has been studiously put off till since I came here, and the villains have sentenced me to pay 5000 dollars damages ! Never mind. They cannot ruin me, while I have my soul left in me. Be not uneasy. We have given bail here, where I have good friends. They will get the money from us in April next. I shall, if I live, be in London in June. You will have many things from me next packet. Washington is dead. Adieu.

" P.S.—When you tell Mr. Gifford this news, assure him that I am not cast down. I will fight as I retreat to the very water's edge. North and the things came safe. Another packet is in, and will leave this in about two weeks. Then you will get the things that I am preparing. Continue my monthly supply, but confine yourself in your letters to mere matters of business. The *Wodrop Sims* is not yet arrived, and, of course, I have not those things. I shall leave an agent here, and a good one ; a good, honest Englishman. Expect to hear from me next packet, and to receive several valuable things, with the plan of my future operations."

From the energy with which Cobbett was laying the foundation of a new business in New York, one is inclined to believe that he did not meditate a

permanent return to England. Sundry advertisements appear, which show that he was desirous of
extending his American connexion. But the idea
of resuscitating *Porcupine's Gazette* was finally
abandoned, and a farewell number was distributed
to the subscribers in January, 1800, in which he
gave an account of recent events, and of his plans
for the future. In February, he commenced a new
periodical under the name of the *Rushlight*, which
was much relished by the public, and had a very
large sale.[4] This was, however, a not very credit-
able publication, being so full of the editor's
personal grievances against the Philadelphians that
there was scarce room for anything else.

In point of fact, the severity of the verdict upset
Mr. Cobbett; he did not recover his equanimity
again. The invitations from England, to come
home, were pressing; there seemed to be far
better prospects for him here, and it is probable
that he found a good deal in New York to make
him dissatisfied with his equivocal position as a
Royalist.

One of the great plans, interrupted by the
breaking up of his Pennsylvanian business, was a
collected edition of his American writings. As
far back as February, 1799, Cobbett had issued a

---

[4] *Vide* Duyckinck, i. 294, art. Rush.

prospectus, announcing the republication of "a new, entire, and neat edition of PORCUPINE'S WORKS," and its preparation was going on during the whole of that year.[5] But the seizure of his goods, by order of the sheriff, included the principal portion of this new "edition," in sheets; and all this was sacrificed. An announcement, therefore, appears on the cover of *Rushlight*, No. II., that PORCUPINE'S WORKS would be published in London.

Orders for English books were invited, and subscription lists opened for the leading magazines and periodicals, during the early part of the

---

[5] A copy of the original circular has fallen into the hands of the present writer. It is dated Feb. 5th, 1799. The volumes were expected to reach sixteen in number, and the price (to subscribers) was to be twenty dollars, or four and a half guineas. The following extracts from this prospectus will give some idea of the extent to which Cobbett's writings had been already circulated :—

"Of each pamphlet, published under my assumed name of Peter Porcupine, about six thousand copies, upon an average, have been printed and sold in America. The sale of those which have been honoured by a republication in England has probably been much greater. All of them, I believe, have passed through three or four, and some, in an abridged state, have attained to ten, twelve, and even seventeen editions. . . . As to the *Gazette*, such has been the increasing demand for it that, though for a long time I laid by a hundred files for sale, I can at this moment make up but three complete for the first year. Thus situated, the orders which I have received from all parts for complete sets of the pamphlets and complete files of the paper have been a mortification to me rather than a pleasure," &c.

year. But it was quite clear that Porcupine was finding himself out of his element. The loss of his immediate neighbours helped to unsettle him, and his best friends were left behind in Philadelphia. That he was making money, and getting a business together once more, is evident from the following note.

"Wm. C. to John Wright, London (May 9, 1800).

" Dear Sir,—I have had the good luck to be able to fulfil my intention of making you another remittance by this packet (which is to sail to-night) in good bills of exchange, which I enclose in this letter, to the amount of 93*l.* 9*s.* 4½*d.* sterling. I have written you a good deal this time, but I cannot . . . . [torn] without once more requesting you not to forget our *order,* because . . . . pends upon its immediate execution. I remain, &c.

" P.S.—If I have not mentioned *Weld's Travels* in my order, send twenty of them, neatly bound."

However, in the course of this month Mr. Cobbett issued a farewell address to the American public ; and, on the 1st of June, set sail for England, taking Halifax on his way.

It was not many years before Cobbett found that his affections were bound up in transatlantic memories. And, although he despised republi-

canism to the last day of his life, he very soon
came to admire much of the American character,
and to follow with deep interest the fortunes of the
republic. A few short years after this date his experience of mankind was getting riper; and his
political education was beginning to enlighten his
mind concerning those objects which are most worth
the struggles of a people.

In a letter to the people of the United States of
America, February, 1803, he says,—

" With some few exceptions, I have long forgiven and
forgotten all the injuries, with which the worst of you, in
your folly and your madness, endeavoured to load me ;
while, on the other hand, I cherish the remembrance of
all those acts of indulgence and of friendship which I
have, in greater abundance than any other person, experienced at American hands. . . . . If no man ever had
more enemies, no one ever had half so many friends, and
these the warmest and most sincere. Never, therefore,
does America, and Pennsylvania in particular, come
athwart my mind unaccompanied with the best wishes
for their prosperity and happiness."

CHAPTER IX.

" MY FAME HAD PRECEDED ME."

THE reader is probably aware, that your "public-instructor" who, at the close of the last century, essayed to lead his fellow-men, had no hold upon the daily press. An occasional jerky paragraph, or covert insinuation, was all that the newspaper ventured upon, when its feelings impelled it to break through the traditions of its calling. Indeed, things were changing at this period, although not so extensively in London as in France and in America ; but the self-constituted leaders of public opinion were, as yet, restricted to the pamphlet, or to the periodical review. The student of history will notice, at least as regards the last quarter of the eighteenth century, that current opinion on politics is fully represented only in these journals. Their influence, however, speedily waned soon after the commencement of the nineteenth century ; and, although the popular review, weekly or monthly, still supposes itself in the van, in our own days, its thoughts and ideas are appropriated, and often superseded, on the morrow of their publication.

The "Monthly Review," redolent of GOLDSMITH and of Griffiths; the "British Critic," and the "Gentleman's Magazine," of high Tory principles: and the "Analytical Review," organ of modern enlightenment,—were the principal publications of this kind, which had the ear of the public, at the period of our history. And we shall be unable to proceed properly with the study of Mr. Cobbett's life, without having first traced, from these sources, the rise and progress of his reputation, ere his return to England.

The "Observations on Dr. Priestley's Emigration," appears to have been reprinted in London immediately after its publication in Philadelphia. Matters were especially troublesome to the ministry just then, and the partisans of loyalty eagerly, frantically, seized upon anything new, in the shape of argument or of declamation, with which to bind up their rotting timbers. Yet, mark the wonderful inconsistency of human affairs! The author of this poor plank, groping after political justice (according to his light), was also the author, or part author, of a pamphlet which was said to be doing infinite mischief among the soldiers and sailors, —a pamphlet against which, *at this very time*, they were actually writing and printing loyal antidotes.

The " British Critic," then, appears to have been the first to draw public attention to the new writer. The number for November, 1794, dedicated several pages to a review of the " Observations," beginning with these appropriate remarks :—

" We sometimes elevate a pamphlet, on account of its importance, to a rank among our primary articles, and this honour is peculiarly due to a stranger, who comes forward to give his decision as an umpire, on points wherein the passions of Englishmen may be supposed sufficiently interested to bias their judgment. Of this nature is the acute and well-written American pamphlet here announced, in which the author, while he addresses himself to Dr. Priestley, as a new settler in the country, speaks very forcibly on many subjects respecting England and its public sentiments and conduct. We do not, therefore, consider the tract as an attack on an individual, but as a decision upon principles."

The writer proceeds to express his opinion that the pamphlet is indeed of American origin, and not fabricated in London. He considers the fable of the pot-shop [introduced into the Observations, being an account of the various articles in a crockery-shop, some formed to honour and others

to dishonour, falling out with each other, and hav-
a general smash] as "strongly in the style of
Swift." He concludes with a pious hope that the
time was coming when, to "excite discontent and
rebellions against government will be universally
considered as a crime too atrocious to be palliated
by any speciousness of theory."

The "Gentleman's Magazine" followed suit in
its number for January, 1795.

The "Monthly Review," well-known for the
flexibility of its opinions, was just then on the side
of toleration, and considered that there could be
no justification for such abuse of Dr. Priestley; it
did not admire the vulgar fable of the pitcher
haranguing the pans and jordans; and concluded :—

"We have no doubt that London has the honour of
being the native place of this production ; although it is
pretended, at the bottom of the title-page, that it was
originally printed at Philadelphia."

The notice taken of the "Observations," on the
part of the "Analytical Review," was in a tone
of the severest condemnation. The writer, also
considering that this was no American production,
but "engendered at home in some murky brain,"
justly remarked that it was unfair to continue the
persecution of Dr. Priestley, after he had left his

native shores. With much ingenuity, the writer proceeded to point out that no American would extol
the English constitution, nor speak of reformers as
regenerated politicians, nor display such jealousy
for the Church of England, nor discourage the
emigrating spirit,—as the author of the "Observations" had done ; and he proceeds to insinuate
that George Chalmers must be the culprit :—

"From the similarity of spirit and style, which we
observe between this production and Oldys's 'Life of
Thomas Paine,' were we to indulge ourselves in conjecture, we should conclude these two pieces to have come
from the same pen. But, whoever be the author of such
gross scurrility, and malignant calumny, it is much to be
wished that he were known to the public, that every
honest man might be able to say to his neighbour,—
"Hic niger est : hunc tu, Romane, caveto."

The "Critical Review," another respectable "defender of morality and taste," did not condescend to
notice Peter Porcupine for several years ; and it was
not till October, 1798, that the "Observations" (4th
Edition) found occupation for its discriminating
pen,—the reviewer having taken up this pamphlet
"to observe scurrility throwing off all disguise."
Of all these public guides, the "Analytical"
appears to have possessed the most talent, and the

" Monthly " to have been the most independent ;
but all were, more or less, ranged on party lines.
According to the political leanings of each writer,
so would go his indulgence toward Peter's forcible
expressions, or his contempt for Peter's vulgar
comparisons.

The " Bone to Gnaw," when republished in
London, was supported by a long preface : " A
Rod for the Backs of the Critics, containing a
Historical Sketch of the present state of political
criticism in Great Britain, as exemplified in the
conduct of the Monthly, Critical, and Analytical
Reviews, &c.   Interspersed with anecdotes.   By
Humphrey Hedgehog.[1] *'Melius non Tangere.'*"
The Historical Sketch (so-called) was a general
attack on revolutionary principles, and their supporters in the press,—with especial reference to
the publications named, which had " reviewed, or
to speak more correctly, *reviled*" the " Observations."   It is not particularly elegant ; and as to
any power, it is milk-and-water against strong ale,
compared with the work to which it is prefixed.
But that was the conceit of this Hedgehog ; who, a
feeble scarabæcide, had just wit enough to fancy
that his little spines gave him a sort of relationship
to him of the quills.

[1] *I.e.* John Gifford.

Peter Porcupine was more fortunate in the advocacy of the " British Critic." That journal, albeit highly prejudiced, was a formidable opponent of the ideas of the day. Intense horror of infidelity, united to warmest loyalty to the Throne and to the Church, pervaded all its articles. It is no wonder, then, that the editor of this review[2] made it his business to patronize the trenchant pen of Peter. On the occasion of noticing " A Little Plain English," the writer records the struggles he has had, to maintain that the new politician was from America,—how " We " were assailed, both in public and private, for "our" supposed credulity. And when the " Life and Adventures " appeared, the satisfaction of the re- viewer was complete. He continued, from time to time, to congratulate himself and the public that he had been the first to discover Peter's merits ; and was by no means disposed to lose sight of him.

" They who chose at that time to doubt of his exist-

[2] The *British Critic* was the joint undertaking of Archdeacon Nares and the Rev. William Beloe, Prebendary of St. Paul's. Both these gentlemen were staunch supporters of Pitt, and received their due reward in this life. They were also accomplished bibliographers and literary students, and rendered great service to literary history. The *British Critic* lived far into the nineteenth century.

ence, would be very glad, if they could, to disprove it now; but to their annoyance, and to the vexation of all Jacobins, he undoubtedly exists; and has done more towards the subversion of the French interest in America, and consequently towards restoring the ancient cordiality between that country and Great Britain, than could possibly have been expected from the efforts of any single writer. Truth,—Truth was with him; and what can long subsist against the powers of Truth and Honesty?" &c., &c.

As to his style, the reviewer is indulgent :—

" That this writer is occasionally a little coarse in his style and expressions, cannot be denied; but, perhaps, he could not easily attain more refinement except at the expense of some strength; his object also appears to be to write in a popular and familiar manner."

On the other hand, the independent and radical reviewers noticed Peter with severe animadversions :—" To look into the writings of this author for *facts* would be a waste of time."—" We meet with a strange *farrago* of petulance, abuse, false reasoning, and absurdity, into which it would be disgusting to enter."—" Absurd comments, gross misrepresentations, and impudent attacks, both upon the dead and the living."—"A writer so weak and infatuated as Peter Porcupine."

But it must be said, that these despisers of Peter had little of argument wherewith to withstand him. His positions were generally just, though sometimes exaggerated ; and his violence was thoroughly consistent from beginning to end,— excepting in this : that he as yet knew nothing of the wicked oppressions which were going on, in some quarters, at home. The "Analytical" justly called him to account for his unfortunate allusions to the freedom of the press in England :— "He complains that he was allowed *only* an hour and a half to go out and find bail. Here, under a similar prosecution, he might have been arrested, and detained for several days, until his Majesty's servants found time to inquire into the securities offered:" with further comparisons of the American and English procedures, very disadvantageous to the latter. But this is almost a solitary example of fair argument ; and it looks very much, upon a reperusal of the various comments which appeared from time to time, that it was only a question of the richness of one's vocabulary, as to who could be the most foul-mouthed in dispute.

But, seeing that sober and respectable SYLVANUS URBAN could uphold Peter thus: "This lively and animated writer, offensive to some of our brethren because he tells the truth."—" Concerning

the writer as the truest patriot in his own country,
and the truest friend to honesty and integrity."—"If
the mercenaries in England and their employers
can confute these just and animated assertions, we
will give them leave to heap harsher abuse than
they have yet done on their natural enemy, Peter
Porcupine:"—we may be fully justified in be-
lieving that his vigour and courage were admired,
on all hands, not less by his adversaries than by
his friends. As long as he appeared to support a
Party this was natural enough ; they could not do
less, at the same time, than attack him with all
the force at their disposal.

There does not appear to be any record of the
actual, direct, means by which Porcupine's writings
were introduced to the British public. The earlier
tracts were printed for John Stockdale, and for the
Rivingtons. The " Life and Adventures " are said
to have been republished at the express desire
of Mr. Canning ; it is probable, therefore, that it
is due to the zeal and acumen of Mr. John Gifford,[3]

---

[3] This gentleman (whose original name was John Richards
Green) had got rid of his patrimony, with the assistance of the Jews,
at an early age. To avoid his creditors, he took the surname of
Gifford ; and, having discovered acuteness and talent in writing, he
soon found himself under the wing of Pitt, and became one of that
statesman's ablest supporters in the press. Having been bred to the
bar, Mr. Pitt was enabled to reward his services by the magistracy
of a London police-court, which he held for many years. Gifford

that Cobbett's writings were discovered to be of incalculable value to the supporters of monarchy. Mr. Gifford was Canning's right-hand man, as editor. On the upper floor of the house of Mr. Wright, publisher, of Piccadilly, a room was rented by the celebrated contributors to the " Anti-Jacobin ; " and here sat Mr. Gifford, conducting the mechanical part of that undertaking. Mr. Upcott, Wright's assistant, was here occupied in transcribing the writings of Canning, Frere, and Ellis, so that their *incognito* might be preserved. And Mr. Wright's bookshop was the constitutional book-shop of the day.

So it came to pass that Mr. Gifford wrote a lengthy preface to " A Bone to Gnaw" (as already mentioned), and henceforward attended to the reproduction of Porcupine's tracts, which were, of course, published at the shop of the monarchical bookseller, at 169, Piccadilly. After the " Anti-Jacobin" was discontinued, Mr. Gifford commenced the publication of the "Anti-Jacobin Review ;" which, supported by Bowles,[4] Whitaker, Dr. Bisset,

---

wrote, besides several other historical works, a biography of his distinguished patron :—" A History of the Political Life of the Right Honourable William Pitt, including some Account of the Times in which he lived " (3 vols. 4to, London, 1809).

[4] John Bowles, barrister, was the author of several anti-gallican pamphlets. In one of these he warmly praises the author of " The

and other Tory writers of the day, became the leading party journal during the remainder of Mr. Pitt's career. The very first article in the new magazine was an elaborate review of Cobbett's anti-republican struggles, founded upon one of his later tracts; and it was succeeded, from time to time, by frequent references to "this staunch friend of social order." The second volume bears the imprint of " W. Cobbett, Philadelphia."

Another celebrity of that day, John Heriot,[5] editor of the *True Briton*, had some interchange of civilities with Cobbett, the latter having desired him to supply his paper regularly to Philadelphia. Here is an extract from Heriot's answer to the application :—

" Permit me now, sir, to return you my best acknow-ledgments for the numbers of your political work, which you did me the favour to transmit. Of the great merits

Bloody Buoy," who had executed a " useful and benevolent, though a most painful and disgusting task."

[5] Mr. Heriot was a Scotchman of great native ability. He had held a commission in the Marines, and subsequently produced a novel and some poems. When the Pitt Ministry resolved to set up a newspaper, the *Sun* and the *True Briton* were established, and Mr. Heriot was chosen editor, and under his management the papers soon reached a brilliant circulation. After his retirement from the press, Mr. Heriot held a valuable appointment in Bar-badoes, and subsequently became Comptroller of Chelsea Hospital, where he died in 1833.

of Peter Porcupine I was not before ignorant. I had
read some of his political works with very high satisfaction. I shall be at all times happy, sir, through the
medium of my papers (for I am proprietor of two), to
recommend writings so deserving to the notice of the
British public, and you will, perhaps, admit I can do this
with some success, when I inform you that the circulation of my two papers extends to nearly 6000 per day.
I had an opportunity lately of making some inquiries
respecting you of a gentleman in my office here, and who
formerly held a high diplomatic mission in America. He
seemed to know you well, and spoke very highly both of
your probity and talents. I have only to repeat, sir, that
I shall think myself highly honoured by your correspondence, and you may at all times rely upon the best
wishes and services of, sir, your most obedient, humble
servant, JOHN HERIOT."

From a letter to Mr. Nichols, printed in the
"Gentleman's Magazine" for September, 1835, it
appears that Cobbett also sought business relations
in that quarter. The letter (dated August 1, 1797)
encloses a file of *Porcupine's Gazette*, and pro-
poses to have a monthly exchange of their respec-
tive publications; adding that the writer would be
willing to promote the sale of the "Gentleman's
Magazine" in America, if he could come to any
arrangement with his correspondent.

The following (unpublished) letter to Mr. T. J.

Mathias[6] will also be of great interest to the reader, as tending to show the authoritative position which he had acquired as a bookseller and publisher :—

"Wm. C. to the Author of 'The Pursuits of Literature : '—

" Philadelphia, 12th Mar. 1799.—Sir,—The 'Translation,' with your obliging note in the blank leaf, is come safe to hand. Nothing that I can address to you can possibly be looked upon as flattery; you will therefore be assured of my sincerity when I say that a testimony of approbation under the hand and seal of the king himself could not have given me greater satisfaction.

" Your matchless poem on the pursuits of literature is become very fashionable in the libraries of the Americans; and, amongst my ' public services,' as you are pleased to think them, I regard my having been the first to introduce this work as one of the greatest. But neither your awful voice nor that of an angel, were one to descend, can save America from another revolution ! Your words will, indeed, be like bread thrown upon the waters; but they will produce no immediate effect here.

" It is with much regret I see the pirating booksellers of Ireland carrying off the profits which, from this country, ought to return into the pocket of your bookseller. They send out cheap editions, by which means they obtain a

6 From a collection of letters received by the publisher of " The Pursuits of Literature," which was formerly in the possession of Mathias, and now in the British Museum (Addl. MSS. 22,976).

preference; and the worst of the business is, they disgrace the work by publishing it incorrectly.

" If you have seen my papers for a twelvemonth past, you will not require from me any additional proof of my respect; the file of papers, which I take the liberty to send you, I therefore beg you to receive as mere vehicles of intelligence. Nothing from this country can be a proper return for your present, unless you will have the goodness to regard as such, the unfeigned thanks of, sir, your most obliged, &c."

Allusion has been made, in a previous page, to the offers made, on the part of the Government at home, to advance Mr. Cobbett's interests. One of his own frequent references to that subject will help to illustrate the subject of this chapter :—

" Mr. LISTON, our minister in America, informed me, in the year 1798, I think it was, that the ministers at home were fully sensible of the obligations due to me from my country, and that, if I would accept of nothing for myself, they wished me to point out any of my relations, in the army or elsewhere, whom they might serve. To which I answered, as nearly as I can recollect, in the following words :—

" 'As to my relations in the army, I can ask for no promotion for them, because I have no opportunity of knowing whether such promotion would be consistent with the good of the service ; and, with respect to my relations out of the army, a sudden elevation might, perhaps, be very far from contributing to their happiness, besides which, though it would be my duty to assist them by means of my own earnings, I should not think it just in me to be instrumental in throwing them as a burden upon the nation.'

"I may now have expressed myself with more perspicuity and conciseness than I did then ; but this was the substance of my answer ; and, if I may judge from what I have since witnessed amongst public writers, I must suppose that Mr. Liston was utterly astonished. It should be observed, too, that, if there was a man in the world, through whom such an offer could have had a chance of success, that man was Mr. Liston—a gentleman for whom I entertained a very high respect, and whose conduct constantly evinced that he was not merely a receiver of the public money, but one who had the interest and honour of his king and country deeply at heart. I had been a witness of his zeal, of his real public spirit, of his unremitted attention to his duty, of the great mischiefs he prevented, and of the great good which he did ; and I respected him accordingly ; but neither that respect, nor any other consideration, could induce me to depart from that line of perfect independence which I had at first chalked out to myself, and from which I never have, to the best of my recollection, for one moment deviated."

CHAPTER X.

"I RESOLVED NEVER TO BEND BEFORE THEM."

THE *Times* newspaper for July 8th, 1800, announced, under date of Falmouth, July 4th, the arrival of the *Lady Arabella* packet from New York, *viâ* Halifax; adding that, "on the 20th, in lat. 50.30, long. 28.10, she was chased by a large vessel, which gained so much on her that she found it necessary to heave her guns, shot, lumber, &c., overboard, by which means she was considerably lightened, and on the following day got so much ahead that the pursuer gave up the chase." Among the passengers, who thus escaped the rigours of a French prison, were "Mr. and Mrs. Cobbet."

The following note is to Mr. Wright, the bookseller in Piccadilly, dated Falmouth, 8th July :—

"DEAR SIR,—I arrived here, with my family, last Friday,

by the *Lady Arabella* packet-boat, and shall set off for London to-morrow morning, travelling by the way of Bath, &c. . . . . in a post-chaise, with Mrs. Cobbett and my two children, so that you may expect to see me in town on Saturday or Sunday next.

"I have taken the liberty to give a draft on you for 20*l.* I brought off only 50*l.* in cash; and, as I have remained here and at Halifax much longer than I thought there would be any occasion for, I was apprehensive I should fall short. Mr. Pellew, of this place, who, by-the-bye, is a brother of the gallant Sir Edward Pellew, offered me whatever I might want, and I gave him the above-mentioned draft. Do not fail to accept it, and I will be careful to lodge the cash with you before the time of payment arrives. Indeed, I will do it immediately upon my arrival.

"Pray make my most respectful compliments to Mr. William Gifford, and believe me, though in haste, your very sincere friend and most obedient servant,

"WILLIAM COBBETT.

"P.S.—That part of my baggage, which I am not able to carry with me, I have sent to a waggon warehouse, directed to your care. I shall, undoubtedly, be in town before it, but if, by some accident, I should be detained longer on the road than the 17th instant, I beg the favour of you to go and claim the things (two trunks, one bale, one deal box, and one band-box) at the Swan-and-two-Necks, Lad Lane."

Mr. Cobbett's arrival in England was early signalized by an opportunity of carrying out his principles, long since determined on, concerning the disposal of the public money :—

" From my very first outset in politics, I formed the resolution of keeping myself perfectly independent, whatever difficulty or calamity might be the consequence of it. . . . With the same resolutionin my mind I returned to England. The first opportunity of putting it in practice was in a little matter with which OLD GEORGE ROSE [1] had something to do. I had brought home with me books, printed in America, enough to fill a couple of large trunks ; and, having been informed by Mr. Pellew, the collector at Falmouth, that as to books *not for sale*, it was usual, upon an application made to the Secretary of the Treasury, to obtain a remission of the duties, I wrote to Old Rose, informing him of the circumstance, and stating to him the ground upon which my claim was founded. George did not ãdmit the claim ; he made

---

[1] The Right Hon. George Rose, M.P., a Government official, and one of the luckiest sinecurists of his day. His " success" in life aroused, alternately, the ridicule and the wrath of his cotemporaries :—

"George Rose, Esq., Secretary to the Treasury, &c., &c., &c., &c., &c., &c., &c."—Mathias : " Pursuits of Literature."

" *Greedy* :—George Rose's moderation, and not satisfied."—Pigott's " Political Dictionary " (1796).

" Who in his lifetime held situations worth 10,000*l.* per annum, and whose family, it has been calculated, received in principal and interest, nearly two millions of the public money."—'' Black Book ; or Corruption Unmasked " (1820).

Mr. Rose was, nevertheless, one of the best public servants this country ever possessed.

some difficulty about it; but, finding that I had, at once, paid the duty, amounting to about ten pounds, perhaps, he caused it to be notified to me that *the money should be returned to me*. This offer I would not accept of, not perceiving how, except by way of a *Treasury gift*, such a return could be made."

Cobbett has made several references to Mr. Pellew, the collector of customs, who appears to have lodged and entertained him, with much attention.

Upon his arrival in London, in the middle of July, Mr. Cobbett took a lodging in St. James's Street, and began to deliberate upon his future. He had scarcely, when everything was counted up, five hundred pounds with which to begin the world anew. But he had not to wait long for a certain sort of encouragement. His fame was very widely spread among the adherents of Government; besides that, numerous gentlemen of Tory principles sought him out. Others, of independent politics, but admiring his talents and his daring, came to pay court. The Government press hailed him, and congratulated their countrymen " on the arrival of an individual . . . . whom no corruption can seduce, nor any personal danger intimidate from the performance of his duty."

Among these visitors were Baron Maseres; Dr.

Ireland (shortly afterwards Dean of Westminster), who was especially gracious to him; the Rev. G. H. Glasse, rector of Hanwell, a well-known pamphleteer of the day, a good scholar, and chaplain to the Earl of Radnor; the Rev. William Beloe; Mr. John Penn, Sheriff of Buckinghamshire (who "took me by the hand the very week I came to England"); &c. So that, along with the immediate officials of Government, there was quite enough to turn Mr. Cobbett's head, had he not been possessed of supreme self-command. At that moment, together with his native and acquired capacities, he had the means and the opportunity, if so disposed, of carving out an easy fortune.

But, of all his admirers, no one seems to have equalled Mr. WINDHAM, in the warmth and eagerness with which that gentleman courted Cobbett's friendship.

The Right Hon. William Windham ("the first gentleman of the age . . . . the ingenious, the chivalrous, the high-souled," according to one of Macaulay's juster judgments) was an enthusiast; and, in the eyes of those persons who shrug their shoulders when a man acts as though he had some faith in his own opinions, *whimsical*. Deeply reverential toward the memory of Mr. Burke, his own genius was not unfitted to bear forth, to another generation, the name and the principles of that great man. Windham was beloved and admired by all persons of refinement and sensibility; and if he has left a name not so widely known as some of his cotemporaries, it must be laid to the account of an extreme self-consciousness, and an honourable delicacy, which prevented him from serving always in the ranks of party with unreasoning devotion.

Mr. Windham's peculiar scare was French Jacobinism; and he, along with the leaders of the party who held similar views, thought that there could be no lasting cessation of hostilities with Buonaparte, whilst the ascendancy of the latter involved the spread of Democratic principles. Mr. Windham was, naturally, a zealous admirer of that arch anti-Jacobin, whose writings had so disturbed the bile of American Democrats; and, upon Porcupine's arrival in London, he immediately sought his acquaintance. With Windham was associated Dr. French Laurence, another intimate friend of the lamented Burke, who also ably represented in Parliament the opinions of that statesman.

Mr. Windham was, at this time, Pitt's Secretary-at-War; and, according to the entry in his diary,[1]

[1] "Council dinner: Hammond, Canning, Frere, Malone; Cobbett, *alias* ' Peter Porcupine,' whom I saw for the first time; Pitt,

he appears to have met Cobbett for the first time on the 7th of August, 1800 (probably at Windham's official residence). Mr. Cobbett's references to this occurrence represent Mr. Pitt as having been very polite to him on the occasion, and as having inspired him with great admiration for his person and manners. He was altogether pleased and gratified by his reception, and by the ready condescension with which the company present conversed with him. But, of course (as he said more than thirty years afterward), "it was natural for Pitt and his set to look at me a little, to see what they could make of so efficient a piece of stuff." Mr. Pitt's habitual austerity and hauteur pretty generally disappeared at the dinner-table; and Cobbett saw him, for the first time, at one of these happy moments. So that, what with his very natural pride at the invitation, and his satisfaction at finding that the King's ministers were such highly-agreeable fellows, he felt more than ever disposed to use his talents in the support of monarchy. He resolved to set up a daily paper; and left Mr. Windham's dinner-table with that resolve uppermost in his mind.

That Mr. Pitt miserably erred, in the prosecution

and George Ellis; Canning's cousin."—"Diary of the Right Hon. William Windham" (Longmans, 1866), p. 430.

of the European war, has long since been established, with all minds not wedded to the notion
that our rulers are of Divine appointment.   What
opposition there was to his ideas, in his own day,
was considered to proceed only from the partisans
of revolution ; and it was easy to apply the term
"*disaffected,*" to humanitarians who hated war, or
to the suffering poor who wanted bread.   But,
notwithstanding that the Government expenditure
was over fifty millions per annum,[3] and that the
ordinary expenses of housekeeping had increased
300 per cent. in seven years, the war was popular
with all classes that had anything to fear from
modern doctrines.   The political ignorance of even
the majority of the House of Commons of that
day would put to shame the very students of our
time.   And it is not too much to say that, had
Lord Grenville been anything of a statesman beyond the name, he would scarcely have treated
Napoleon's overtures for peace, made at the close
of the year 1799, with mere contempt, and allowed
a fair opportunity for a general pacification to pass
away because he must have, as a basis, the re-
instatement of the Bourbons upon the throne of
France.   Ministers wanted to come out of the

[3] The total population, at the same time, being less than *eleven*
millions.

contest, in point of fact, with GLORY ; and any peace, which did not involve the attainment of the objects with which the war was, professedly, being carried on, was certain also to involve their prestige, if not their places. This may be said without any disparagement to their honour. Mr. Pitt, Mr. Windham, Lord Grenville,—all of them and their supporters, honestly believed that their mission was, not only to keep French principles out of England, but to smother them throughout Europe. Sternly, earnestly, they kept to their purpose ; forgetting, or, more probably, never having taken to heart, the prodigious expansion which the eighteenth century had produced in the human mind, and the certainty of its development in the line of liberty ; whilst confounding, in one heterogeneous estimate, the unstable Gaul, the restless Pole, the high-spirited Celt, and the conservative Briton.

So Mr. Pitt's supporters in the press, reflecting the fearsome notions of their chief, and dreading, as from the Evil One himself, the faintest breath of democracy, could only regard the " masses " as unfit for more than the mere semblance of political rights. The impossibility of phlegmatic JOHN BULL ever permitting, on his own soil, such follies

and excesses as the French Jacobins had perpetrated never entered their minds. "Law and
Order," as personified in George III. and his
ministers, was the only antithesis to "Anarchy."
Some of these writers lived to see the perilous
consequences of the repressing system ; and a few
survived to note the blessings which flowed from
general political enlightenment. Some, to the
very last, shut their eyes to the inevitable, and
could prognosticate only decay ; others, sooner or
later, discerned the signs of the times, and served
worthily in the van of progress. Of these latter,
one of the first, one of the most earnest, one of the
bravest, was Mr. William Cobbett.

And it is not uninteresting to note that, on the
very morrow of Mr. Windham's dinner-party, the
dimness began to clear away from Cobbett's mind.
Better and nobler hopes for the future of England,
founded upon something more solid than class-
prescriptions, unfolded themselves ; the veil began
to part, behind which was hidden the framework of
misgovernment alike with the skeletons of its
framers ; a glimmer of dawn, the expansion of
which was soon to light up a path, so startlingly
and unexpectedly distinct from his previous conceptions, appeared,—a path, not upon the mossy turf
of favour and privilege, leading on to other mossy

turves, but one trending up-hill, among stones and briers—which stones would, at last, beaten down into the earth by later footsteps, provide a firm foot-hold—which briers, refreshed by successive showers, would yet emit a sweet and blessed odour!

Here is his own account; and the man, or the woman, who can read it without emotion, need scarcely go on with this history :—

"When I returned to England, in 1800, after an absence from the country parts of it of sixteen years, the trees, the hedges, even the parks and woods, seemed *so small!* It made me laugh to hear little gutters, that I could jump over, called *rivers!* The Thames was but a *creek!* But when, in about a month after my arrival in London, I went to Farnham, the place of my birth, what was my surprise! Everything was become so pitifully *small!* I had to cross in my post-chaise the long and dreary heath of Bagshot; then, at the end of it, to mount a hill, called Hungry Hill; and from that hill I knew that I should look down into the beautiful and fertile vale of Farnham. My heart fluttered with impatience, mixed with a sort of fear, to see all the scenes of my childhood; for I had learnt, before, the death of my father and mother. There is a hill, not far from the town, called Crooksbury Hill, which rises up out of a flat, in the form of a *cone,* and is planted with Scotch fir-trees. Here I used to take the eggs and young ones

of crows and magpies. This hill was a famous object in
the neighbourhood. It served as the superlative degree
of height. '*As high as Crooksbury Hill*' meant, with us,
the utmost degree of height. Therefore, the first object
that my eyes sought was this hill. I could not believe
my eyes! Literally speaking, I, for a moment, thought
the famous hill removed, and a little heap put in its
stead; for I had seen, in New Brunswick, a single rock,
or hill of solid rock, ten times as big, and four or five
times as high! The post-boy going down hill, and not
a bad road, whisked me in a few minutes to the Bush
Inn, from the garden of which I could see the prodigious *sand-hill* where I had begun my gardening works.
What a *nothing!* But now came rushing into my mind,
all at once, my pretty little garden, my little blue smock-
frock, my little nailed shoes, my pretty pigeons that I used
to feed out of my hands, the last kind words and tears
of my gentle and tender-hearted and affectionate mother.
I hastened back into the room. If I had looked a
moment longer, I should have dropped. When I came
to reflect, *what a change!* I looked down at my dress—
what a change! What scenes I had gone through!
How altered my state! I had dined the day before at a
Secretary of State's in company with Mr. Pitt, and had
been waited upon by men in gaudy liveries! I had had
nobody to assist me in the world—no teachers of any sort
—nobody to shelter me from the consequences of bad,
and no one to counsel me to good, behaviour. I felt
proud. The distinctions of rank, birth, and wealth, all
become nothing in my eyes; and from that moment (less

than a month after my arrival in England) I resolved never to bend before them."

The determination to start a daily paper was wise on the part of Mr. Cobbett, as far as his experience in Philadelphia had shown how possible it was for him to entertain a large circle of readers; but unwise, in that he had scarce capital enough with which to print the numbers for a single week. Yet the opportunity for carrying out his plan without risk was placed at his disposal ; and there are few incidents in Cobbett's whole career which redound so greatly to his credit as the refusal of this offer. The pride with which, in after-years, he told and retold the story, may be estimated very differently by different minds; but the spirit with which the refusal was made is unexceptionable. There was no other way out of it, if he meant Independence. If glimpses of grandeur had really not contaminated that honest heart, nor weakened the impulses of that patriotic soul, how should he live, and move, and work, and fight, with his hands not free ?

And this is the story [he is addressing Mr. George Rose] :—

" John Heriot was at that time the proprietor of two

newspapers, called the *Sun* and the *True Briton*—the former an evening and the latter a morning paper. I had heard that these two papers had been set on foot by *you*, who were then one of the Secretaries of the Treasury, and that, when set on foot, the profits of them had been given to Heriot. Now mark, that Mr. Hammond, who was then Under-Secretary of State in the Foreign Department, offered to me the *proprietorship* of one of those papers *as a gift;* and I remember very well that he told me that this offer was made in consequence of a communication with you, or your colleague Mr. Long, I forget which. This was no trifling offer. The very types, presses, &c., were worth a considerable sum. Mr. Hammond, who was a very honest as well as a very zealous and able man, had behaved with great kindness to me ; had invited me frequently to his house, where I dined, I recollect, with Sir William Scott, with Lord Hawkesbury (now Lord Liverpool), and several other persons of rank ; and, in short, had shown me so much attention, that I felt great reluctance in giving the following answer to his offer :—' I am very much obliged to you, and to the gentlemen of whom you speak, for this offer; but, though I am very poor, my desire is to render the greatest possible service to my country, and I am convinced that, by keeping myself wholly free, and relying upon my own means, I shall be able to give the Government much more efficient support than if any species of dependence could be traced to me. At the same time, I do not wish to cast blame on those who are thus dependent; and I do not wish to be thought too conceited and too confident of my own powers and judgment to decline any advice that you, or any one in office, may at any time be good enough to offer me ; and I shall always be thankful to you for any intelligence or information that any of you may be pleased to give me.' Mr Hammond did not appear at all surprised at my answer ; and I shall always respect him for what he said upon hearing it. His words were nearly these :— 'Well, I must say that I think you take the *honourable* course, and I most sincerely wish it may also be the *profitable* one.' I ought not, upon this occasion, to omit to say that I always understood that Lord Grenville, who was then Secretary of State for Foreign Affairs, was not one of those who approved of the baseness and dependence of the press."

He also ventured to remind Mr. Hammond

"of the fable of the wolf and the *mastiff,* the latter of which, having one night, when loose, rambled into a wood, met the former all gaunt and shagged, and said to him, 'Why do you lead this sort of life? See how fat and sleek I am ! Come home with me and live as I do, dividing your time between eating and sleeping.' The ragged friend having accepted the kind offer, they then trotted on together till they got out of the wood, when the wolf, assisted by the light of the moon, the beams of which had been intercepted by the trees, spied a *crease,* a little *mark,* round the neck of the mastiff. 'What is your fancy,' said he, 'for making that mark round your neck ? '

'Oh!' said the other, 'it is only the mark of my collar that my master ties me up with.' 'Ties you up!' exclaimed the wolf, stopping short at the same time; 'give me my ragged hair, my gaunt belly, and my *freedom ;*'— and, so saying, he trotted back to the wood."

Opportunities for reflecting upon the comparative states of dependence and independence crowded apace. He could scarcely turn, among his new circle of friends, without discovering some new Government parasite, some new candidate for ministerial favour, some new office-hunter or aspiring sinecurist. Mr. Pitt disdained the society of newspaper-people, but was only too willing to pay them for their praises. And it must not be left unnoticed that the practice of liberally rewarding this class of writers has often been justified by circumstances. The case in point, viz. the fight which was going on against democracy, required that the enemy should be fought with his own weapons; only it very unfortunately happened that all the talent was on the other side, and, where quality was lacking, the fight must needs be kept up with the aid of gold and silver. Mr. Cobbett would, indeed, have been worth buying, if his price could have been named ; while there was a Paine, or a Thelwall, or a Godwin to be withstood.

The following brilliant and humorous passage of Cobbett's, written in his old age, will complete our illustration of this topic:—

"At the time of my return, the great Government writers and political agents were John Reeves, who had been chairman of the *Loyal Association against Republicans and Levellers;* John Bowles; John Gifford; William Gifford; Sir Frederick Morton Eden, Bart.; the Reverend Mr. Ireland, now Dean of Westminster; the Reverend John Brand; the Reverend Herbert Marsh, now Bishop of Peterborough; Mallet Du Pan; Sir Francis D'Ivernois; and Nicholas Vansittart. These were all pamphlet-writers, supporting Pitt and the war through thick and thin. They, looking upon me as a fellow-labourer, had all sent their pamphlets to me at Philadelphia; and all of them, except Marsh, Vansittart, and the two Frenchmen, had written to me laudatory letters. All but the parsons called themselves 'SQUIRES in the title-pages of their pamphlets. Look at me now! I had been bred up with a smock-frock upon my back; that frock I had exchanged for a soldier's coat; I had been out of England almost the whole of my time from the age of [twenty]. We used to give in those times the name of 'SQUIRE to none but gentlemen of great landed estates, keeping their carriages, hounds, and so forth: look at me, then, in whose mind my boyish idea of a 'SQUIRE had been carried about the world with me: look at me, I say, with letters from four 'SQUIRES and from REVERENDS on my table; and wonder not that my head was half turned! Only think of me (who, just about twelve years before, was clumping about with nailed shoes on my feet, and with a smock-frock on my back) being in literary correspondence with four 'SQUIRES, two REVERENDS, and a BARONET! Look at me, and wonder that I did not lose my senses! And if I had remained in America, God knows what might have happened.

" Luckily I came to England, and that *steadied* my head pretty quickly. To my utter astonishment and confusion, I found all my 'SQUIRES and REVERENDS, and my BARONET too—all, in one way or other, dependents on the Government, and, *out of the public purse, profiting from their pamphlets.* John Reeves, ESQUIRE, who was a barrister, but never practised, I found *joint patentee of the office of King's Printer*—a sinecure worth, to him, about 4000*l.* a year, which he had got for thirty years, just then begun. John Bowles, ESQUIRE, (also a briefless barrister) I found a *Commissioner of Dutch Property;* and the public recollect the emoluments of that office, as exposed in 1809. John Gifford, ESQUIRE, I found a *Police Magistrate*, with a pension of 300*l.* a year besides. William Gifford, ESQUIRE, I found sharing the profits of Canning's anti-Jacobin neswspaper (set up and paid for by the Treasury), and with a sinecure of 329*l.* a year besides. My BARONET I found with rent-free apartments in Hampton Court Palace, and with what else I have forgotten. My REVEREND John Brand I found with the living of St. George, Southwark, given him by Lord Loughborough (then Chancellor), he already having a living in Suffolk. My REVEREND Ireland I found with the living of Croydon, or the expectancy of it, and also found that he was *looking steadily at old Lord Liverpool.* The REVEREND Herbert Marsh I found a pension-hunter, and he soon succeeded to the tune of 514*l.* a year. Mallet Du Pan I found *dead*, but I found that he had been a *pensioner*, and I found his widow a pensioner, and his son in one of the public offices. And Nicholas Vansittart, ESQUIRE, who had written a pamphlet to prove that the war had enriched the nation, I found, O God ! a *Commissioner of Scotch Herrings !* Hey, dear ! as the Lancashire men say ; I thought it would have broken my heart !

" Of all these men, REEVES and WILLIAM GIFFORD were the only ones of talent—the former a *really learned* lawyer, and, politics aside, as good a man as ever lived —a clever man; a head as clear as spring water; considerate, mild, humane; made by nature to be an English judge. I did not break with him on account of politics. We said nothing about them for years. I always had the greatest regard for him; and there he now is in the grave, leaving, the newspapers say, *two hundred thousand pounds*, without hardly a soul knowing that there ever was such a man ! The fate of WILLIAM GIFFORD was much about the same : both lived and died bachelors ; both left large sums of money ; both spent their lives in upholding measures which, in their hearts, they abhorred, and in eulogizing men whom, in their hearts, they despised ; and, in spite of their literary labours, the only chance that they have of being remembered, for even ten years to come, is this notice of them

from a pen that both most anxiously wished to silence
many years ago.   Amongst the first things that Reeves
ever said to me was : 'I tell you what, Cobbett, we have
only two ways here ; we must either *kiss*,—or *kick* them ;
and you must make your choice at once.'   I resolved to
kick.   William Gifford had more asperity in his temper,
and was less resigned.   He despised Pitt and Canning
and the whole crew; but he loved ease, was *timid ;* he
was their slave all his life, and all his life had to endure
a conflict between his pecuniary interest and his conscience.

"As to the rest of my *'Squires* and other dignified
pamphleteers, they were a low, talentless, place-and-
pension-hunting crew ; and I was so disgusted with the
discoveries that I had made, that I trembled at the
thought of falling into the ranks with them.   Love of *ease*
was not in me ; the very idea of becoming *rich* had never
entered into my mind ; and my horror at the thought of
selling my talents for money, and of plundering the
country with the help of the means that God had given
me wherewith to assist in supporting its character, filled
me with horror not to be expressed."

CHAPTER XI.

"I TOOK THE LEAD, IN SINGING THE PRAISES OF PITT."

MR. COBBETT'S facile pen could not remain completely at rest, whilst the project of a newspaper was yet only in the bud. On the 30th August he issued a sixth (and final) number of the *Rushlight*, wherein he reviewed the circumstances of his career, and the tenor of his writings in the United States. This fugitive number is not only very temperate in style, but elegant, unless exception be taken to its strong anti-gallican spirit; calling, as it does, upon the Americans to shun "all connexion with that den of monsters, France." With reference to his own war-whoop, he says,—

"I studied the interests of my country. To make the name of Englishmen a friendly sound, to recommend an imitation of our Government, our fashions, our propensities, and finally to make them pay a tribute to

England, through the medium of her manufactures, was the object nearest my heart."

At last, in the course of the ensuing month, an advertisement appeared of the projected newspaper; and the public were invited to ask for a prospectus at the house of William Cobbett, at No. 18, Pall Mall. It was to be called THE PORCUPINE, and to appear every morning at the office, No. 3, Southampton Street, Strand.

The prospectus of the *Porcupine* was on the lines of anti-Republicanism. The editor confessed that it was with the utmost astonishment and indignation that he found a portion of the press endeavouring to bring down upon his native country the calamity and disgrace attendant on revolution ; still preaching fanaticism and infidelity, and " still bawling for that change which they have the audacity to denominate Reform." It was not for him to fold his hands and tamely listen to the insolent eulogists of republican governments, who had seen republican officers of state offering to sell their country for a few thousand dollars, who had seen republican judges become felons, and felons become judges, &c., &c. The paper should be distinctly anti-gallican :—

" The intrigues of the French, the servile, the insidious,

the insinuating French, shall be an object of my constant
attention. Whether at war or at peace with us, they still
dread the power, envy the happiness, and thirst for the
ruin of England. . . . . Had they the means, they would
exterminate us to the last man ; they would snatch the
crutch from our parents, the cradle from our children ;
and our happy country itself would they sink beneath
those waves on which they now flee from the thunder of
our cannon. . . . While we retain one drop of true British
blood in our veins, we never shall shake hands with this
perfidious and sanguinary race, much less shall we make
a compromise with their monkey-like manners and tiger-
like principles."

The *Porcupine* would also resist the mischievous
portion of the press, and pay much less regard to
the feelings and interests of fanatical and factious
booksellers than to the cause of religion and
loyalty. The editor held it to be the duty of men
in power to employ the pen, as well as the sword,
in defence of Government, yet,—

"The peculiar circumstances, under which I now
come forward, demand from me an explicit and solemn
assertion of my INDEPENDENCE. My undertaking is my
own; it was begun without the aid, without the advice,
and even without the knowledge, of any person either
directly or indirectly connected with the ministry; if,
therefore, I hope to yield some trifling support to that
ministry, it is not because I have received, or ever shall

receive, any gratification at their hands; but because I am most sincerely persuaded that, next to the virtues of His Majesty and the general loyalty of his subjects, this country owes its preservation to the wisdom and integrity of Mr. Pitt and his colleagues."

But all this should never make the *Porcupine* "the blind instrument of party, the trumpet of indiscriminate applause." The prospectus concluded with further references to the writer's long-continued solicitude for the happiness and glory of England.

The first number of the *Porcupine* appeared on Thursday, Oct. 30th, and the price was 6*d.* It bore the motto—FEAR GOD, HONOUR THE KING. The proprietor had received five columns of advertisements, notwithstanding a previous announcement that the "obscene and filthy boastings of quackery" would, on no consideration whatever, be admitted. So the paper had a very fair start. In the third week, the early numbers were being reprinted; and on the 9th December, the circulation had reached 1500. Also,—

"The Porcupine cannot boast of being seen in the numerous pot-houses of this metropolis: but we have the superior advantage of being generally read by persons of *property*, *rank*, and *respectability*."

This was probably the case, for the *Anti-Jacobin Review* condescended to back up Mr. Cobbett thus :—

". . . . A daily paper, under the title of the *Porcupine*, has been most deservedly admitted as a desirable appendix at the breakfasting-table of every *true* friend to their *king*, to their *country*, and to *decency*."

Mr. Pitt's resignation of office, early in 1801, although ostensibly caused by his difference with the king upon the Catholic question, had for its .object, more probably, the substitution of a minister who could consistently negotiate with Buonaparte. This was suspected by many ; and it appeared conclusive, upon the almost incredible announcement that Mr. Addington was to take the helm of affairs. That arch-mediocrity, owing his promotion entirely to royal favour, had filled the Speaker's chair with tolerable credit, but was without any of the gifts entitling him to rank among statesmen ; and, until it was discovered that Mr. Pitt was still chief wire-puller, the nation could hardly credit the appointment ; and, as far as can now be judged, it was the beginning of a more widely-spread distrust of Pitt.

The *Porcupine* had consistently praised the " heaven-born" minister, and continued to do so, more or less, during its whole career. It began to diverge in opinion on the day of the above announcement. It was high time "for all true Englishmen to rally round the Throne," for the granting of the proposed concessions to the Catholics "would undermine and finally overthrow," &c., &c., according to the long-buried tenets of High-Toryism. A few weeks afterward, some sarcasm, directed toward Pitt's paper-financing, appeared, but was disavowed next day by the editor, who had not seen the paragraph before it appeared in print, and who continued to entertain, "in common with a vast majority of the nation, the highest opinion of that gentleman's talents as a financier." Upon a report that Mr. Pitt was intending [July] to sell Holwood, he remarked that "we shall ever continue to think that to suffer a man, who has rendered such services to his country in particular, and to Europe in general, to feel the consequences arising from a confined income, is to incur a national disgrace." But, by the end of the year, Mr. Cobbett was in opposition, along with the new party under Mr. Windham's leadership.

Before dismissing the *Porcupine* newspaper, the reader will be entertained with a few characteristic illustrations. The editor very early began to display his pugnacity toward the opposition press. Not that he was singular, but that he excelled all his cotemporaries in the art of hitting straight when attacked. The newspapers of that day were largely occupied in throwing dirt at one another,[1] and one column was often taken up by a string of paragraphs, containing laboured sarcasms directed toward public men or the other public prints. The *True Briton* was especially industrious in this way. But here is *Porcupine :*—

"The DETECTOR.—Under this title, it is our intention to devote a column or two of our paper, once a week at least, to the detecting and exposing of the ignorance, perverseness, and falsehood of the Jacobinical and stock-jobbing prints, which, to the great scandal and reproach of the nation, are not only tolerated, but *read*. From our experience, acquired in a country where the spirit of Jacobinism is, if possible, still more daring and violent than in England, we are convinced that, to succeed in a warfare such as we have commenced, defensive measures will not do," &c.

"The *Times* calls the *Chronicle* the 'leading print of

---

[1] A practice which lasted, however, until a recent generation ; *e.g.* see the following tit-bits from the *Times* of July 26th, 1838 :— Of the *Morning Post*—"this kitchen-stuff journal ;" "this cockney out of livery ;" "flippant and foolish as its brother blockheads.'' And of the *Courier*—"that abject slave and unprincipled tool of the Ministers." The *Post* is also said to "proceed the entire swine," &c.

Opposition,' which compliment the *Chronicle* returns by styling the *Times* the 'leading print of Government.' . . . . What can entitle them to the epithet '*leading*,' we are at a loss to discover, except it be their superiority in point of turpitude . . . . if falsehood and hypocrisy ad-mit of degrees of comparison, we are rather disposed to give the *Times* the scandalous pre-eminence."

"The *Morning Chronicle* was yesterday seized with the horrors," &c.

"To Correspondents.—Nimrod is surprised that we should have condescended to notice the *Oracle*, and advises us to pursue a nobler game ; but he should do us the justice to recollect that, when *game* are not to be found, sportsmen sometimes amuse themselves by de-stroying *vermin*."

"Ignorance and perversity : For these two amiable qualities the *Morning Post* and the *Times* are eminently distinguished."

(The *Observer*): "The occupation of this print is to scrape together the orts of the week, and hash them up," &c.

"The *Monthly Magazine*, a periodical miscellany, which we have already mentioned with due abhorrence."

"The *Morning Herald*, in the delirious enjoyment of its puns and conundrums."

"Profound *Morning Post !* poor innocent ! what does it know of the existing differences between this country and America ? No more, we dare engage, than do the footmen and chambermaids who read its conundrums with such delight. . . . . We would indeed earnestly recommend the *Morning Post* to avoid politics altogether. Its company will always be welcome in the kitchen, and sometimes in the nursery."

The *Porcupine* had the smaller difficulties to contend with; as when several country subscribers complained of "other papers being foisted on them;" and "the flagrant imposition of some of the hawkers in Wimpole Street, who have charged eightpence for the *Porcupine.*" In fact, there was a little too much communicability on the part of the editor toward his correspondents, at the same time that correspondents were permitted to be very plain-spoken. One of them suggested that satire would be more keen if conveyed in the most polished language: he thought that "the comparison, some days ago, of *the dog returning to his vomit*, or any ideas or expressions bearing upon coarseness, offend the more refined inhabitants of this kingdom."

In inviting correspondence for his paper, Mr. Cobbett adopted a course which is not usually taken, viz. that of requesting that communications be *not* accompanied with the real name of the author. He was, besides, much plagued with unpaid letters—a circumstance which he had often to complain of both before and after this period.

Some of his correspondents were people of real distinction, among them being Lord Grenville, who wrote letters under the name of SULPICIUS. Jeremy Bentham, also, contributed a long article upon the projected Population Bill ; which appears in the *Porcupine* of Dec. 1st, 1800, and is reprinted in Bentham's collected writings.

Toward the close of the *Porcupine's* career, the negotiations for peace came to a conclusion, and that paper stood almost alone in opposition. The perilous task of boldly attacking the First Consul was pursued :—

" We request our readers to observe that henceforth we shall be very particular in what we say about the most illustrious sovereign, Consul Buonaparte. Oh, how we shall extol him ! We shall endeavour to give our readers the earliest information when he rises, breakfasts, dines, sups, and spits."

And, as all this was in direct violation of the popular feeling of the moment, a catastrophe occurred which, in all probability, contributed to bring the *Porcupine and Anti-gallican Monitor* to an untimely end. Mr. Cobbett was repeatedly urged to bend before the blast, but that was not in him.

The story appears to be this. Lauriston, the

bearer of the despatches containing the prelimi-
naries of peace, received an ovation from the
mob, immediately upon his landing. On his reaching London, "a vile, degraded rabble, miscalled
BRITONS, took the horses out of the carriage," and
dragged the vehicle round the parks and the West-
end in triumph.

The *Porcupine* was horrified: this was all in
the French style, and the nation was prostrate at
the feet of Buonaparte. But, among all reflecting
politicians, the peace was derided; and, several
persons declining to light up their windows in token
of rejoicing, had the mortification of seeing them
broken. On the 7th October, all the windows on
the east side of Berkeley Square were damaged;
and Bond Street and the neighbourhood displayed
similar evidences of popular displeasure. On Saturday, the 10th, a general illumination took place;
and there were few who dared to run the risk of being
counter to that displeasure. Among those few,
however, was the publisher of the *Porcupine*, who
had in the morning's paper reiterated his objections
to the proposed treaty; and now, in the evening,
resolutely kept the windows in darkness, both of the
house in Pall Mall, and of that in Southampton
Street. Of course, both houses were sacked, the
cheerful rabble keeping up a siege of six or seven

hours' duration,—the person in charge, at the newspaper office, narrowly escaping with his life.

There was a great demand for this Saturday's
paper. On Monday, however, the editor was
"under the necessity of apprising his readers that
the publication of the *Porcupine* must cease until
the 'delirium of joy' shall have subsided." This
interregnum lasted two days. On Thursday commenced the publication of a series of letters, addressed to Lord Hawkesbury, "on the peace with
Buonaparte." They were signed WILLIAM COB-
BETT, and continued to appear at intervals until
the 4th of November.

But the *Porcupine* was doomed. In spite of an
increasing circulation, the paper was a financial
failure ; it was interfering with the bookselling
business in Pall Mall, and the proprietor was
getting dissatisfied with the annoyances entailed
upon him. " He who has been the proprietor of
a daily paper for only one month wants no Romish
priest to describe to him the torments of purgatory." So, in the course of November, the paper
became the property of Mr. John Gifford ; and on
the 1st of January, 1802, it finally disappeared,
being merged in Heriot's paper, the *True Briton.*

The "Letters to Lord Hawkesbury" have been
highly extolled, and not without reason, for they

practised, and I still do practise, industry and economy to their utmost extent."

This plan was communicated to Dr. Laurence, and to several other gentlemen of the new opposition, by Mr. Windham. It was warmly adopted ; the money was immediately raised, and the new journal started. The first number appeared in January, 1802, and bore the title of " COBBETT'S POLITICAL REGISTER."

CHAPTER XII.

"THE THOUGHTS OF THE NATION ARE LIKE A CORK IN THE MIDDLE OF THE OCEAN."

WILLIAM COBBETT was now in his fortieth year,[1] in the prime of life, blessed with unfailing health, unimpaired talents, and habits of industry, and a sturdy sense of his independence. At this beginning of the year 1802, he could command anything he chose—not the least matter being the ear of thousands of ready listeners. It is very easy to understand and account for the immediate success of the *Political Register.* The plan had long been in Cobbett's mind. It partook of the qualities of his Philadelphia *Censor,* joined to those of a weekly newspaper: parliamentary debates, public official

---

[1] A portrait (*vide* Frontispiece), engraved by Bartolozzi, appeared at the close of 1801. Cobbett appears in the surtout and neckcloth of the period, and has sufficient dignity of mien, notwithstanding his light hair and round face, and one's impression that he would look as well in a smock-frock.

documents, foreign intelligence, weekly prices-current, and diary of the weather, &c., along with the editor's summary of politics, made up such a journal as was wanted—not only for periodical instruction, but that might furnish a ready means of reference. As projected and as carried out for the first two years, the *Register* was far in advance of anything that had been hitherto attempted. About three hundred subscribers were found, to start with, the price being 10*d.* per number, fortnightly. But the two numbers for January were so far successful, that February 6th saw the commencement of a weekly issue.

From this date until June, 1835 (excepting a break of three months, April—June, 1817), the famous *Register* appeared uninterruptedly. Its form changed from time to time; but its valiant, its unconquerable editor was the ruling spirit and the chief contributor during the long period of thirty-three years. Its readers, its patrons, its friends, its enemies, its own views upon public characters, its own assertions as to the tendency of events, its own beliefs—all changed from time to time. But, with the vicissitudes amid which its intrepid career was run, there was one principle underlying the whole—one foundation from which it was never removed. That was a strong conservative attachment to the constitution of the country, allied to deep affection for its people—sentiments which were never more necessary to be proclaimed than during the hideous misgovernment of the first quarter of this century, and sentiments which were never more constantly proclaimed than through the lips, or by the pen, of William Cobbett. The reader may, in the course of this entertaining history, be able to satisfy himself how true—how *very* true—is this standpoint.

Meanwhile, let us take a few soundings at the outset ; let us see what bottom the lead brings up ; steering will then be an affair of confidence—such perplexities as do arise depending mainly upon the conditions of wind and storm, tide and current, and not upon unknown conditions existing beneath the waters. Here, then :—

[1802] "The throne on which God has placed our Sovereign, and our own prosperity, freedom, and public happiness, which have no other basis but that throne, are our first and greatest care. . . ."

[1817] "A thousand times over have I said that we wanted *nothing new.* I say so still. We want the laws of England. We want no innovation. We want to destroy neither Kings, Nobles, nor Church. We want the laws of England, and *the laws of England we will have.*"

[1820] "My principles, then, are as follows :—I hold that it is the duty of us all to do our utmost to uphold a Government in King, Lords, and Commons. That, as to religion, opinions ought to be left as God has made them in our minds, perfectly free, and that persecution on account of religious opinions is of the worst and most wicked kind. That no man ought to be taxed but by his own consent, agreeably to the law of the land. That elections ought to be free. . . . That the affairs of the nation ought to be so managed that every sober and industrious and healthy man ought, out of his own wages, to be able to support himself, wife, and family, in a comfortable and decent manner. . . . That it is the weight of taxes which produces all the miseries which this nation now suffers. . . . That the Debt and other fixed expenses are a mortgage on the labour of every man, woman, and child, in the country. . . . That, unless a great change speedily take place, this nation will become feeble and contemptible as well as enslaved ; and that its capital will be conveyed away to enrich and to give power to rival nations."

[1833] "I hold that this, which we have here, is the best sort of Government in the world."

At the commencement of the year 1802, that party represented by Mr. Windham and his friends honestly believed that England was at the feet of Buonaparte ; and, so strongly did they urge their opinions, that the advocates of peace were beginning to talk again of war, "should it be found necessary," even before the definitive treaty arrived in London, in April. Mr. Cobbett's view was that we were "a beaten and a conquered people;" that John Bull was only a spaniel after all. Not that "Boney" was so much to be feared, as the spirit of the French Republic, which was sapping the foundations of English loyalty. Anti-Gallicanism seemed dying out. Noble sentiments were being overpowered by effeminacy, cant, and the love of money. Loyalty had become "a matter of expedience rather than what it used to be—a principle of equal force with filial affection or the love of life."

But Mr. Addington and his ministry are pledged to peace, and peace must be tried, if only to expose its inutility. So, while the ministerial papers blow peace-bubbles, and leave off, for a while, calling "Boney" wicked names, Mr. Cobbett sighs to think how the paths of glory do indeed lead but to the grave : for England is approaching her final doom.

The first-fruit of all this is ruffianism in the shape of newspaper abuse and of mob-tyranny. For the time being, Mr. Cobbett is the most unpopular man in London, and he knows it—and he defies it :—

"The alliterative words, *peace* and *plenty*, sound well

in a song, or make a pretty transparency in the window of an idiot ; but the things which these harmonious words represent are not always in unison."

Which means, of course, that he will certainly not illuminate his windows on the forthcoming celebration of the signing of the Definitive Treaty. His *Register* is occupied with more letters to Lord Hawkesbury, written, too, in magnificent style, and furnished with arguments which might be refused a hearing, but could not be gainsaid.

So the peace-proclaiming cavalcade approaches; the order for illumination goes forth ; and the windows of No. 11, Pall Mall, are once more shattered, and the ornamental " Crown and Mitre " once more dashed to the ground.

This time, however, it was a more serious matter for the assailants. Cobbett had expected something of the kind, and removed his wife and family to the house of a friend ; he gave notice to the police, and was resolved to reach the culprits, if possible—which he did, for "six of the villains " were brought up to Bow Street next morning. They were all in a respectable station in life, two of them being clerks in the Post Office, and one of these a son of the Rev. William Beloe, who had formerly been one of Porcupine's warmest admirers.

In the end these young men were tried at the sessions, and heavily fined.

But the incident furnished Cobbett with material for sarcasm, which was freely dealt out at intervals. He " would rather be *compelled* to illuminate than have a choice, and so have his house demolished by Government reptiles." On the king's birthday (4th June) the people were not illuminating, as "the practice seems discredited on account of recent occurrences." And in the following year, when things were going wrong again, and the decks were once more being cleared for action, he ventures to remind Lord Hawkesbury (who had "smiled " at the affair) that there was a time to weep as well as a time to laugh.

The alternations of tone, on the part of public writers and speakers of this period, with reference to Buonaparte, are very amusing. They had called him a tyrant, a despot, a cut-throat, a murderer, an assassin, a poisoner, a monster, an infidel, an atheist, a blasphemer, a hypocrite, a demon, a devil, a robber, a wolf, a usurper, a thief, a savage, a tiger, a renegade, a liar, a braggart, a cuckold, a coward, and a fool.

They now extolled his character: " his courage, his magnanimity, his wisdom, and even his piety."

A few months later, he was "the most abominable miscreant that ever breathed."

No wonder, then, that the man, who had been consistent all through, and was found to be right at last, must be put down. If there is anything the average specimen of John Bull hates, it is the man who has caught him tripping. Hence, from this time, Mr. Cobbett found he had the bitterest enemies on his native soil. Early in the year 1803, Otto, the French ambassador, wanted the Government to prosecute him, along with Peltier. Mr. Windham was exhorted to disavow him. The "British Critic," which had suckled Cobbett's infant reputation, now felt "diffident" of much that it had said on his behalf; and the Addington ministry had their eye upon him. As for his rivals in the press, it must be said that their conduct was unhandsome. Here was the very first man who had succeeded in obtaining an independent position for the craft ;[2] yet the mere fact of his having rejected the arts of Treasury corruption was sufficient to rouse their envy. There was Mr. Heriot, for example, who was getting fat and rich, and was looking forward to some snug berth to which he might retire, could not bear to see Mr. Cobbett getting

[2] *I.e.*, independent, not only of subsidy, but of the shackles of party.

fat and rich on independent principles. So far did this feeling extend, that a very sad affair presently ensued.

There had been a debate in the House of Commons upon the Defence Bill, on which occasion Mr. Sheridan had taunted Windham with his connexion with the *Political Register*, and insinuated that the editor of that journal had incited the sailors to mutiny. This latter was not only a flat misrepresentation, but such a thing was totally contrary to Mr. Cobbett's habit of mind : if there was a thing he was specially earnest about, it was the condemnation of resistance to lawful authority —more especially with regard to the military and naval services. Mr. Windham answered with spirit, and, for once, spoke with almost as much humour as Sheridan himself; concluding in the following terms :—

"As to the weekly publication to which the hon. gentleman has alluded, I entertain all the sentiments of respect which he supposes me to entertain, both for the work and for its author, of whom I had a high opinion long before I personally knew him. I admired the conduct which he pursued through a most trying crisis in America, where he uniformly supported all those principles upon which the happiness of mankind depend ; where he uniformly opposed all those principles (including such as were formerly professed by the hon. gentleman) which tend to sap the foundations of civil society, and to spread misery and wickedness through the world; and where, by his own unaided exertions, *he rendered his country services that entitle him to a statue of gold.*"

This was too much. Aristocratic and plutocratic animosity had been growing fast enough, and would have been harmless, even with the aid of Mr. Sheridan's gay disingenuousness; but now, this was too much for the journalists who were struggling (where they were not subsidized) for ministerial favour. So they echo Mr. Sheridan, and return to the charge; the *True Briton* going a little farther than is needed, and indicating the appropriate punishment:—

"Mr. Windham professes himself to be the *Soldier's Friend.* We cannot suppose, however, that his attachment to a certain *American scribbler* arises from his being the writer of a work at the beginning of the French Revolution, bearing that title, because that work had for its object *to excite the soldiery to mutiny,*—to which, it seems, the same patriotic writer now endeavours *to instigate the navy.* We speak merely from what has been said in the House of Commons, for we think no true Briton can read the works of the person alluded to with any kind of temper. The *pillory* or the *gibbet* we think a more appropriate reward than that which Mr. Windham has suggested for a writer of such a stamp."

Now, all through Mr. Cobbett's long life, there was nothing roused his ire so much (in the way of personality) as the charge of sedition ; and all through his life he was justified in repudiating it. It was not his way. He was a man for facing his adversaries. And, to the end of his days, whatever his other errors, he could never be reproached with the arts of covert warfare. So Mr. Cobbett was nettled ; and,—

"in less than three hours after the libel was published, the libeller, Mr. Heriot, received personal chastisement in the very apartment where he had fabricated the libel."

The reader, who may feel interested in the full details of this squabble, will find Heriot's version in the *True Briton* of August 15—22, and Mr. Cobbett's account in the *Political Register* for August 20, 1803. It is sufficient to record here, that Mr. Heriot brought an action for assault, and did not appear to prosecute ; and that "focus of accumulated infamy, the *Political Register*," went on its way.

Just before the above incident occurred, circumstances had led to the production of an article in Cobbett's *Register*, which should now be mentioned, as indicating, probably, the extremest point of time at which he gave uncompromising support to the Government.

War had been declared in May, and the nation was again regarding the quality of its bayonets, and the condition of its belts and its gaiter-buttons. The fear of invasion was uppermost in the minds of everybody who had anything to lose, so the "people" must themselves be roused. Mr. Cobbett therefore prepared a manifesto, and placed it (through Mr. John Reeves) at the disposal of the ministry. The paper was not only accepted, but printed and sent round to all the clergy in the kingdom ; accompanied by an official circular, directing them to post it on the church-doors, and to "deposit copies in the pews, and distribute them in the aisles," and amongst the poor, &c.[8] This appeal to the British nation is a grand piece of writing, in Cobbett's best style. And no reader will wonder at the power which he was acquiring over the public mind, after perusing the following extracts :—

[8] It appears in the *Political Register* for July 30, 1803, and may be found sometimes in old collections of pamphlets and broadsides.

" Important Considerations for the People of this Kingdom.

"At a moment when we are entering on a scene deeply interesting, not only to this nation, but to the whole civilized world; at a moment when we all, without distinction of rank or degree, are called upon to rally round, and to range ourselves beneath, the banners of that sovereign under whose long, mild, and fostering reign the far greater part of us, capable of bearing arms, have been born and reared up to manhood; at a moment when we are, by his truly royal and paternal example, incited to make every sacrifice and every exertion in a war, the event of which is to decide whether we are still to enjoy, and to bequeath to our children, the possessions, the comforts, the liberties, and the national honours, handed down to us from generation to generation by our gallant forefathers; or whether we are, at once, to fall from this favoured and honourable station, and to become the miserable crouching slaves, the hewers of wood and the drawers of water, of these very Frenchmen, whom the valour of our fleets and armies has hitherto taught us to despise; at such a moment it behoves us, calmly and without dismay, to examine our situation, to consider what are the grounds of the awful contest in which we are engaged; what are the wishes, the designs, and the pretensions of our enemies; what would be the consequences, if those enemies were to triumph over us ; what are our means, and what ought to be our motives, not only for frustrating their malicious intentions, but for inflicting just and memorable chastisement on their insolent and guilty heads." [Here follows an account of the events which had brought Europe to its present disastrous enslavement, and Napoleon to his present height of power. Concluding with an eloquent reference to the results of the invasion of Germany in 1796-8, the writer winds up with the following appeal.]

" Such are the barbarities which have been inflicted on other nations. The recollection of them will never be effaced : the melancholy story will be handed down from generation to generation, to the everlasting infamy of the Republicans of France, and as an awful warning to all those nations whom they may hereafter attempt to invade. We are one of those nations ; we are the people whom they are now preparing to invade. Awful, indeed, is the warning, and, if we despise, tremendous will be the judgment. The same generals, the same commissaries, the same officers, the same soldiers, the very same rapacious and sanguinary host, that now hold Holland and Switzerland in chains—that desolated Egypt, Italy, and Germany—are at this moment preparing to make England, Ireland, and Scotland, the scenes of their atrocities. For some time past, they have had little opportunity to plunder: peace, for a while, suspended their devastations, and now, like gaunt and hungry wolves, they are looking towards the rich pastures of Britain. Already we hear their threatening howl; and if, like sheep, we stand bleating for mercy, neither our innocence nor our timidity will save us from being torn to pieces and devoured. The robberies, the barbarities, the brutalities they have committed in other countries, though at the thought of them the heart sinks and the blood runs cold, will be mere trifles to what they will commit here, if we suffer them to triumph over us. The Swiss and the Suabians were never objects of their envy; they were never the rivals of Frenchmen, either on the land or on the sea; they had never disconcerted or checked their ambitious projects, never humbled their pride, never defeated either their armies or their fleets. We have been, and we have done, all this : they have long enter- · tained against us a hatred engendered by the mixture of envy and of fear; and they are now about to make a great and desperate effort to gratify this furious, this unquenchable, this deadly hatred. What, then, can we expect at their hands? What but torments, even sur- passing those which they have inflicted on other nations? They remained but three months in Germany : here they would remain for ever; there, their extortions and their atrocities were, for want of time, confined to a part of the people; here they would be universal : no sort, no part, no particle of property would remain unseized ; no man, woman, or child would escape violence of some kind or other. Such of our manufactories as are mova- ble they would transport to France, together with the most ingenious of the manufacturers, whose wives and children would be left to starve. Our ships would follow the same course, with all the commerce and commercial

means of the kingdom. Having stripped us of everything, even to the stoutest of our sons and the most
beautiful of our daughters, over all that remained they
would establish and exercise a tyranny such as the world
never before witnessed. All the estates, all the farms, all
the mines, all the land and the houses, all the shops and
magazines, all the remaining manufactories, and all the
workshops, of every kind and description, from the
greatest to the smallest—all these they would bring over
Frenchmen to possess, making us their servants and their
labourers. To prevent us uniting and arising against
them, they would crowd every town and village with their
brutal soldiers, who would devour all the best part of the
produce of the earth, leaving us not half a sufficiency of
bread. They would, besides, introduce their own bloody
laws, with additional severities; they would divide us
into separate classes, hem us up in districts, cut off
all communication between friends and relations, parents
and children, which latter they would breed up in their
own blasphemous principles; they would affix badges
upon us, mark us in the cheek, shave our heads,
split our ears, or clothe us in the habit of slaves! And
shall we submit to misery and degradation like this,
rather than encounter the expenses of war; rather than
meet the honourable dangers of military combat; rather
than make a generous use of the means which Providence
has so bounteously placed in our hands? The sun, in
his whole course round the globe, shines not on a spot so
blessed as this great and now united kingdom. Gay and
productive fields and gardens, lofty and extensive woods,

innumerable flocks and herds, rich and inexhaustible mines, a mild and wholesome climate, giving health, activity, and vigour to fourteen millions of people : and shall we, who are thus favoured and endowed : shall we, who are abundantly supplied with iron and steel, powder and lead : shall we, who have a fleet superior to the maritime force of all the world, and who are able to bring two millions of fighting men into the field : shall we yield up this dear and happy land, together with all the liberties and honours, to preserve which our fathers so often dyed the land and the sea with their blood : shall we thus at once dishonour their graves, and stamp disgrace and infamy on the brows of our children ; and shall we, too, make this base and dastardly surrender to an enemy whom, within these twelve years, our country-men have defeated in every quarter of the world ?   No ! we are not so miserably fallen : we cannot, in so short a space of time, have become so detestably degenerate ; we have the strength and the will to repel the hostility, to chastise the insolence of the foe.   Mighty, indeed, must be our efforts, but mighty also is the meed.   Singly engaged against the tyrants of the earth, Britain now attracts the eyes and the hearts of mankind ; groaning nations look to her for deliverance ; justice, liberty, and religion are inscribed on her banners ; her success will be hailed with the shouts of the universe, while tears of admiration and gratitude will bedew the heads of her sons who fall in the glorious contest."

The wonderful activity of Cobbett's pen, at and

after this date, can only be appreciated by a
glance at the volumes of his celebrated journal.
On every topic that arose he had something to say.
Much of what he said was accepted by the reflecting
part of the public ; many of his predictions were
verified, and many falsified by events ; and many
of his opinions he learned to alter. But under-
neath the whole lies a burning desire for English
prosperity, unimpaired by the faintest token of
self-seeking. To enumerate the topics of the day
would involve the delineation of his opinions
thereon. They will have to be studied by the
future historian.

It will be sufficient for our purpose to note,
therefore, that the *Political Register* had already
become the vehicle for the ventilation of most of
the questions which were agitating the public mind,
from invasion down to vaccination. Often loaded
with prejudice, but very generally pervaded with
liberality, the views of his correspondents partook
of his own ardent spirit, contributing largely to the
enlightenment of the public mind.

That topic which most of all contributed to
revolutionize his relations with his early political
friends was the question of Finance. He began to
examine this subject in the year 1803, after having
read Adam Smith, Chalmers, and others in vain,

and at last lighted upon Mr. Paine's "Decline and Fall of the English System of Finance." This pamphlet, he says, was the means of opening his eyes; and from May in this year he began to urge a reduction of the interest on the national debt, and the policy of discovering some means of redistributing the wealth of the country.

But that which, for the time, influenced Cobbett's career, was his unsparing criticism upon the ministry of the day. Mr. Addington had been an object of ridicule from the moment of the first rumour of his appointment as premier; and his puerile efforts at statesmanship only served to confirm the original verdict of the public. Narrow-minded and presuming, he was utterly unfit for a position of authority, in which he would have to pass beyond the mere traditions of office. As a personal favourite, however, of the king he was endured for a while, until his obvious incapacity rendered it imperative that the destinies of the country should be entrusted to other hands. The want of decision and energy in the conduct of the war, and the waste and mismanagement of the military and naval resources of the country, were highly disappointing to a people whose patriotism for two whole years was artificially stimulated by rumours of invasion. "Another inactive and in-

glorious year sunk the British nation in her own
eyes, and in those of Europe." [4] This is the
general verdict of the cotemporary chronicler, on
reviewing the circumstances which led to Mr.
Pitt's resumption of office in May, 1804. Until
near the period, however, when the crash came, the
self-conceit of this clever ministry was superior to
any free comments ; they seemed fated to bring
upon themselves overwhelming disgrace. It is true,
there was opposition in Parliament (as well as in
the press), but opposition was ascribed to anything
but its real cause, and was treated with disdain.
Upon the report of the address, when Parliament
reassembled in November, 1803, Mr. Windham
ventured to express his dissatisfaction with the
incompetency of the ministry, but "no reply was
made to him." [5]

So the *Weekly Political Register* was in its glory.
The editor was determined to contribute his share
of effort toward relieving the country from the
benefit of Mr. Addington's services, and transmit-
ting his name to posterity "with all the contempt
it deserved." [6]

[4] "Annual Register," 1804.
[5] Lord Colchester's "Diary," i. 463.
[6] A very funny pamphlet appeared about this time, which may be
noticed as the first one of its kind, aimed at Cobbett's *Register*. The
title is "Elements of Opposition" (Hatchard, 1803), and it consists

It is not surprising, then, that Mr. Cobbett was now being closely watched, in order that an opportunity might arise for retaliation. Mr. Cobbett was helping to ruin the king's ministers ; the ministers would try and settle Mr. Cobbett. But it must be on some side issue ; there was no need for poor Mr. Addington's name to come in. There would soon be rope enough, one way or other.

The affairs of Ireland were again in a muddle. Robert Emmet's insurrection had just occurred, and martial law was eventually proclaimed. Mr. Fox protested in vain against the system under which that country was governed, as also did the *Political Register.*[7] A correspondent (Mr. Robert Johnson, a Judge of the Irish Common Pleas) sent some letters, signed " JUVERNA," containing an able, but rather bitter, series of comments upon recent events, to which the editor gave a prominent place in his journal (November—December, 1803). These letters opened the flood-gates of

of a series of rules, founded upon the opinions of Cobbett :—" How to describe a prime minister ;" " How to be outrageous for the public good ;" " How to talk of what you do not know," &c., &c. The pamphlet went through several editions.

7 " It were idle trifling to impute the distractions and general backwardness of that country to any other cause than the circumstances in which she has been placed, and the example or wish of those to whose management she has been entrusted."—" Annual Register," 1804.

wrath; and Mr. Cobbett was, accordingly, prosecuted in the following May for publishing
"certain libels upon the Earl of Hardwicke, Lord
Lieutenant of Ireland," and others.

"Juverna" had stated, among other matters, that
"the government of a harmless man was not
necessarily a harmless government;" that Lord
Hardwicke "was in rank an earl, in manners a
gentleman, in morals a good father and a good
husband;" that "he had a good library in St.
James's Square," and was "celebrated for understanding the modern method of fattening sheep as
well as any man in Cambridgeshire;" and he
wanted to know if the Viceroy was "one of that
tribe who have been sent over to us to be trained
up here into politicians, as they train the surgeons'
apprentices in the hospitals, by setting them at
first to bleed the pauper patients?"

Against Mr. Justice Osborne (of the Irish King's
Bench) the insinuation of "Juverna" was that he
had *wrongfully* stated, in a recent charge, that
the progress of crime in Ireland had been
effectually checked by the "well-timed efforts and
strenuous exertions of a wise and energetic government."

Lord Redesdale, the Irish Chancellor, was
sneered at in general terms; and alluded to as "a

strong chancery pleader," not entitled to claim one particle of trust or confidence from the public.

The trial was like all the political trials in those days:—imputations of the worst motives, insinuations of motives undreamt-of, graced the Attorney General's speech for the prosecution; Lord Ellenborough anticipated the decision of the jury by calling the words libellous: what more was to be expected than a verdict of guilty? [8]

The defendant's witnesses to character were all eminent men: Mr. Liston, Lord Henry Stuart, Mr. Windham, Mr. Charles Yorke, the Earl of Minto, and Mr. John Reeves, successively testified

---

[8] Jeremy Bentham, in an article on "The Elements of Packing, as applied to Juries," comments on this affair. Had he been upon the jury, he "should not have regarded it as consistent with his oath and duty to join in a verdict of guilty." Bentham, also, has a capital note on the impunity of men of family, and the punishment due to men of *no* family, called forth by a question of the Attorney-General. It certainly was an unnecessary piece of meanness on the part of Perceval to ask, "Gentlemen, who is Mr. Cobbett? Is he a man of family in this country? Is he a man writing purely from motives of patriotism?" &c.—"Works," v. 66, 80, 106, &c.

The end of this affair was the prosecution of Judge Johnson himself, in the following year. Cobbett had delivered up the anonymous MS., with the admission that the envelope had the Dublin post-mark. The hand-writing was then traced to the worthy judge. The newspapers which were not slavish supporters of Government greatly disapproved of the affair; the *Morning Chronicle* being especially bold in the expression of its contempt. The judge retired in 1806, upon a pension of 1200*l.* a year.

to his loyalty, and thereby practically supported the non-libellous view of the matter. The defendant's counsel, Mr. Adam, pointed out that the avowed object of the writer was "the support of good government in Ireland, and the removal of the present administration." But in vain.

On the next day a civil action for damages was tried in the King's Bench, brought by Mr. Plunkett, Solicitor-General for Ireland, on a passage in one of Juverna's letters ; the ground was all gone over again, and with a similar result. Mr. Erskine led the prosecution.

From this day Mr. Cobbett had a handle to his name, which his unreasoning and malicious foes—his envious, his beaten foes—could flourish at will. He was now a "Convicted Libeller." And when you can call a man a convicted libeller or a convicted anything, you may fill the office of ass to the sick lion, not only with impunity, but with credit and distinction to yourself. You will even find many base admirers.

CHAPTER XIII.

"I SAW THINGS IN ANOTHER LIGHT."

THE unmistakable success which had attended the publication of "Mr. Windham's Gazette" (as the *Register* was nicknamed) soon made a revolution in Cobbett's plans for the future. It had been his cherished thought to resume a semi-rural life, visiting London once or twice a week, in the case of being enabled to relinquish the bookselling business.

It was not until 1805 that a permanent removal was made out of London ; meanwhile, however, the shop in Pall Mall had long been relinquished. In March, 1803 (according to a notification in the *Register*), it appears that Mr. Harding had just taken the business over,[1] whilst John Morgan had also returned to Philadelphia to recommence book-

---

[1] Harding was succeeded by John Budd before the year was out.

selling there. Besides the ordinary trade, the firm
had produced the long-promised "Selections from
Porcupine's Works," issued in May, 1801, and
dedicated to John Reeves. The list of subscribers,
printed in the first volume, includes the Royal
Princes, the chief supporters of Government, and
about 750 other names in England and America.
A second edition of his translation of Martens'
"Law of Nations" was also published in June,
1802, with the treaties brought down to the current
date. It is pretty certain, therefore, that the business in Pall Mall was a flourishing concern.

Among other labours, independent of the *Register*, were, a translation of "L'Empire Germanique,"
a tract of the period,² accompanied by a memoir on
the political and military state of Europe; and a
reproduction of the "English Grammar for Frenchmen." And, as though he were not yet fully
occupied, Mr. Cobbett must needs undertake one
more grand scheme.

This was nothing less than a plan for publishing
the parliamentary debates. The inadequacy of the
existing reports had long since attracted Mr.
Cobbett's notice, and he had endeavoured to supply the need by printing the bulk of the debates
in the early supplements to the *Political Register*.

² Also printed in the Supplement to vol. ii. of the *Register*.

At last, toward the close of the year 1803, he resolved to issue, periodically, full and accurate reports, giving as his reason that the debates, "as at present communicated to the world, reflect very little credit on the nation."

Accordingly, on the 3rd of December, 1803, appeared the first number, price one shilling, of "Cobbett's Parliamentary Debates."[1] The person who was selected as reporter and editor was a man very well qualified for the task—no other than Mr. John Wright, formerly bookseller in Piccadilly. He had failed in 1801, and his bankruptcy was attributed by Cobbett, partly to taking "more delight in reading of books than in selling of them," and partly to "the misfortune of being bookseller to Messrs. Canning, Frere, Ellis, and the other Anti-Jacobins, by whose works, though such a puffing was made over them, he lost many hundreds of pounds." . . . . "Seeing him once more ready to begin the world afresh, I proposed to him the editing of the parliamentary debates, of which we have now [1810] continued the publication since the year 1803."

[1] This undertaking has long since made the name of Hansard famous ; but this is the place to remind the reader, that its origin, and successful issue for a number of years, is one of the long-forgotten public services of William Cobbett. The original form is still retained.

One more enterprise remains to be noticed. In February, 1803, was published the first number of " Le Mercure Anglois de Cobbett," containing a "translation of such parts of the *Register* as may be thought useful or interesting to politicians on the continent of Europe." There does not appear, however, any trace of the publication of more than three numbers of this " Mercure."

Upon leaving Pall Mall, Mr. Cobbett took a house in Duke Street, Westminster. His country trips were few, for his work did not at present give him opportunity to escape from town for any lengthened period. But, in 1804, the occasion of a visit to Hampshire was prolonged so far as to revive his ardent wish for a permanent rural life. Mr. Wright (who occupied apartments at a tailor's, at No. 5, Panton Square) was getting increasingly useful to him, and their mutual confidence was now of the closest character. And it is due to this friendship, and its ultimate rupture, that we are indebted for an ample insight into Mr. Cobbett's personal and domestic history during the succeeding years.[4]

A letter, dated 9th August, from Lord Henry

[4] Addl. MSS. 22,906-7, in the British Museum, is a collection, formerly in the possession of the late Mr. Dawson Turner, from which some of the interesting letters in the text addressed to Mr. Wright are derived. The cause of their preservation will appear in the sequel.

Stuart's seat, at the Grange, near Alresford, announces the arrival of the family there, and requesting attention to some business matters, particularly the despatch of a parcel of London newspapers; then very full of the famous Middlesex election, in which the contest lay between Sir Francis Burdett and Mr. George Mainwaring. On the 13th he writes from Southampton :—

" . . . I received the newspapers and your letter safe. By the enclosed you will perceive that I mean not to go up for this next *Register.* The reason is, I have not got Mrs. Cobbett and the children settled to my mind; and, besides that, I want to take them all to the pony-races at Lindhurst, on Friday next. They have begun *to breathe.* We have seen the school at Twyford. The master is a noisy hawbuck. He is a Burdettite, and so is his wife. I like the place very much, and none the worse because it is that very identical school that Pope first went to. Of this circumstance the master failed not to apprise us. The boys are all very well, and very desirous to see you—William in particular, who says you must come and see him every Sunday. The pony is an excellent bargain. I shall take the whole off from here, bag and baggage, next Saturday, and go to Wickham; and on Sunday night, or Monday morning, I shall leave Wickham for London, where I shall stay during next week, and then set off to fetch home the brood for the winter. I am in the midst of a pony country, and I think I shall pick up another to take home with me. I shall write to you again to-morrow with another parcel, and again on Wednesday, so .that you will have all my copy by Thursday's post ; and that you may know how to calculate, I now inform you that my copy will make exactly twenty-five columns, or twenty-six at most. I have several interesting articles, and they all must come in. I shall touch the Middlesex election; the miscreants shall not escape. . . . If there be anything worth relating, pray give me a line upon it. My address is at Mr. Harris's china warehouse, Southampton. D—— the china ware ! William was out walking with me by the beach yesterday morning, and after a long and pensive silence, he said, ' Pa, why do you have a china-shop in your house ?' He is by no means reconciled to the crockery-ware yet. . . .''

This period (the summer and autumn of 1804) is also to be noted as that during which Mr. Cobbett's political opinions underwent a change. Much twaddle has been written and uttered, during the last seventy years, upon this celebrated " change." The present biographer, heedless of all that has been said, does not intend to argue out any calumnies, from beginning to end of the story ; but it is necessary here to note the first appearance of the change in question, because the selection from the correspondence, which will now be placed before the reader, makes occasional reference to

Mr. Cobbett's growing animosity to "the race that
plunder the people," to the "court-sycophants,
parasites, pensioners, bribed senators, directors,
contractors, jobbers, hireling lords, and ministers of
state," which, he was now beginning to discover,
were not the people of England, in the strict sense
of the word. He had been leading the opposition
to Mr. Pitt for a year or two past, and was now for
the first time showing an inclination to break altogether from the shackles of party.

During his absence, Mr. Wright acted as sub-
editor of the *Register;* and it will be seen that
even his labours could not have been light. Nearly
every letter to him, enclosing copy for the *Register*, implores him to read the MS. carefully, and
"make corrections as to grammar or phraseology,
and supply omissions; for I cannot read a word
of it."

[Wm. C. to J. Wright.] . . . "I thank you for sending
the selection of newspapers. They afford me excellent
matter for comment. I think I have posed them about
the car project.⁵ They know not what to say. There
are some very good things in the *Chronicle* upon this
subject. The little letter in Wednesday's paper is de-

⁵ A curious device of Mr. Pitt's, by which 10,000 men could be
transferred, in a few hours, to any part of the coast. It provoked a
good deal of current satire.

licious. The Methodist meeting [6] is not less so. That's
the tone to take. I cannot enough abhor the wretches
who would revive, at this critical moment, the hideous cry
of Jacobinism. This is a subject upon which the selfish
dogs ought to be incessant lashed, till all the nation
hates them—and the time is most proper for it. I wish
you would endeavour to inculcate this notion with all
whom you know. Nothing would tend more to the sub-
jugation of the country than the revival of this most
mischievous cry. I shall not cease my endeavours; but
do you use yours also.

"Before you come down, which will be about the 7th
of September, I suppose, I will tell you what we do
about leaving the house. I like your idea very well.
In order that you may be quite clear by Saturday, or the
Friday afternoon, you shall have the last of my copy for
next *Register*, on Wednesday morning. But you must
read the proofs. . . ."

". . . I beg you not to be out in the evening, lest
some robbery should be committed. If anything should
be the matter of James, pray send to Mr. Teggart immediately. . . ."

". . . Urry received his money. And you will send
me another just such sum by next post. I have had
entrance money and fees to pay for seven children,
clothing, trunks, &c., &c., to pay for; and we have been
obliged to buy table and bed linen for ourselves, together with a suit of clothes for John and another for

[6] In support of Mainwaring's candidature for Middlesex.

me, lest people should take me for *a heathen philosopher.*
. . . We go to church here.   I hope the saints will not
be jealous at this !"

" . . . My articles do not make so much as I expected I should have time to write.   I began yesterday
at nine o'clock, and I finish now at six for the post—
thirty-three hours, including eating, drinking, and sleeping
time. . . . Pray read the whole with great care, before
and after it is set up.

" We went our journey yesterday, and it is now fixed
that Nanny goes to school at Winchester, and the boys
at Twyford, on Saturday the 22nd instant.   We shall
stay at Botley till about the 2nd or 3rd of October, and
then we shall go and cram ourselves into the cursed
smoke again.   It is just possible, however, that we may
stay in the country till near the middle of the month. . . .
In addition to the things mentioned in my memorandum,
I request you to send the following by the mail-coach, in
a new parcel :—

" My famous breeches.

" A new pamphlet of Lord Lauderdale, in answer to
the Edinburgh reviewers, just advertised.

" Montesquieu's Spirit of Laws ;—in the bookcase, I
believe."

" . . . Now, as to the school project, it has failed.
William tells me that something is continually making
him cry.   When he saw me, he was ready to burst   He
is going back, but the others will stay.   You have helped
to make him so in love with home, and you must have
the teaching of him another year or two.   His mother

cannot live without him yet, and they must be humoured.
. . . Am I never to have my fine breeches, or did you
mean only to tantalize me?"

". . . I am alarmed that you have inserted HIBER·
NICUS [7] without my seeing it. I hope there is nothing
violent or personal? Send me, in the parcel with the
population abstract, the letter from MONTROSE; and
pray put in nothing without my seeing it. A trip at this
time would be ruinous. I am very uneasy till I see
Hibernicus. . . . As the air of Botley is so favourable
to the Muses, I shall write two more *Registers* in it. Indeed, we cannot quit it sooner. I think I shall, in my
letters to the Grand Charlatan, make good ground for us
all to stand upon. The first point, the corner-stone, is
well placed.[8] . . . Mrs. C. sends her compliments. The
boys want to see you again. There is, we think, a large
day-school mixed with boarders in Dean's Yard, Westminster, for William—will you ask? He is too young
and weak to be taken from our table to sup upon bread-
and-cheese and water!"

". . . Observe well, that two words in Mr. Bonney's
letter must be left out—the word 'excellent' in the
first sentence, and the word 'pensioned' in the last.

---

[7] On the Irish Additional Force Bill, in *Register* of Sept. 29.
The letter was not absolutely free from provocable matter.

[8] The first of a series of letters to Mr. Pitt, on the "Causes of
the Decline of Great Britain." Cobbett upbraids the heaven-born
minister with having deserted his own principles, and thus exposed
his former staunch supporters (among whom is C.) to the charge
of having deserted *him.*

The word 'pensioned' would not be safe; the word 'excellent' is an injury to B.'s letter, and is, on every account, much better left out; as, indeed, compliments to myself always should be, appearing as I do in my own name, and not as an editor. Take care that they are both left out. . . . Insert the article upon the stamp duties, but be very careful of the words."

The foregoing extracts, from letters written in September and October, 1804, throw some light for the first time on Cobbett's happy domestic circle; they are dated from Itchen and from Botley, at either of which places the family were then visiting. The affectionate tenderness towards his children is here shown to have been an active principle, and we shall have further glimpses as we proceed. But the most striking thing here apparent is his sensitiveness on the score of personal offence, on the part of himself or his correspondents. The galloping pace at which he wrote, and his negligence as to reviewing what he had written, were sufficiently perilous; and another " Juverna " affair was not to be thought of.

Other extracts might be made; but the references to current politics would be too obscure, without much detailed explanation. The following will show, however, the general drifting of Cobbett's views :—

". . . I am happy to think that I am likely to be of some use in uniting men in support of the throne, the Church, and the real liberties of the people, against the conspirators of loan-makers and directors, directors of all sorts, I mean ; East India as well as Bank . . . whether I shall draw them out at last I know not. I wish I may. But they have now such a load to toil against, that I am apt to think they will desist, and by-and-by glance at my present writing as a proof of my disaffection and abandonment of principle. If it please God to give me health, that shall not serve them, though. Pray keep a good look-out, for, if they say only a word, I wish to meet it instantly."

". . . Is it really true that the cowards have given up Malta? Why, they went to war for Malta ! ' Malta,' said Dundas, in his villainous brogue, ' Malta ! Malta ! en parpatooaty, es tha trewly Breetush oabjuct of ware !' And now he gives it up! For God's sake look at his speech, *Reg.*, vol. iii. p. 1662. But be sure not to talk of it to any one, as I should then be anticipated."

". . . Have you seen Reeves ? I think I must come to a plain understanding with him ; for I hate cold half-friendships. I think my two last numbers must have staggered such people."

Mr. Cobbett is in town in November to attend Judge Johnson's trial ; but he is at Botley House again in January. Mr. Wright pays them another visit, too, having been desired to bring a fine large twelfth-cake, also " the portfolio with all the boys' pictures in it."

That some people were getting " staggered," as Cobbett says, is by no means unlikely. He has been publicly called upon to " defend himself from the charge of not having joined the opponents of Sir Francis Burdett ; " when, lo ! it is discovered that an acknowledgment must be made, of at least some claim, on the part of the latter, to represent the Middlesex constituency, as against his oppo-nent :—

" The former sentiments and expressions of Sir Francis Burdett were not, for the most part, so wrong in them-selves as in the season of their application. Some of them, indeed, were such as no time or place would justify. . . . His language, and many of his acts, during the former election, as well as previous to it, were sedi-tious to a degree bordering upon treason ; they did, in my opinion, totally incapacitate him as a member of Parliament. . . . He chose to disgrace himself and his cause by an appeal to the worst passions of the worst part of the people.   But if nothing of a seditious nature has appeared in the conduct of Sir Francis Burdett since that election, upon what principle will his opponents justify their resentment against him, whilst they are so ready to overlook the political sins of others ? "

A few months earlier in this year, the ministerial part of the press had classed Burdett and Cobbett together as "a party endeavouring to create despondency." This appears to have been the beginning of it ; and Mr. Cobbett, on looking more dispassionately into Burdett's claims as a politician, finds that the leading objects of both their minds are the same,—

"It will be recollected that, on the 2nd of July last, application was made to Parliament for a grant of 591,842*l.*, wherewith to pay off the arrears of the Civil List ; . . . Sir Francis Burdett took the liberty to say a few words to the *thirty or forty persons* who were about to grant this half-million of money, which was to be raised upon the people. . . . He objected to the ground upon which the minister had made this application, and could not see, he said, why the rise in prices and the consequent abridgment of every man's comforts should be urged as a reason for augmenting the amount of the Civil List. He complained that there was a waste of the public money. . . . He did not declaim against taxes, but against their too great amount, and against the misapplication of them. . . ."

and protests that none but a contractor, a farmer-general, a paper-money maker, or a hired author, could find anything objectionable in the sentiments

thus expressed. In short, Mr. Cobbett has discovered that the advocates of parliamentary reform
are not, necessarily, a faction seeking to subvert
the throne. He has had his grievance, some ten
or a dozen years, against the "public-robbers;" but
he has groped about, in pursuit of them, in crooked
bye-ways: has even rubbed shoulders with them
without knowing it: has now come in sight of
the highway along which are running other pur-
suers, whose distant shouts have, till now, been
unmeaning, because misunderstood.

He looks with abhorrence at the prospect of a
revival "of those political animosities which were,
during the last war and at the last peace, so fruit-
ful in national calamity and disgrace, which destroyed all freedom of discussion and almost of
intercourse; and which, while it sheltered all the
follies and faults of the minister even from inquiry,
exposed every word and act of every other man to
misrepresentation and suspicion."

Here, then, we have Mr. Cobbett fairly started
upon his mission. Parliamentary opposition,
hitherto, had meant a struggle for power and
place, with the biggest share in the nation's loaves
and fishes; it would henceforth signify a determination to watch the grasping hand, to restrain the
thirsty leech. And Mr. Cobbett will, at any cost,

keep the nation on the alert concerning the proper disposition of its resources.

In the hope which Cobbett now indulged, of arresting, if possible, the enormous growth of the public debt, he began to advocate a union of the two opposition parties. We find him, then, about this time, obliged to defend himself from the charge of supporting Mr. Fox, whose " seditious ravings " it had once been "impossible to hear without indignation." And the charge would naturally be indefensible on the part of a hireling. But the C. J. Fox that was now praised was not the C. J. Fox who once coquetted with Jacobins. In Cobbett's eyes, Jacobinism was now dead and buried. The risk of anarchy had departed from British shores. The peace of Amiens had proved a failure ; and the Whigs, who had opposed that treaty from one point of view, were beginning to coalesce with the Windhamites, who had opposed it from another. For some time past there had been hopes of a union of all the great men of the country, in a strong, "broad-bottom'd" administration, as the only means of restoring public confidence.

So, although Mr. Cobbett is ready to admit the claim of the heaven-born minister to a place among the great, he now declines any longer to

support him, as hitherto. Not only that : he proceeds to instruct Mr. Pitt on the causes of his
failure as a statesman. Rather cool, this, for the
quondam ploughboy ! But he must needs prove
that Mr. Pitt has deserted his principles, in order
to justify his own new position. As to the charge
of versatility, he thinks that "inconsistency" means
" the difference between profession and practice."
The best exposition of this "difference" is found
in an article of the *Register*, toward the close
of the year 1805 :—

"If I praised Mr. Pitt, it was Mr. Pitt the 'heaven-
born' minister, with regard to whose character I had
participated in the adoption of those notions so prevalent
amongst the ignorant crowd about twenty years ago. It
was Mr. Pitt the corner-stone of the confederacy against
republican France : Mr. Pitt who had openly and
solemnly vowed never to make peace with France till
the political balance of Europe should be completely
restored, and till safety and tranquillity could be obtained
for England ; it was this Mr. Pitt that I praised, and not
the Mr. Pitt who advised, who defended, and who extolled the peace of Amiens. The Mr. Pitt that I praised,
as a financier, was the Mr. Pitt who, in the year 1799,
declared that he would carry on the war for any length
of time without the creation of new debt ; and not the
Mr. Pitt who, in less than two years afterwards, justified
the peace as necessary for the husbanding of our re-

sources, having, in the interim, created new debt to the amount of about seventy millions sterling. If I praised Mr. Pitt, as an upright public man, as a real patriot, it was the Mr. Pitt who began his career with professions of incorruptible purity, and who, in the warmth of his zeal, had proposed to reform the Parliament itself, rather than not cut off the means of corruption; and not the Mr. Pitt who procured to be passed the bill relating to the Nabob of Arcot's debts (of which bill I had never yet heard); nor the Mr. Pitt who, notwithstanding the information of Mr. Raikes, suffered the practices of Lord Melville and Trotter to go on unchecked ; no, no; not the Mr. Pitt who lent forty thousand pounds of the public money, without interest, to two members of Parliament—never making, or causing to be made, any record or minute of the transaction, and never communicating any knowledge of it even to the cabinet ministers. . . . . The English Constitution that I extolled was that Constitution which, to use the words of Mr. Pitt himself (in his early days), carefully watches over the property of the people; that Constitution which effectually prevents any misapplication of the public money, or severely punishes those who may be guilty of such misapplication; and which, above all things, provides that the money raised upon the people, by the consent of their representatives, shall not in any degree, or under any name, be *given* to those representatives by the ministers of the crown, and especially in a *secret* manner. This Constitution I hope yet to see preserved in its purity; and were it not for that hope, neither hand nor pen would I move in its defence. But it will be so preserved, or we are the most base of mankind."

A number of persons were now ready to support these views of Mr. Cobbett ; and a still greater number, animated by fear, or by envy, assailed him with the utmost virulence. His friends told him that the circulation of the *Register* would be diminished if he persisted in opposing Pitt ; that the advocacy of Burdett would operate unfavourably upon its reputation. He assured them all, however, that he was receiving better support than ever, and that the great majority of his correspondents acknowledged, that conviction of the truth of his reasonings, and of the rectitude of his motives, was stealing into their minds.

If there was one man who could stand up before the country with pure hands, that man was William Pitt. But it was not given to him to inspire other men by his example in this matter. The system of political corruption was too strongly holden for the best-intentioned reformer to undertake its reduction, without risking his political existence. The creed, common to Whigs and Tories, that the king and the country were to be ruled for the exclusive benefit of the "ruling" families, was the basis of the system ; and only a SAMSON, who should himself perish amid the wreck, might essay its destruction.

As early as 1802 Mr. Cobbett had ventured upon a sarcasm with reference to the clerkship to " the Pells." This celebrated sinecure, worth 3000*l.* a year, was in the power of Pitt to take to himself without reproach : as is well known he declined, and it fell into the hands of Addington, who bestowed it upon his son, then only twelve years of age. Cobbett thought this was setting decency at defiance ; seeing that the immaculate minister, about this time, persecuted a poor trades-man of Plymouth[9] for doing what everybody around was doing.

A stray shaft or so was discharged from time to time ; but not till three years after did the fight really commence. At last, in 1805, with the exposure of Lord Melville's naval mal-administration, the whole matter was ripe for discussion ; and in August of that year appears the first of those curious pension-lists,[1] which were, for the ensuing

[9] One Hamlin, a tinman, who had offered Addington a large sum of money for an appointment in the Customs. He was prosecuted, fined, and imprisoned, although he solemnly declared his ignorance of the crime, having seen for years Government places publicly advertised for sale, besides having probably received money for his vote from the agents of the Government itself.

[1] After Cobbett's first list of pensions, &c., the plan was copied

quarter of a century, the stock-in-trade of radical grievance-mongers. It was now open war. Mr. Cobbett, for the second time in his life, found himself *standing alone*. Aristocratic friends were deserting him, whilst the new ones were yet only gathering. As for the abuse, with which he was favoured by his opponents, it was as unreasoning as it was disgraceful.

by others, and the lists at last swelled, under different hands, to a volume of several hundred pages :—"The Black Book ; or, Corruption Unmasked. Being an Account of Places, Pensions, and Sinecures, the Revenues of the Clergy and Landed Aristocracy ; the Salaries and Emoluments in Courts of Justice and the Police Department ; the Expenditure of the Civil List ; the Amount and Application of the Droits of the Crown and Admiralty ; the Robbery of Charitable Foundations ; the Profits of the Bank of England, arising from the Issue of its Notes, Balances of Public Money, Management of the Borough Debt, and other Sources of Emolument ; the Debt, Revenue, and Influence of the East India Company ; the State of the Finances, Debt, and Sinking Fund. To which is added Correct Lists of Both Houses of Parliament, showing their Family Connexions, Parliamentary Influence, the Places and Pensions held by Themselves or Relations ; distinguishing also those who Voted against Catholic Emancipation, and for the Seditious Meeting and Press Restriction Bills. The whole forming a Complete Exposition of the Cost, Influence, Patronage. and Corruption of the Borough Government." (London, John Fairburn, 1820.) This interesting volume kept increasing in bulk until the æra of the Reform Bill.

END OF VOL. I.

GILBERT AND RIVINGTON, PRINTERS, ST. JOHN'S SQUARE, LONDON.

www.ingramcontent.com/pod-product-compliance
Lightning Source LLC
Chambersburg PA
CBHW020948030726
47496CB00005B/1401